NO SAINTS
AMONG US

No Saints
Among Us

Ivan Zador

East of the Mountains and West of the Sun™

RHYOLITE PRESS LLC
Colorado Springs, Colorado

Zador, Ivan
No Saints Among Us / Ivan Zador
First edition, April 1, 2023

ISBN 978-1-943829-46-0

Library of Congress Control Number: 2023935427

Publisher's Cataloging-in-Publication data

Names: Zador, Ivan, author.
Title: No saints among us / Ivan Zador.
Description: Colorado Springs, CO: Rhyolite Press LLC, 2023.
Identifiers: LCCN: 2023935427 | ISBN: 978-1-943829-46-0
Subjects: LCSH Physicians--Fiction. | United States. Central Intelligence Agency--Fiction. | Immigrants--Fiction. | Czechoslovakia--Fiction. | Psychological fiction. | Historical fiction. | BISAC FICTION / Psychological | FICTION / Historical / 20th Century / Post WWII
Classification: LCC PS3626. A36 2023 | DDC 813.6--dc23

Published in the United States of America by Rhyolite Press LLC
P.O. Box 60144
Colorado Springs, Colorado 80960
www.rhyolitepress.com

Cover design, book design and layout by Donald Kallaus
Front cover background courtesy: Julian Mora-Unsplash

To Manci and Bandi

ACKNOWLEDGMENTS

My heartfelt thank you to my friend Elliot Cohen and to Horst Richardson for helping me make the right connections. To my editor Maryann Miller and to my publisher Don Kallaus of Rhyolite Press. And to my wife Sandy and my friend Livia Luce for invaluable advice.

CHAPTER 1

"IN THE EVENT OF GENERAL MOBILIZATION, you will report to The Square of The Fallen Soldier. You will bring your identification card, your driver's license if you have one, your party membership card if you have one, toiletries, utensils, and provisions for one day. If you do not report immediately after the declaration of general mobilization, you will be dealt with according to the law."

Roman Hollander stared incredulously at the plain red card he had just removed from the mailbox. He turned it. Yes, it was addressed to him. He reread it. "Report to The Square of the Fallen Soldier." Was there intentional irony and derision in the choice of the gathering place, or was it unwitting prescience?

This would not be Roman's war to fight. He knew he had to leave. He had to break out before it was too late.

HE CLEARLY REMEMBERS THAT SPRING AND SUMMER back in nineteen sixty-eight, although he was only twelve then. Smiles enlivened people's faces, laughter echoed, hope was heady. Small crowds assembled on street corners, students collected signatures for petitions, barefoot girls with daisies woven in their hair were milling around in the main square. His father, for the first time Roman could recall, read out loud from the newspaper at the dinner table, revelations from the past flooding the pages like the water mass from a breached dam. An American poet was passing through town, they made him King of May, carried him around with a crown on his head. Writers huddled at their country retreat, composing a manifesto. There were fresh faces, fresh voices on the small gray screen flickering in the living room. Then an open letter coming from afar, from the boundless East, "Friends everlasting, dovelets," it read, "we will not abandon you. We will be at your side forever."

"That's a threat," he told his father. "They will be rolling in. The invasion is coming."

"Don't worry, son," Dad reassured him. "The boys across the ocean won't allow it." And a month later, in the early morning, screeching noises coming from above woke him. He lay still and listened. What was it? Airplanes flying low? A few minutes later, thunderous thuds causing the windows to rattle made him jump out of bed. Artillery, he concluded. Then rapid, short, ominous bursts of machine gun fire, sounding like knuckles rapping on a hollow door, joined the blasts. He ran out of his small bedroom into the hallway. Dad and Mom were already up, pacing in the living room in their pajamas. The phone rang, and they both lunged for it. Dad made it first and picked up the handset, and he almost whispered as he was hanging it up a short while later. "This was Pepa. It is what we thought. They invaded. We are under attack." Then he screamed; "Bastards! Motherfuckers!" and raised his fists, his face twisted into an angry grimace. Mom hugged Roman. "You predicted it, child," she said, shaking her head in disbelief. She turned to Dad; "Let's pack our bags and run, like we did thirty years ago," and they laughed bitterly because they knew it was too late, they were not young any more, not adaptable like they used to be.

There was smoke and fires outside. Low leaden sky. Tanks rolling through the streets, hammer and sickle painted on the turrets. Soldiers in bulky, dirty, dark-brown uniforms, burgundy berets, confusion on their faces, "These are children, for God's sake," Mom exclaimed. "Everybody to the Central Radio Station!" Roman heard people shout. "We have to defend The Radio!" Dad turned and Mom grabbed him by the lapels of his jacket, "Don't go," she cried out, and he pushed her hands away and took off running downtown toward a thick cloud of smoke rising above the buildings, toward the sounds of machine gun fire.

A FEW HOURS LATER, after the airwaves turned silent, his father came back, his clothes torn, covered in blood, knuckles scratched and bruised. "Not mine, the blood is not mine," he gestured when he saw the panicked look on their faces. "It was the man standing a couple of feet away from me. They mowed him down, and the man next to him too."

They hugged him. "It could have been you," Mom whispered. "How many dead?"

"Hard to say. Many. A few guys threw Molotov cocktails. Other than that, we had only stones and tram tracks. Plenty of those. Against tanks and machine guns. We built barricades from overturned trams. All of us were civilians. No army, no police joined us. Total shame. Total betrayal." He left to wash up and to change his clothes. Then they all sat down around the table, gloomy, quiet.

"It's over." Dad broke the silence. "The dream is over."

LEAVING CZECHOSLOVAKIA permanently for the West is not allowed. One way to escape without accepting the risk of being killed at the border is to receive permission, in the form of an exit visa, to travel to the West on vacation and once there, to make the decision not to return. This permission is predicated on the approval by the secret police, officially called the State Security, the feared investigative arm of the communist dictatorship.

Roman's odds of getting the visa were low: his sister Hana had defected several years earlier; he had his own share of encounters with the State Security; he was a Jew, and Jews were not the communists' favored people. On the other hand, Roman reasoned, the State Security probably wished that all the local adherents of the Mosaic faith would just disappear. Perhaps he had a chance.

"How long will it take before I'm notified of the decision?" Roman asked the surly older woman in a gray uniform sitting behind a plexiglass window. He had just applied for the exit visa. "Come back in two months," she told him, and here he was again, looking at the same woman, giving her his name, straining to conceal his agitation.

"Hollander, Roman."

"What an odd name." She pulled out a cardboard box with alphabetically filed documents and very slowly sorted through them. Finally, she picked one out, glanced at it and handed it over. It was a one-time exit visa for a two-week trip, valid for six months.

"What? I got it?" He had difficulty controlling his excitement.

"Why are you so surprised?" she inquired with a suspicious glare, her severe eyebrows asymmetrically raised.

"No, not surprised at all. Just pumped up about the vacation," he said as he darted out, squeezing the permit in his hand. Either there was a miscommunication between the secret police and the passport department, or they truly wanted to get rid of him. It didn't matter. He was determined not to let this opportunity slip away.

ROMAN STARTED PACKING his luggage. Taking more than one bag for a two-week excursion and bringing anything other than summer attire would raise suspicion. He stared at his leather jacket. It was the only one he had ever owned. Its chestnut-colored surface was still smooth. It had an inner cotton lining and was quite heavy, not something to wear in warm weather. Roman held it in his hand. He laid it down on the sofa. Then he picked it up again. In the end, he put the jacket in the suitcase on top of the already packed items and closed the lid. He took a tiny ring binder, his address book, out of the desk drawer and started turning the pages. The data in it had to be completely innocuous. Wolfgang Pernsteiner on 25 Friedrichstrasse, the Czech émigré Marie

Rezek whose phone number should be listed in the Ostbaum phone book, the town of Gerstand where the refugee camp was located, all this information would have to be etched in memory. He placed the address book in a small backpack, together with a passport, his exit visa, the wallet with one hundred American dollars that his uncle had sent him from Paris, and the train ticket with a reserved seat.

He walked through the two rooms of the minuscule apartment. He was not leaving much behind because he had very little. A few items that had some significance or value had already been taken by his parents for safekeeping. The apartment was the property of the city, and whatever remained in it after he was gone would be misappropriated. He looked out the window. Two young men stood in the doorway of the building across the street, drinking bottled beer, smoking, laughing. He lay down on the sofa and lit a cigarette. If he makes it across the border, he will never see these pale-blue walls again, he will never again sleep on this couch, this squeaky bastion of respite and carnal gratification. It was four in the afternoon. He will be leaving from the Main Railway Station in two hours.

THE TRAIN BARRELED ACROSS THE EVENING countryside, and the reddening sun was spreading its rays over the hilly, wooded landscape. Roman stepped out of the compartment into the aisle, pulled down the window and let the strong warm wind blow across his face. The train made a stop in Pilsen, and then continued to an area at the Western border that he had come to know well during his despised compulsory army service two years before. There was the city of Protěž with a large border patrol base, the quaint spa of Janovice, and Křemen, the town nearest to the military post where he had been stationed. Křemen had two bars, a hospital, and a church. The church was a small baroque structure surrounded by an empty lot with overgrown grass. He still remembered the day he had passed by it on his rare leave, his few hours of a deceptive sense of freedom, because for conscripts the military service was fundamentally a low-security prison with an occasional furlough. A

Mass had been taking place inside the church. Strong orange and yellow lights spilled out through the open doors, contrasting against the grass and trees in the distance like big chunks of thick, oily, shiny paint roughcast on the background of an emerald-colored canvas. The rich tones of the organ, the singing, and the smell of incense saturated the air; and the church, its black steeple outlined sharply against the dark sky and the grass around it rippling in the mild breeze, seemed to be floating above ground in dreamy rapture, transfigured ephemerally into an airy mystical edifice of deliverance.

THE REGULAR RATTLE OF THE TRAIN wheels gradually slowed until it stopped with a drawn-out groan. Looking out his window, he could read the sign "Cheb" on the dirty tiled wall of the dimly lit railway station. Cheb was a city on the frontier with West Germany where border patrol agents were conducting inspections. Soon enough, he heard the pounding of heavy boots in the aisle and opening and closing of compartment doors. He was astonished how quickly warm, calm, confident hands could transform into clammy hands of trepidation.

He shared the compartment with two young Americans who, judging by their huge rucksacks and a tired, disheveled appearance, must have been partaking in a backpacking trip across Europe. "Passport control," announced a gruff voice that belonged to a tall border guard with a narrow face and tiny penetrating eyes. The two Americans handed him their passports. He stamped them and returned them without a word. "Your luggage, please," he said after checking Roman's passport and the visa. Roman rose, took the baggage off the shelf above his seat and opened it.

"A leather jacket, huh. Isn't it too warm for the summer?"

"I am planning to go to the Atlantic coast. It's chilly out there, especially at night."

The man ignored Roman's comment and continued to look through his belongings, eventually completely unpacking the valise and putting all the items on an empty seat. He asked for Roman's backpack and quickly located the notebook. He went through each page individually. Nothing earth-shattering to be found there, Roman thought. The two Americans were watching with their mouths agape, eyes wide. "Who is Pavla Machová?" the guard suddenly asked.

Oh shit. Pavla was a friend of his who defected to France right after graduating from high school. He must have overlooked her name when he was checking the booklet for potentially suspicious information. "Pavla Machová?" he repeated, pretending surprise and ignorance, trying to buy time, thinking frantically about what to answer.

"Yes. There is a Paris address with her name. And the phone number does not look like a Czech one to me," the guard said with feigned amusement.

"Ah. Yes, yes. She is an old woman who has lived in Paris since before the war. She's a former girlfriend of my uncle. They recently split up. She found herself a younger man, but they are still on good terms. In fact, she is the contact person in case something would happen to him. That's why I have her address and phone number." Roman began to sweat.

"You have an uncle in Paris?"

"Yes, he is listed on my exit visa. He has lived there for fifty years. He is an old man."

"Looks like a bunch of fossils vegetating there in Paris. Should I call the old woman?"

"Feel free, go ahead. I have to warn you that she is a very nasty woman whose Czech is almost non-existent."

"That is OK. I'm not afraid of very nasty women, and I speak French." The guard walked out with the notebook. Roman was certain that the man was bluffing about the phone call and his linguistic prowess, but he may have gone to check Pavla's name against a database of recent émigrés, if such a database existed. His stomach was in knots but he forced himself to smile. "Sorry for the delay. Not my fault," he said to the Americans. They didn't answer and looked away. After a while, the border guard returned, gave the notebook back, and left without a word. Roman was not sure how to interpret this. Then, in about fifteen long minutes, the train started moving, first very slowly, then gradually gaining speed.

They were crossing the border into Germany.

THEY WERE TRAVERSING the Bavarian countryside, and only then did Roman fully realize that in the next few hours he would have to arrive at a decision that would irrevocably affect the rest of his life, the most important decision he ever had to make. It was the choice to either continue his trip to Paris, spend his vacation there as formally intended, and come back, or to leave the train in Ostbaum, in Germany, parting with his previous life.

When he had been granted the visa, when he had said good bye to his parents, when he had boarded the train, there had been no doubts about what he would do. Now, he found himself reanalyzing his plans, but all he could produce were jumbled thoughts, an ineffective, anxiety-provoking, painful mental clutter. Finally, a half hour into agonizing ruminations, he came to the realization that, after months of having his mind set on leaving, he preprogrammed himself to execute his plan if an opportunity arose, and no arguments, rational or irrational, could change that now.

THE NIGHT'S DARKNESS made room for a timid dawn, a dawn he wanted to delay if he could. He knew from a trip taken long ago that within minutes the train would make a stop in Ostbaum. He grabbed his luggage and the backpack in automatic stilted motions, moved to the coach exit, and when the train came to a halt, he pushed the heavy door open and stepped down onto the platform, having just made the fateful leap from tyranny to freedom, from dreariness to light, from stale predictability to uncertainness, from having basic guarantees to surrendering them. The gravity of the circumstance left him dazed, paralyzed. Eventually he mustered enough resolve to find a money exchange booth to buy German marks for dollars. The next step was to call Marie Rezek.

CHAPTER 2

·····················

IT HAD BEEN ABOUT TWO MONTHS EARLIER, in the late spring, when a stranger rang the bell of Roman's apartment. A trim middle-aged man in a well-fitting knee-length black coat, with a thick moustache and straight long gray hair, was standing at the door. Too fashionable for a Czech. Must be a Westerner.

"Roman?" asked the man and continued in English with a strong German accent, "can I come in?"

He hesitated for a moment. Was this a trap set up by the police? But Roman was insignificant to them, a small-time troublemaker. "Yes, I am Roman. Come in." He stepped aside so that the man could enter, then closed the door.

"I am Wolfgang Pernsteiner. Your sister asked me to stop by." They sat down in the tiny living room. "I am from Ostbaum. I met Hana and Martin through a mutual acquaintance when they lived in Germany before leaving for the States. I am a businessman, and I travel often between Ostbaum and Prague. Your sister called me several days ago and told me you may be making plans to leave the country. She thought I could help you, at least with some aspects of your journey."

Roman was still suspicious of a set up. If Pernsteiner was an agent, he would have been able to glean some information about Hana from her limited communications with her family that stayed behind, and possibly also from her direct contacts in Germany. But again, Roman was a small fish. He decided to trust the unannounced guest. "Yes, Wolfgang, I want to leave. I will take a two-week vacation in August. Officially, I will be traveling to Paris to visit my uncle. That is the extent of my planning so far."

"I am not very well versed in the current situation of refugees from the East, but I can tell you that your best bet would be to get out of the train in Ostbaum and head to the refugee camp in Gerstand, a few kilometers outside the city limits. It is a huge camp, one of the largest in Europe as far as I know. I would not go all the way to Paris if I were you. Germany is much more supportive of refugees than France. There is a lady in Ostbaum, Marie Rezek, she is Czech but she has been living in Germany since nineteen sixty-eight. She has helped many of your countrymen find their bearings once they escaped to the West, including your sister. She is a little neurotic, and she can be fickle, but she's willing to lend a hand. I would contact her right after getting off the train. Her number is listed in the phone book."

"I will somehow have to get my medical school diploma brought out of the country. Without it, I would not be able to reenter my profession. I am reluctant to take it with me. They may search me at the border and I'd be in dire straits if they discovered it."

Wolfgang thought for a moment, then said. "I know most of the border policemen at the Cheb crossing because I go back and forth so often. They haven't searched me yet. I feel comfortable bringing it to you. Once you get settled at the camp, come and see me. My office is on 25 Friedrichstrasse in Ostbaum. This way I'll know you've made it to Germany, and when I am back in Prague again, I will get the diploma from your parents, and I will fetch it for you. What do you think?"

Roman considered it a realistic plan. Still, it was fraught with peril, and he was impressed by Wolfgang's willingness, without much hesitation, to go through with it. Judging by his forthright demeanor,

Roman was confident that the man meant what he said. "I will gladly accept your offer," he told Wolfgang, shaking his hand.

"Next time we'll be meeting in Ostbaum. Best of luck," Wolfgang stated straightforwardly and stood up to leave.

Rezek's number was in the phone book as Pernsteiner had promised, and Roman closed the door of the phone booth and dialed it. A high-pitched female voice answered, uttering a few words in German. An unpleasant tone, he thought. That is not a propitious portent. He replied in Czech, apologizing for calling so early in the morning, explaining who he was and awkwardly, he felt, informing Marie, assuming that it was her, that he had just disembarked the train from Prague and that his intention was not to return. He mentioned Wolfgang, and his sister Hana.

There was silence on the other end of the line. "I am not helping refugees anymore," Marie finally said.

"I don't think I'll need much help. Maybe some advice. Maybe a place to store a few things."

"Sorry, Roman, I decided to stop helping refugees. I have enough of my own troubles. I don't need anyone else's. I can't help you. I am so sorry."

"But Marie..."

"I am sorry."

Roman paused. It was useless to continue. He was only making a fool out of himself. He was ready to hang up but then, as if in a paradoxical effort to allow her to perhaps be of a little bit of assistance, he asked for directions to the Gerstand refugee camp.

"Take the subway to Ehrlichstrasse," she told him." Then board the train to Gerstand. All the best."

He stepped out of the booth, stunned, humiliated. A young family passed by him, the parents, pulling wheeled suitcases behind them, and two blond elementary school-age girls, skipping, fencing with badminton rackets, giggling happily. He did not need anything specific from Marie at this stage, yet he fully counted, mistakenly and naively he now knew, on her support, and with that expectation dashed, he felt he was losing the ground under his feet.

He glanced toward the platforms, and he just now took note of the bright sunny morning, heralding, in all likelihood, a warm, pleasurable day. By this time, the train that had brought him here was approaching Stuttgart and in a few more hours it would make its final stop at Gare de l'Est in Paris and the travelers would alight from the carriages to be absorbed by the broad, white, tree-lined boulevards and avenues and by the labyrinthine tunnels of the Métro, and to be surrounded by the tastes and smells of buttery croissants, and caramelly flans, and Camembert, and Panaché, and he was standing in the arrival hall of the Ostbaum train station at the beginning of a long road, and he decided that it was an auspicious morning after all. He lifted his luggage and headed for the subway.

THE MAIN GATE OF THE GERSTAND REFUGEE CAMP was locked. Through gaps between the posts of a metal fence he could see a sizeable concrete yard bereft of vegetation. Farther down, multiple cuboid two- or three-story tan-brick buildings occupied the expansive lot. Few people were outside as it was still fairly early on a Sunday morning. There was a police station across the street, a uniformed cop was standing nonchalantly in the doorway, exposing his face to the sunrays. Roman approached him and stated simply: "I want to defect." For him, this terse sentence was the momentous culmination of all that preceded it, the planning, the hope, the decision, the doubts, all contained in these four words.

For the policeman, his utterance was much less consequential.

"Come back tomorrow," he grinned. "No one's in the camp to process you today. They will be opening at eight in the morning. There are several places to stay overnight on the main avenue if you want to stick around town."

Roman picked up his suitcase that was getting heavier by the minute, trudged to the center of town, and checked into the first hotel he caught sight of. He hauled his luggage to the second floor and fell on the bed, exhausted. He lay there on his stomach, his face in his palms, until he drifted into a restless sleep. When he woke, the briefly suppressed reality vengefully returned making him break out in a cold sweat. He got up, strode across the room, and peered outside. A man and woman were standing at one of the windows of the apartment building on the other side of the street, the man with his arm around the woman's shoulders. After a few seconds they disappeared behind the curtains. The evanescent scene and the cozy air of his hotel room made him acutely and agonizingly aware of the fact that the next day he would be swallowed by the camp machinery and his privacy would be gone, likely for a long time, that he would be entering a period of life filled with unpredictability, that the road ahead would be hard and the future uncertain. He was unsure to what extent he would be able to influence the events that were about to come to pass. That is, unless he changed his mind. He still had plenty of time to do that. Officially he was still on vacation. It was his decision to take this path, and it was in his power to reverse it. But, like on the train, he realized that he was not able to. That, frankly, he did not want to.

With dull pressure building up in his chest and behind his eyes he decided to leave the hotel and take a walk through town. He strolled past brown clapboard and red brick houses with manicured lawns, a neo gothic stone church, restaurants and cafes with ornamental hanging signs and outdoor seating, where waiters with serious countenances, dressed in white shirts and black aprons, were preparing for the diners, past a park with a pond and ducks and geese and benches and weeping willows, past flawlessly aligned rows and rows of fruits and vegetables without blemish displayed on racks in front of the grocery store. All that he saw was in soothing harmony, choreographed by middle-class capitalist prosperity. East of the border, no such harmony existed.

There are many facets to freedom, mused Roman, and this quaint town, through its orderliness, cleanliness, plenitude and conservatism, was expressing freedom's calm, sober, everyday proud version.

*   *   *

HIS PARENTS. When will he see them again, if ever? He'd dropped by their apartment right after he had left the passport office, the fresh exit visa in his pocket. "Show me your mug," Mom said after they drank up their coffee at the kitchen table. She was fond of reading the future from the pattern of the coffee grounds left at the bottom of a cup. "I see travel in the offing. The shapes look like continents. The edges are pretty jagged, though. Seems like rough going."

"I've got the visa."

"Oh, yeah? The coffee dregs hit the mark again. Then you are leaving and not coming back, huh?" Mom said, putting the cups in the sink and filling them with water. Dad did not speak, he just lit up a filter-less Sparta, that raw and bitter symbol of life under communism, and inhaled deeply.

"I think so. It's time. The bottom line is, the commies are not going anywhere. I don't want to end up in jail. I was too close once already. I don't like the threat of mobilization. I don't like that it's nineteen eighty-four. I have a very uneasy feeling, a premonition of sort."

"Have you thought it out?"

"Yes. I have an outline of a plan, but first I have to contact Hana. I'm worried about you, though. You'll be here all alone if I leave." He listened to his words and they sounded hollow.

"We will be fine, son," Dad said. "We raised both of you to despise the Bolshevik so we should not be surprised. Hana left first, now you. We kind of expected this, right, Simona?"

Mom let out a sigh. "We did. But it's the right thing to do, Roman." She gave him a kiss. "Hana left with Martin. You will be going it alone, I assume."

"Yes."

"It will not be easy. Especially in the beginning."

Roman looked at his parents with concern. They were used to dealing with adversity starting at a very young age, but at this moment, their faces seemed a little worried, a little downhearted. "We will miss you, son." Dad patted him on the shoulder. "I know you will be alright."

"I'll write to Hana," Roman said. The mail coming from the West was routinely censored and before his sister left, they had come up with a few code words for future contingencies. Their code word for defection was pigeon. Prague was full of waddling fat pigeons blanketing the city with their tooth-pasty excrements, including on the narrow, claustrophobia-inducing balcony of their parents' apartment, so they thought the pigeon predicament would be a reasonably legitimate yet inconspicuous enough topic to bring up in a letter.

He moved to the tranquility of his parents' study. Its heavy window curtains were always partially closed, the chandelier lights always dimmed. Two massive dark-brown maple-wood bookcases filled with tomes of encyclopedias, literary theories, history books, poetry, and fiction, were standing along the walls. His parents were artistic translators, and they were bibliophiles. Roman grew up reading; reading in the small faux leather chair in the corner of the study, reading on the softly padded linen sofa in the living room, reading stealthily during family meals in the kitchen from books stashed in the small hiding space under the table top, reading past midnight in the brass-framed bed in his constricting bedroom. He read on trams, always sitting in the very last seat by the rear window, riding from terminal to terminal, the continuous hustle and bustle around him conferring an added sensory dimension to the text. Sometimes, after hours of devouring line after line, page after page, he would become overwhelmed by a peculiar euphoric heaviness, by an intoxicating yet oppressive sense of complete engulfment by the story, by the words, and in those moments, in a perceived self-preservation effort, he would slam the book shut and disassociate from it, only to return to it a short while later, the behavior of a veritable addict.

He read *The Three Musketeers* when he was eight and reread it multiple times, and he fell in love with all that was French, and he sobbed with disappointment when Mom and Dad explained to him that he would never become a French nobleman. He consumed the four volumes of *War and Peace* at twelve. Prowling through the pages of *The Decameron* occasioned a recurrent hard-on that he was pleasantly bothered by and did not know how to handle. Later, he progressed to Joseph Ks and Swanns and Leopold Blooms, the realm of word-bending complexity dueling with astonishingly clever lucidity, and all these oeuvres were on his parents' shelves.

Little did he know that years later, after his father died and his mother became very ill and had to leave the apartment, the furniture would be reduced to a pile of wood and, together with all the books, that precious collection that personified his parents and had been gathered over a lifetime, would be loaded onto the bed of a diminutive truck and dumped into a landfill at the edge of the city.

LATE MORNING THE NEXT DAY he was back at the refugee camp gate. The guard asked for his passport and transcribed the information from it into a thick logbook. He told Roman which building and which room number to go to. "There are some free beds there, just take one." He opened a binder, studied the pages for a while, wrote a few notes. "Tomorrow at nine you will have an interview with the intelligence services and at ten with the immigration agent. All that will be on the first floor of the administration building. Follow the signs and be on time." He scribbled the information on a small piece of paper and handed it to Roman. "Food is served three times daily. Tomorrow you will get an ID card that will allow you to go in and out of the camp. We prefer that you stay in Gerstand. I'll keep your passport for now. You'll get it back later." They preferred, not demanded or ordered. Benevolence that he had not experienced before. He doubted that this preference was strongly enforced.

The room was large and surprisingly light, with several rows of wooden bunk beds. Roman noticed a lower-level bed that appeared unoccupied, and he put his luggage on it.

"Newcomer?" he heard a voice coming from the top cot. He looked up and saw a young man with a pleasant face and long curly auburn hair.

"Yeah, just moving in. From Czechoslovakia. How about you?"

"I am from Albania. I've been here for a while." He glanced at his watch. "Ah, it's almost noon. Lunchtime. Do you want to get some food? We can talk on the way."

The hefty cafeteria door was still closed, and Roman and the Albanian joined the back of a line that wound from the door all the way to the top of a long staircase. Roman looked around. It was a colorful crowd. African women in long, brightly patterned skirts, some in turbans, their men in black tee shirts and gold-color chains around their necks. Pakistanis and Afghans in flowy beige and blue pajama shirts, wide pants and flip flops. Latin Americans and Eastern and Southern Europeans. He recognized the sound of Polish being spoken, and he could hear some other Slavic languages he was not able to accurately identify.

"How did you get out?" he asked the Albanian.

"I ran across the Yugoslav frontier to Austria. From there I made my way to West Berlin. I worked there in a pizza shop. Life was good. But then I was caught by the immigration police and they shipped me here. Now I am trying to get my status formalized."

Loud noises emanated from the front of the line. Two men were engaged in a fist fight, the crowd forming a circle around them.

"I will probably apply for asylum in the States," Roman said.

"Tough to get there. The Germans are a little easier."

The screams coming from the cafeteria door grew louder. One of the men was brandishing a long knife. The circle around the two widened considerably, but the onlookers, with their arms folded on their chests, appeared amused.

"Does this happen often?" Roman gestured to the fighting men.

"It happens," the Albanian said. "This is a restive bunch. Many of them came from wild places."

The ring of gawkers split as an athletic middle-aged man, dressed in a gray suit and a purple shirt, rushed toward the fellow who was wielding the knife. He stopped in front of the brawler, and for a few seconds both men stood motionless, staring at each other, trying to anticipate the opponent's next move. Then the dapper fellow dashed forward, quickly disarmed the scrapper with just bare hands and put him in handcuffs. At the same time the cafeteria door swung open and the throng plowed in like a roaring avalanche.

Fifteen minutes later, with food on their trays, Roman and the Albanian found an empty table next to several young men involved in a loud conversation. "These are the Tamil Tigers," Roman's companion said in a low voice. Roman looked at the men making sure they were paying no attention to them. They were not.

"Those fearsome warriors from Sri Lanka?"

"There are quite a few of them at this camp. Apparently, they first went to East Berlin, but the communists did not want them. They loaded them on a subway train and sent them to West Berlin. Let the capitalists enjoy their company. From there, they wound up in Gerstand."

"Are you married?" the Albanian asked after a brief pause in the conversation.

"Single. You?"

"I am single, too. I like men. Young men, like seventeen, eighteen. I like them with barely any facial hair, no body hair. In other words, you're not my type. I used to date girls, but then I tried it with a boy, and I liked it. I still go out with girls, but I prefer guys. What about you?"

"I prefer women."

Roman looked up from his plate. Two uniformed cops walked through the door and headed to a table in the back of the room that was occupied by three large, bearded men. "I have an interview with the spies coming up tomorrow," Roman said. "Any advice?"

"The best is to be truthful. You'd be surprised how much they know about you already."

IT WAS THE MIDDLE OF JANUARY in Prague, his last winter in the city before the defection. The temperature hovered below freezing, low enough to cause a sneaky chill that crawls under the skin and stays there and makes one want to go somewhere inside for a glass of warm grog. Roman was walking across Kampa, an island in the river with its untended old mansions and its weedy lawns now covered with gray slush. He was passing by a neglected yellow building standing on the bank, a building he had noticed before because of its squat loneliness, it's just that on this particular day he saw a large "*Read 1984!*" inscription painted in dark-blue letters on its front wall. There are still a few brave souls living among us, Roman thought and, buoyed by this uplifting realization, kept his mind occupied for the rest of his trudge across town by conjuring up the image of the gritty person who accomplished this mission.

He could picture a man, standing on a foot stool or a small ladder, under the imperfect cover of a cold night, writing a message to his countrymen to wake up, risking prison. He must have come to the island at around three or four in the morning, when it was less likely that he would run into cops scouring the streets, and when it was too late for the alcoholics to still be out, and too early for working folks to be leaving home to earn their daily living. He drove there in a small car, Roman imagined, a second hand Škoda or the cardboard Trabant, parked in a nearby small square, assembled his gear, and walked to the house shivering in the freezing darkness. He drew the numbers and letters in thick paint, stopping several times to look over his shoulder, finishing in five minutes. Then he hurried back to his vehicle and took off, driving fifteen miles to the suburbs where he lived, where rows and rows of gray high-rise apartment structures loomed; they called those projects The Moonscape. He opened the front gate of his building on the second try, turning the key with difficulty because his fingers were stiff in the cold. The elevator was not working, so he threw the ladder over his shoulder and climbed up to the eighth floor.

Inside the apartment, he quietly took off his coat and shoes and tiptoed to the bedroom. His young wife was asleep, and he hoped he had not woken her up earlier when he was leaving. He carefully lifted the blanket and lay down next to her, feeling her warmth. He covered his face with his hands, closed his eyes and let out a deep breath. *Well done.* He had an hour of rest before the alarm clock would ring.

CHAPTER 3

THE ROOM THE RECEPTIONIST ushered Roman into was small, windowless, with an olive-green linoleum floor, bare beige walls, and two yellowish tube lights on the ceiling. The intelligence officer, a man probably in his forties, with a ruddy complexion and a thick blond moustache, was sitting behind a rectangular desk with a gray laminate top. He was leafing through the questionnaire Roman had filled out in the waiting area.

"Do you speak German?" he asked in a gravelly voice after Roman took a seat on the opposite side of the desk.

"No, but I speak English."

"Have you ever been a member of the Communist Party?"

"No. Never."

"Your parents. Have they ever been members?"

"Never."

"Were you a police informant?"

"No." Roman shook his head.

"Both of your parents escaped Czechoslovakia right after the war broke out and joined the French partisans, the Maquis, to fight the Nazis. That's where they met, in Southern France, correct?"

"You seem to know a lot about my parents. Perhaps more than I do." *Is he just trying to demonstrate to me that he is omniscient, or is he heading in a specific direction?* Roman thought.

"Your dad has some Hungarian background. Do you speak Hungarian?"

"Rudimentarily."

"What about Russian?"

"I had to learn it in school. I hated it. Why this interest in my linguistic abilities?"

"Just wondering."

The agent paused and gazed into Roman's eyes. "You are an educated man. I also happen to know that you are a courageous man. You don't speak German, but I have no doubt you would quickly learn. What do you think about working with us against the communists?"

Roman raised his eyebrows. He did not answer.

"You know from firsthand experience," the man continued, "how despicable that regime is. Now you would have an opportunity to help us fight against it. We need native speakers of East European languages. We need people familiar with the surroundings. We need people who are determined. You would be immediately granted asylum in Germany. You would get a place to live right away. What do you say?"

Roman should have been prepared for this request, but he was not. Yes, the officer was right, it was a nefarious regime, but Roman's current intention was to get away from it, not to battle it.

"Look, Mr – "

"Guntherschön."

"Mr. Guntherschön, I don't think I would be up to the job. Also, my hope is to continue my career in the United States if at all possible." He expected an annoyed reply but his questioner remained composed; he must have been used to getting rejected. His lips curved into a barely perceptible smile. "Take my business card in case you change your mind. Here's your passport back."

HIS NEXT APPOINTMENT, in a room across the hallway, this one with a window, was with the immigration agent, a young Czech woman with short auburn hair and heavy blue eye shadow.

"So," she smiled at him, "based on the information you filled out, your intention is to apply for asylum in the United States, true?"

Roman nodded. She had a pleasant voice, and he started feeling more at ease.

"The outcome can be unpredictable. Not everyone gets in. The Americans tend to be picky. Obtaining asylum in Germany should be much less complicated."

"I still want to pursue it."

"Alright," she said. "If that is what you wish, I'll direct you to a Czechoslovak refugee fund agency that can handle your asylum request." She reached to one of several stacks of forms that were towering on her desk. "Here is their application."

It was a thick form. Roman glanced at the pages. *This is a gargantuan questionnaire.* His look must have betrayed his frustration, because the woman let out a good-natured laugh. "It's long, and it's byzantine. I know. But don't be intimidated. Fill it out as soon as possible, and mail it in, so that the process can start. Again, no guarantees. I wish you good luck."

Good luck alright. The direction is set.

He walked out of the building, to the camp yard full of exiles lingering in groups under the warm August sun. A young Polish lad sat on the sidewalk, dark blood flowing in a steady stream from his heel. He had a dirty scarf wrapped around his ankle, tied with a knot. It was pushing deep into the skin. A man and a woman were standing beside the boy. Roman slowed as he came near.

"What happened?"

The woman looked at Roman. "He stepped on a big shard of glass. He is still bleeding. For some reason the scarf is not stopping it, even though we tied it as tight as possible."

"The scarf is making it worse," Roman said. "Try to undo it."

"What are you, a doctor?" the fellow standing next to the youngster scoffed.

"Just give it a shot."

"OK, let's try it," the woman said. "I hope it works."

She knelt down and carefully released the knot. It did not take long before the flow of blood slowed to a trickle and then stopped altogether. The boy smiled, wiped his heel with the scarf, and carefully stood up.

ROMAN WAS A RELATIVELY RECENT medical school graduate. The six years at the university had gone by enveloped in a cloud of excitement and exhaustion that sometimes moved at a whirling speed, sometimes stood still, and in which a multitude of memories were stored. One of them was nostalgically attached to the most immutable of settings, the large reading room in the library of a former Jesuit college where he'd spent many an hour reading. A dark, cold and musty hall, with a disused tall fireplace with sky-blue ornamental tiles standing in isolation at the entrance. A single fireplace, notwithstanding its loftiness, could not have been enough to heat the vast space. Perhaps there had existed additional ones that were since removed, or it could be that the Jesuits just abided the cold; they were known for abnegation.

Deeper into the room were rows and rows of wooden desks with glaucous-colored waxed canvases covering their tops, each equipped with a small brass lamp emitting a feeble orange light, and chairs with unyieldingly hard seats. Baroque stucco reliefs decorated the walls, and ceiling frescoes depicted events in the life of Ignatius of Loyola; the future saint hanging his sword and dagger at the altar of the Black Madonna of Montserrat, parting with his military path and dedicating himself to the service of the Lord; Ignatius a beggar; Ignatius and his followers taking vows of chastity and poverty.

A thick anatomy atlas spread on the desk opened to the page illustrating a long bone with its grooves and curves and angles and tuberosities that will all have to be seared into memory. Sometimes his buddy Honza Nečas, a fellow student, joined him, a big curly-haired kid, a fine piano player. They quizzed each other in front of the acrid restrooms on the basement floor or, on warm spring evenings, in the courtyard flanked by the gray walls of surrounding buildings covered with creeping tendrils and leaves of ivy. They tested their understanding of bone surfaces and muscle attachments, of nerve pathways crisscrossing the forests of the brain, of rivers of blood running through the body, of the indefatigable heart, with its reservoirs and gated dams, that contracts roughly three billion times during an average lifespan, and after the closing hour they habitually relocated to one of the nearby bars to cement their freshly acquired knowledge with a few pints of ale.

Honza was a dependable friend. Roman once needed a high-quality turntable, a mixer, and a pair of large speakers for a house party he was in charge of organizing. Honza owned such equipment and loaned it to Roman without any vacillation.

The bash itself, when it took place at a house in a hamlet a few kilometers North of Prague, was unfolding propitiously until about eleven at night when Roman, relieving himself in the basement bathroom, heard loud thumps upstairs, and then shouts and screams, "Secret Service. Line up facing the wall. Hands up!" There was stomping and more thuds. *They must be searching for something*, Roman thought as his agitation grew, *they are probably patting people down.* He had four samizdat copies of Havel's *The Power of the Powerless* stuffed in the large inside pockets of his jacket. He'd intended to pass them on to certain friends at an opportune moment and was glad that he had not yet done it. He took the copies out of the coat and began tearing up the pages and flushing the shreds down the toilet as fast as he could.

"Where is Hollander?" *Shit.* So they were looking specifically for him. One more copy to dispose of as the stomping was getting nearer. The men were now in front of the bathroom, they banged on the door, rattled the knob, then kicked the door in. A bruiser in a black leather coat forced himself into the small space, his face twisted with rage. "Are you Hollander? Are you hiding in here destroying the evidence?"

"No, I'm sick. Vomiting." Roman wiped his face and pushed his hand against his stomach.

"Shut up." They pulled him out, threw him against the wall, ripped off his heavy jacket, searched it, patted him down and added a few hard blows. They did not find anything. The copy remnants were floating safely in the sewers.

The agents grabbed him, and the host, Petr Holík, a thin freckled young man whose usually pale face turned crimson during the assault, crammed them into an unmarked Škoda and drove them through the black streets of Prague. They stopped at the Hospital Row in front of a free-standing pseudo-Gothic low brick building, the capital's only drunk tank which had the unique added feature of medical supervision.

"These two juiceheads need a place to stay for the night," one of the cops said to a tall big-boned woman in a blue nurse's uniform who stood at the entrance of the triage room.

"We're not drunk," Petr protested. "This is abuse."

"Shut your cake hole, or we'll take you straight to jail."

"For hosting a party?"

"Don't tempt me, punk."

The area was large, chaotic, pandemonic, a distillate of Prague's worst dissipation. A twitchy muscular gray-haired man with wild roving eyes was squirming in a chair next to a wall with peeling white paint. A nurse was cautiously counting his pulse, and a cop stood behind him, his enormous fingers on the man's throat, ready to squeeze the trachea if he attempted a wrong move. A few feet away, two policemen and a young man in white uniform, an orderly or a medical student, were struggling to restrain a chubby fellow in a black suit. "Grab him by the wrists, not by the arms," one of the panting cops instructed the guy in white.

"You're in deep shit," the chubby man hollered, "I am a member of the Central Committee. You'll suffer for this!"

"I don't give a fuck," the cop yelled back, "I don't give a fuck, do you hear me?"

An older man, shirtless, in blue overalls, his toes pushing through holes in his grimy sneakers, was leaning against the wall, raising and shaking his enfeebled fists. "I used to be a boxing champion. You should've seen my glorious chest. My arms. Cunts were dripping wet when I was in the ring. Now look at this. Look at me." Then, perhaps realizing how aptly and truthfully he was able to express and summarize in his intoxicated state the pitiful progression of a life, he started to cry in large, heaving sobs.

A tall gent with straight dark hair, wearing glasses with sleek black frames and an olive-colored sports jacket, strolled across the room, a pipe in his mouth, surveying the commotion with a blasé expression on his face. Roman recognized him. He was a psychiatrist, a lecturer at the Medical School. The big-boned nurse examined Roman's and Petr's gait and she had them touch their noses with their index fingers. "They don't seem inebriated, comrades," she said, turning to the policemen.

"They are staying," the lead cop barked back. "We'll drop by later to make sure they are still here. So don't try to pull any tricks."

An orderly took them to the basement area, to a capacious dimly lit room with multiple rows of mattresses covered with grayish sheets, most of them occupied by drunks sleeping off their intoxication. The air was supplanted by alcoholic vapors. Roman and Petr took two of the remaining empty pads. A couple of men with red, scarred faces and tousled hair, sat in the middle of the room in chairs equipped with bizarrely long, spidery metal legs. They were recovering alcoholics whose treatment program required them to participate in operating the drunk tank in order to witness the ravages of the bottle from the outside. Roman knew this because a few months earlier he had spent several hours there as part of his psychiatry rotation. The men were overseeing the miserable drunken mass that produced a cacophony of snoring with multiple wheezy sounds contained in a single snore, and gasping, groaning, screaming, burping, farting, crying, retching, moaning—a spontaneous disharmony so marvelous, so stunning that Samuel Barber would have been in envy of it.

The one person who knew that he was in the possession of the samizdats, Roman contemplated while listening to the limitless improvisations performed by the drunks, was Honza Nečas, and he was beyond suspicion. Or was he? And Věra Nosková knew, the slender, transparently pale redheaded woman whose husband, a rocker and a poet, was in prison again, this time for subversion. Věra passed the samizdats on to Roman. She was only a casual acquaintance. What if she herself was an agent?

The man next to Roman suddenly sprang up like a released coil, bellowed "*L'Assommoir*! Never again!" and collapsed back into the mattress.

AT SEVEN IN THE MORNING Roman and Petr were discharged from the drunk tank. The police were not around. They walked for five minutes to the nearest tram stop and parted there. Petr rode straight to work at a construction site, and Roman went to class.

ROMAN AND HONZA NEVER SAW EACH OTHER or spoke again after graduation. Honza took the position of a general practitioner in a small town in Eastern Bohemia. Before relocating, he shared with Roman his new address, but the two letters Roman wrote to him, and several phone calls he made, were left unanswered.

ROMAN RECEIVED HIS GRADUATION DIPLOMA from a purple-faced gentleman in a bright-red cloak, a four-cornered black hat, and a golden Rod of Asclepius in his hand, *A dissipated university bureaucrat in a Satanic disguise,* Roman imagined. It was a solemn ceremony in the venerated inner chambers of the University seat. Soon after that, he started toiling humbly in a small hospital located in the outskirts of Prague. In the mornings, he had to fight his way in and out of trams packed with commuters like pickled herrings in a barrel to catch the hiccupy bus reeking of gas that dropped him off about half a mile from the facility after a forty-minute ride. He did not mind that the last leg of his daily journey was on foot. The narrow road to the clinic led through a wooded area that was dark-green and luxuriant during the spring and summer months, and on his walk, he was usually able to shake off the jolt of the morning's travels and clear his brain before the true explosion of the day.

He typically had over thirty people on the wards to take care of. With only one physician on duty after hours and no back up, call nights could be baptism by fire for doctors fresh out of school. The institution was not equipped to handle the very ill, but, since there was no other hospital nearby, anyone who was sick enough was brought in regardless of what ailed them, and those who were not sick enough were brought in too, just to play it safe. Folks with asthma attacks, infections, diabetic comas, infarcts, heart failure, strokes, victims of mushroom poisonings and car accidents, and malingerers, drunks, hypochondriacs, fugitives from justice looking for a place to keep out of sight, crazies; each day a procession of humanity at its most vulnerable passed through the hospital entrance door. In the beginning, Roman felt like he was on the ropes almost every night when he left the hospital, but he kept stubbornly returning in the mornings, until he gradually fell into a relative routine, and the days started changing, a fast-flowing river with a few unexpected turns replacing long rows of steep, jagged peaks.

THE HOSPITAL CHIEF, Petr Svoboda, was a lean man with a long, slightly crooked nose giving his narrow face a virile, ruggedly attractive look, his starched white uniform flawlessly ironed, his blond hair carefully combed, particularly on the afternoons of family visitations when inducements were pouring in. He was a legendary miser who would wait in underpasses to catch a car ride to the clinic with young doctors so he could save on fuel. He used to work as a physician for the airline company, taking care of the flight attendants' sniffles, before his wife put her foot down and made him change course.

His deputy, Milan Stránský, a spindly fellow with thick horn-rimmed glasses, a stethoscope with azure-color tubing habitually hanging around his neck, had served prison time in his previous life. He worked at one of the best clinics in the city, Pinnacle Health, when he was arrested. After they released him, he was exiled to the small hospital in the periphery as a continuum of his punishment. His aptitude for medicine returned quickly; Roman happened to be at Stránský's side when he pulled a man straight out of the jaws of death after everyone else had given up on him. "Don't worry, you'll get better at it," Stránský told him then, noticing Roman's overwhelmed look. "It all comes with experience."

Whenever Roman asked for advice, Stránský gave it without posturing. That was uncommon in the competitive medical world, and Roman considered him a friend. Roman once asked him why he had served time. The reticent Stránský shrugged. "Those communists, they haven't got any sense of humor."

ABOUT A MONTH AFTER Roman left Prague, he went to see Wolfgang Pernsteiner. His office was in downtown Ostbaum, in the pedestrian zone with blue flagstone-paved walkways, tidy shops, cafes, pubs, galleries, offices, medical practices, all housed in esthetically coordinated low, cream-colored buildings lining the streets that bordered on a city block full of porn parlors and prostitutes.

"Is Mr. Pernsteiner in?" Roman asked the girl at the front desk and before she could respond, the office door opened and Pernsteiner stepped into the hallway. He recognized Roman immediately. "*Grüss Gott,*" he welcomed him and motioned for him to come into the office where they both sat down. "I've been waiting for you to come. I just returned from Prague. I brought the diploma."

"You did?" Roman almost shouted in surprise, his excitement contrasting with Pernsteiner's stoic demeanor.

"Yes. I decided to stop by your parents' apartment. We had a good conversation."

"How are they holding up?"

"They are adjusting to the new reality, let's put it this way. They were already called to the police station where they were told you would be tried in absentia for defection. The good news is that it doesn't look like they will have any difficulties themselves. They are both retired so the authorities will leave them alone. I asked your folks for the diploma, and they gave it to me."

"Any hurdles at the border?"

"None. I put it on my back, between the shirt and the sweater, just to make sure."

"You are a good man, Wolfgang," Roman said. "I owe you."

Wolfgang waved a hand understatedly. "That's alright. Where are you going to keep your diploma? You need a safe place. Documents like these get stolen. They have a high value on the black market."

Roman had not thought of that, but he had no doubt that Wolfgang was right. "Would you be willing to keep it for now?"

Pernsteiner hesitated. "Too many people pass through my office and even through my house. None of them are criminals, at least as far as I can tell, but you never know. What about Marie Rezek. Have you had a chance to contact her?"

Roman told him about his telephone encounter.

"I am not that surprised. She can be moody. Apparently, she's been also having some marital difficulties. You may want to call again. She may be more receptive the second time around. Storing your diploma temporarily at her place is the least she could do for you."

For some reason, he clearly did not want to take the responsibility for keeping the document, but that did not change Roman's respect for him, and his gratitude.

"Roman, you have a long road ahead of you," Pernsteiner said. "I wish you all the best. If you need anything, you know where to find me."

CHAPTER 4

THERE WAS A POINT, in the early summer, when Roman thought that his defection plan would be derailed. It was after he had obtained the exit visa, after he had bought a train ticket to Paris, that he received a summons for a ten-day military exercise for reservists. His date of departure to the West was in six weeks, and he was certain that they would not let him travel out of the country if he were to learn any secrets of import during the maneuvers. The great escape may not happen after all. But his fears were quickly assuaged when he arrived at the training location. It was near the city of Jarovice, about ninety miles north of Prague. Around two hundred reservists were assembled on a meadow by the railway station. Two young professional soldiers, both military physicians with the rank of captain, were explaining the purpose of the exercise to the men ranging in age from mid-twenties to mid-forties, a largely passive-aggressive bunch in rumpled ill-fitting swamp-green uniforms, with facial expressions varying from amused to disgusted.

"Soldiers, comrades," one of the captains started, a heavy-set man with widely-spaced teeth, "you are being trained to function as a front-line medical unit. In real combat conditions you would last for about fifteen minutes."

There was laughter among the reservists.

"Yes, you would be wiped out very quickly. This train behind us," and the man pointed to the railway wagons standing on a side track, "represents a mobile medical unit. The train will also serve as your sleeping quarters."

"There will be discipline," the other captain took over, the shorter of the two, with bodybuilder shoulders. "No fights and no drinking while we are here. We," he motioned to his colleague, then to himself, "will leave every evening for the night and we'll come back again the next morning. We don't really give a fuck about what you do here after we are gone. The reserve officers will be in charge in our absence."

There were about fifteen reserve officers there, Roman included, but they clearly commanded little respect because the rows of privates were writhing with laughter, howls, and whistling after the announcement. There was no doubt it would get rowdy here after hours.

TIME WAS PASSING SLOWLY. Heavy wooden boxes full of medical equipment and drugs were moved from one place to another without a purpose. Field latrines and makeshift showers were built. Grunting pot-bellied dads carried each other on stretchers around the meadows blanketed with the ephemeral cottony whiteness of dandelion seeds. Limbs were immobilized and arteries compressed, understanding that in real time it would all be over within fifteen minutes.

They made regular trips to the woods to cut trees for fuel. On one of these excursions, they drove by a Russian military base, a quadrangle of one-story barracks of indeterminable color. Privates stood at attention in a single row on the lawn near the road, an officer was slowly walking along the line with his broad torso bent forward and his large head close to the soldiers' faces, his mouth moving and his hands folded behind his back. Suddenly, he stopped in front of one of the conscripts and thrust his fist in the soldier's face with full force. The youngster wobbled but managed to stay on his feet. A stream of bright red blood gushed out of his nose. The rest of the men kept standing at attention. The officer resumed his strut, his hands comfortably behind his back again.

THE SMOKY, DIRTY RAILWAY STATION watering hole filled up completely each evening after the captains left. Officers and regulars were sharing tables. A very large muscular man sitting next to Roman was not a lumberjack in civilian life, he was a psychologist who went by the name of Vlastimil. He carried on a monologue about psychometric testing but after a few pints of beer, listening to him, or rather to his pleasant baritone, was not entirely unenjoyable to Roman. Then, suddenly, the man changed the subject. "Doc, I suffer from severe anxiety when I am around guns or gunfire. If I have to go to the shooting range or to practice throwing hand grenades, I may do something unpredictable. I may go apeshit. I may actually unintentionally kill someone."

"You sound like you are speaking from experience. Did it ever happen? That you killed someone?"

"Hasn't happened yet. Doc, if we go shooting, I will have to have an excuse."

"I think we can do that," Roman told him. He did not believe Vlastimil's story, but he was impressed by the man's pacifistic fear of guns, and he was certainly eager to avoid any accidents even if their chance was unlikely.

"Today, I had a bad headache after chopping wood. I was diagnosed with tension headaches in the past," the psychologist continued. "The pain is gone now. The beer is helping. But I can't drink beer all day long, can I? So, if we have to cut wood again, or if I don't feel well for some other reason, I may show up asking for an excuse for that reason too."

Roman took a big gulp from his mug and made no comment. He was not a friend of the little soldier game they were involuntarily partaking in, but he was not a fan of malingerers, either. This man looked like one, and Roman had to assume that the purpose of his initial affable behavior was to get on his good side so it would be harder to resist his demands later. The guy was, after all, a psychologist.

Next morning, Roman was not surprised to see Vlastimil walking to the makeshift medical office located in one of the train coaches. *Here comes trouble.* Four men, all physicians, were in the carriage that day. Vlastimil's head was turned to one side, his forehead was furrowed, nose wrinkled, upper lip raised, mouth open. He was rubbing his temple with his right hand; his left hand was supporting his lower back. His whole body was an epitome of pain. He climbed the steps of the wagon with considerable effort. He quickly glanced around and once he saw Roman, he shouted, "Roman, I hurt!"

"I can see that, Vlasta," Roman said. "I thought the beer last night was supposed to help. What hurts?"

"My head hurts. My back hurts. Everything hurts, dude."

Roman tried to gently rotate the man's head but Vlastimil immediately screamed out with pain and pulled away. "Okay, I will give you two aspirin tablets and have you lie down and relax a little bit." Roman pointed to a soft pad in the corner of the carriage. "We'll see how you feel in an hour."

"Two pills and an hour of lying down will not do. I need to be in horizontal position for a couple of days."

"Vlasta, why don't you just try what I recommended?" Roman asked. But the psychologist quickly became angry.

"You were fine talking with me yesterday, sipping on your beer like an infant and enjoying the conversation, weren't you? Today, you act like we've never met!" His face was contorted into sharp lines.

"Calm down Vlastimil. I will help you. But let's work together, alright?"

"No, not alright. I don't feel well, and I want to be excused from everything."

Roman sat on a folding chair in the back of the carriage, and Vlastimil stood in the middle of the floor several yards from him. He now moved closer, clenching his fists. Roman debated whether he should stand up, but he decided to remain seated to try to avoid an escalation of an already precarious situation. He held up one hand.

"Please take it easy. I will give you an excuse if you don't feel better, but let's try something first."

But his effort to calm the man down was futile. Vlastimil quickly surveyed the carriage and, noticing a long metal bar lying on the floor, he swiftly bent down, grabbed it and raised it to shoulder level. He did not seem to be in any pain while making these swift moves. Roman and the two men sitting next to him, Tonda and Fanouš, rose with their arms in front of their faces in a defensive position. The fourth doctor, a surgeon called Karel, was standing behind Vlastimil.

"Don't do anything stupid, buddy. You have only a few more days before this war game is over, and you will be going home. Put that rod down," Roman urged Vlastimil in a tense voice. From the corner of his eye, he could see Karel quickly opening a wooden box with a red cross painted on it. Karel pulled out a syringe, attached to it a long large bore needle, then took a small ampule and drew up its whole contents into the syringe. Vlastimil stood in a fighting position with his left leg forward, his face raging, ready to pounce. He lifted the bar slightly higher. The three doctors attempted to back away, but they were already at the end of the compartment, and there was nowhere else to retreat. By this time Karel was ready. He moved closer to Vlastimil, stretched out his arm, rammed the large needle in his ass and pushed the plunger. The psychologist froze for an instant, then screamed and turned to face Karel. At that moment the three men lunged forward, forced the metal bar out of his hands and wrestled him to the floor.

"Karel, that was some quick thinking," Roman told him between heavy breaths. "What did you give him?"

"Valium. A truckload of it. It should kick in any second." He was right. Vlastimil's efforts to throw them off grew rapidly weaker, and soon he was lying on his back motionless, snoring loudly. His face was now smoothed out and peaceful; he looked like a giant sleeping baby. At that point, the wagon door flew open and the two captains rushed in.

"What is going on?" they both exclaimed in unison. "We were walking by and we heard screams," the broad-shouldered one added.

"Everything is OK now. But this guy almost killed us," Roman said. "He is a psychologist with huge anger issues and a complete lack of self-control. We need to get him out of here as soon as possible. We could call the cops but since he is drugged up, it may be better to call for an ambulance to take him to a psychiatric hospital. The hospital can then contact the police. Are you in agreement?"

"Yes comrade, excellent plan. We'll get the operator to place the call right away," the heavy-set captain said. The other one nodded, and they ran off.

"I hope you do it fast, you dimwits," Fanouš scoffed.

They must have done it fast indeed because thirty minutes later a beige ambulance pulled up in front of the carriage.

"Went crazy? Couldn't take the hardship of military life?" the driver asked, laughing.

"He got pretty threatening. Here's the report." Roman handed over a sealed envelope.

The doctors had to help the crew put Vlastimil on a stretcher and load him into the van. He was still dozing, but, in a smart move, the paramedics preemptively restrained him.

THEY WATCHED THE AMBULANCE drive off the meadow and onto the dirt road. In unison they all lit a cigarette with trembling hands.

"That was something," Tonda spoke up for the first time since the incident." That dude was nuts. I wonder if they do any health-record screening before they call people up."

"Psychologist, you said. Helping others with their emotions. A little irony there," Fanouš laughed.

"That's what he told me," Roman said. "He knew about psychometric testing. Maybe he used to be one and got fired. Who knows? In the bar he shared with me that he could kill someone if he was forced to be around guns because they freaked him out. It looks like he could kill someone for not getting a doctor's note. He seemed fixated on getting an excuse."

"He sure was. Give me an excuse or die." Karel reached under the cot and pulled out a case of beer.

CHAPTER 5

"**WELL, HERR DOCTOR, HOW ARE YOU?**" Marie Rezek's voice was hesitant, but she was a bit more pleasant than during their initial conversation. She spoke Czech with a faint German accent.

"I didn't think it would be a stroll on the beach, Marie. But things have been progressing according to expectations. You can probably hear the trepidation in my voice, but there is something I'd like to ask you. I have my medical school diploma with me, and I don't have a secure location to store it. I was wondering if you would be willing to temporarily safeguard it."

Her answer came after a brief pause. "I don't think that should be a problem. Bring it over."

She gave him directions to her apartment.

THE REZEKS LIVED IN A FASHIONABLE CONDOMINIUM building on a quiet street canopied by overhanging branches of massive oak trees. On the other side of the lane was a small park with an oval-shaped pond. The living room was spacious, full of light. A white Bechstein grand piano stood by the wall next to a glass sliding door that opened into a large balcony. Floors were laid with porcelain tiles with a gray base and a swirling turquoise pattern. Marie Rezek was a tall woman, probably in her early fifties, with hollow cheeks, blond hair and eyes with a seductively rich azure color but empty, without a spark. Her face was still showing traces of past beauty, but heavy lines around her eyes and the corners of her mouth gave her a sorrowful, resigned look.

"Are you hungry?" she asked.

He nodded. She gestured to a barstool in the dining area, and she took a McDonald's hamburger and a can of Coke from the refrigerator. She warmed the hamburger in a microwave oven. "See, the whole world is getting Americanized. But the hamburgers are tasty. No one can argue with that."

Roman looked again around the living room, and only then did he notice a young woman sitting on the far side of a beige leather couch in the shadow of a large bookcase. She was striking, with long brown hair, dark eyes and white skin, and a serious, contemplative expression. When she became aware of his gaze she stood up and slowly walked over to him.

"This is Evelyn, my daughter," Marie said, then turned to the young woman. "This is Roman Hollander. He defected from Czechoslovakia a few weeks ago."

"Welcome to Ostbaum," she said in a deep quiet voice. She did not smile. "I wish things would change so that there was no more need for defections."

"That is not going to happen any time soon, Miss."

"We emigrated in sixty-eight," Marie said." My husband was an internist with quite a few years of practice when we came here. Since then, he has done well for himself, and for us, as you can see." The daughter turned and went back to the couch. "He is not around much these days," continued Marie, with an apologetic smile. "He befriended one of his assistants, and he mainly spends time at her place."

Roman finished eating the hamburger. It was indeed tasty, in a plain, straightforward sort of way. Marie touched his shoulder. "Okay Roman. Let's tend to the matters you came here for."

She took him gently by the elbow and led him to the foyer. She opened the door of a wall cabinet and lifted a safe box from its lower shelf. She unlocked the safe, put the folded diploma inside and locked it again. "Your diploma will be protected here. Once you are ready, you can pick it up."

"Marie, who has access to the key?" Roman asked.

"Only family members. You can be sure that your document will be secure here."

"I have no doubt that it will be. You've been of great help."

He was eighteen years old. They met on the highest floor of the City Hall tower, the tower in front of which a throng gathers every hour on the hour to hear Death ring the bell, and to clap on the sight of the squat somber wooden apostles filing rigidly behind two narrow windows above The Astronomical Clock. He was there to fill in time, she was there for a summer office job. She tripped on the steep marble staircase and dropped a large stack of documents, and he helped her get up and gather the strewn sheets one by one.

Her name was Irena, same age as him. They struck up a conversation about the mushroom-picking season that was soon approaching, and their secret mushroom-hunting spots in the forests, and about an intricate mesh of trails in the woods north of the city leading to a flooded surface mine with secluded pebbly nudist beaches. They talked about Renata, the skinny pale kid from a provincial town, with braided blond hair and weird clothes and a voice like Janis Joplin's, who took the musical scene by storm like a whirlwind coming out of the blue. The only true Czech rocker.

Roman waited for Irena in the square under the green statue of the reformist priest burnt at the stake after having declared that truth would always win, and when she was finished with work, they went to see Blind Pepa Zelenka, an avant-garde musician, as Irena characterized him, playing in an obscure building in a room with uneven wood floor and a few shaky tables and folding chairs. Blind Pepa was not only blind, he was also paralyzed from the waist down.

He reached the podium by pushing himself up against the platform floor with his arms, rising straight from his wheelchair. He slithered to the piano bench like a lizard. After a few moments of groping and another upward thrust, he was comfortably situated on the stool and randomly mashing the keys, discharging a torrent of atonal dissonance.

"You're a fraud, Pepa," someone shouted from the audience.

"Shut up, you're squelching my inspiration," he yelled back.

"You just have to liberate your mind and your senses, then the harmony will slowly creep in," Irena said.

"This guy must be well connected to be able to express himself so freely," observed Roman.

"Yes, I think his daddy is in the Politburo," Irena laughed.

"Why are we here then?"

"Cause there is nothing else going on as far as I know."

"Let's go to Etna, they play jazz there occasionally."

They sat down at a table in the far corner of the room. "All coffeehouses are full of State Security," Irena declared.

"How do you know I am not one?" Roman asked.

"I don't know if you're not, and you don't know if I'm not. Should we presume for tonight that neither of us is one of them?"

"Let's."

Five respectable men were playing homegrown staid jazz, only brass instruments. He remembered a jazz festival down South two years before. He had hitchhiked to the location. A couple with a daughter about his age gave him a ride for the first half of the trip. Throughout the whole time in the car, the girl was smiling at him shyly, but she and Roman did not say a word to each other, probably because of the intimidating presence of the parents. The next person who picked him up was a man in a cowboy hat, with a huge beard, who drove barefoot. He was a large-animal veterinarian. Roman learned from him, among other tidbits about veterinary life, that IV injections in cows and horses are given in the jugular vein, and that during a rectal exam, the whole arm goes in.

The festival was taking place outdoors on a large meadow, cattle grazing in the background. That was some jazz. Trumpets, sax, guitars, piano, percussion, the audience ballooned into a sea of people, too big for the Bolsheviks' comfort. A man in a white shirt and a tie and a dark-blue suit emerged on the stage and announced that the concert was over. The crowd booed and stayed put. Cops moved in with tear gas and batons, people panicked and ran, some climbing over fences into private yards, villagers came out with dogs and axes, and police vans were waiting on the county road, scooping up hapless jazz aficionados. Roman crawled into a culvert and stayed there until it was quiet, then hid out in the woods for the rest of the night.

"I'm wondering what the future holds for Renata," Irena mused.

"She is unbridled, like a hurricane. She has a substantial following. The authorities won't tolerate her for long. She'll either have to conform or they'll throw her in jail or kick her out of the country."

THEY FINISHED THEIR GLASS OF WINE, left Etna and walked to the waterfront. It was getting dark. The river with its stony banks, the looming edifices, and the sky were all fused into one breezy gray mass. A lonely barge was sailing downstream, its blue and red shimmering lights guiding it to its destination, to a nearby port or to the shipyards at the Baltic Sea hundreds of miles away.

"I love rivers," Roman said, and they stopped for a moment and listened to the soft ripples of the water. "There is something about the meanders and the shores, and the unrelenting flow, and the endless travel."

"My dad's a journalist," Irena said, "or was a journalist, rather. One of the gigs he had was writing for the travel column in *The People's Newspaper*. He composed some captivating river tales."

"He *was* a journalist? Not any longer?"

"He did not toe the line after the invasion. They fired him. Now he's shoving coal into a metal beast in the basement of an apartment building."

"The usual story. How is he handling it?"

"What do you think? It was hard initially, from a journalist to a stoker, but he learned to look at the upside. He calls himself Hephaestus and wants us to treat him with deference, like a deity. Cockroaches keep him company. He likes to pour beer into a little glass bowl for them. He can read as much as he wants. Nobody bothers him, unless one of the articles of his that he still writes and keeps in his drawer for better times, mysteriously finds its way into a samizdat publication. Then he gets dragged to The Tiled Cage[1] for a long, friendly chat. He thinks one of these days he's going to get arrested. He has a tooth brush and a comb and a few other personal things all packed in a plastic bag and ready, in case there is banging on the gates at four in the morning."

"He's a hero, one of the few who are not afraid to resist. If it ever changes here, which I doubt will happen in our lifetime, he'll be hallowed."

"Don't bet on it. People like him are quickly forgotten. Vultures run the show in any system."

They climbed up the granite steps back to the city streets.

THAT WAS TEN YEARS AGO, a summer romance, a wonderful fling. Where is she now? Where's her dad? The system is still there. It will be there for time eternal.

DAYS DRAGGED ON at the refugee camp. Roman filled out the documentation to initiate the American asylum request and mailed it to Munich. Fall was approaching, but the days were still warm. His Albanian room-mate was cruising the streets of Gerstand in the passenger seat of a BMW convertible with a sultry brunette behind the wheel. Working on formalizing his status, notwithstanding his sexual preferences. Who could blame him?

On an early afternoon, an afternoon he will remember forever, it was drizzling outside, and a group of quiet, slight young men in kaffiyehs had just moved in and took up the bunk beds by the large window, a camp guard came to the room. "Hollander," he called out, "you have a visitor. A woman. Seems pretty anxious."

Coming near the gate, he could already see Marie Rezek, dressed in a black pantsuit and high heels, shaking with sobs. Roman rushed to her.

"What happened, Marie?"

"You would not believe it, Herr Doctor. The diploma... it's gone!"

"What? Gone? How is that possible? Did someone break in?"

He must have come across quite upset because Marie took a few steps back.

"No break in. I opened the safe this morning just to make sure the diploma was there. I don't even know why I did it. It must have been a premonition. It was gone."

"Who else knew that it was in the safe?" Roman shouted.

"Evelyn knew," she said with a low moan. "She would never take it. But," Marie thought for a moment, "she has a boyfriend. Albert. He is kind of a scoundrel. A con artist. I don't like him. They recently came back from a month-long excursion to Africa, to the safaris in the South. I heard him complain that the trip cost too much money, and that he was strapped for cash."

"Do you realize how important this document is? Did you know someone had to smuggle it out of Czechoslovakia, taking a big risk by doing that? I trusted you!"

She did not answer. She just whimpered.

"Did you report it to the police?"

"Yes, right after I found out it was missing."

"Did you tell them about the boyfriend?"

She nodded. "The person I spoke with was Detective Unterholz. He said he would be looking into it."

Roman turned around. A shrill, perfunctory, "I am so sorry," a fake appeal for absolution, pierced his ears as he was walking away.

For an hour, he was furiously and desperately pacing the streets. He should have kept the diploma in the suitcase or in the train station locker. The presumably safest location had proven to be the least secure of all. His plan for the future was unraveling. The diploma was his only proof that he was a physician.

There was no doubt in his mind that the family was involved in this. It could have been the daughter helping her boyfriend get his finances in order, but Marie herself may have been part of the act. Maybe it was revenge for Roman's insistence that she help him, notwithstanding her assertion during their first exchange that she was not keen on doing that. This can't be real, Roman thought, his face flushed and his temples throbbing. But it was.

DETECTIVE UNTERHOLZ WAS A STOCKY MAN wearing a wool sweater and umber corduroy pants. "I feel bad for your loss, young man. Unfortunately, I've got no leads."

"Did you speak with that man, Albert, Evelyn's boyfriend?"

"I did, to both of them. They denied any involvement."

"They denied it and that's all? You will take their word for it?"

"What do you want me to do? I can't beat them. We'll continue to look, but the diploma is probably long gone. Whoever took it most likely quickly sold it, and I am sure it changed hands multiple times since then. So, by now it is untraceable. These things can go for five thousand dollars or more. I don't think they can be easily put to use in Europe or North America. But in parts of Asia, Africa, or Latin America, a reasonably smart crook with some medical background could hang a shingle with the help of a stolen diploma."

"That is encouraging. So, in addition to the fact that my career is effectively ruined, there is this wonderful notion of another doctor Hollander practicing fake medicine somewhere."

"I will get in touch if we have any news," Unterholz ended the conversation. A refugee's stolen medical diploma was probably the least pressing issue on his mind.

CHAPTER 6 ......

OR THE NEXT FEW DAYS Roman was drowning in bouts of helpless anxiety and raging anger at himself and the likely culprits. If Marie was at least partially truthful, Albert must have had something to do with the theft of the diploma. Based on his conversation with Unterholz, Roman thought he could safely assume that the investigation was closed, which meant that if Albert did it, he was able to get away with the crime scot-free. That was infuriating.

The more he was ruminating about the incident the more Roman wanted to confront Albert. He realized that there was no proof that Albert had committed the theft. He knew that it was an emotional reaction, an attempt to settle the score, and that the interaction would most likely be very unpleasant; but that did not prevent him to take off one warm fall afternoon and ride the train to Ostbaum and walk slowly to Marie Rezek's apartment building. He had no plan in mind other than to sit on a park bench facing the front door of the building and watch the people who were entering and leaving it. He would recognize Evelyn and if there was a man with her, he would assume that it was Albert. Roman accepted that he might not encounter them that afternoon, but he was prepared to come another day if that were the case. He had time on his hands.

He waited for several hours. The large glass door opened a few times but there was no sight of Evelyn with a male companion. The sun started to set but the temperature was still balmy. The street was quiet. Then a young woman opened the door and held it ajar for someone. The woman was Evelyn. A broad-shouldered man followed her out of the building. Evelyn waited so that he could catch up to her, and she reached out for his hand. That's it, Roman said to himself. He was not sure what he was going to tell them. He was nervous, and he was afraid, but he rose and walked up to the couple. "Albert?" he said.

They stopped. The man had the expression of a person who was confident in his ability to handle any situation. "How can I help you," he answered in a perfunctorily affable voice, eyebrows slightly raised.

"I am Roman Hollander. I am sure you know my name. What happened to my medical school diploma?"

Albert shrugged. "I am sorry. I don't know what you are talking about." Evelyn was standing behind him, looking at Roman with a fixed gaze.

"I think you do. I think you do because you took it."

"Says who?"

"Well, Marie was suspicious. Perhaps me, you, and Evelyn can have a conversation about it right here."

"Listen, foreigner." Albert's voice was raised but still measured. "I suggest you stop harassing us and get on your way. As I said, I have nothing to tell you."

"Not so fast. You took my diploma. You didn't care about destroying a person's future. You are a thief." They were now standing just inches away from each other. Albert was much bigger than Roman but the size discrepancy made no difference at that point. Roman pushed him and Albert swung at Roman, hitting him in the eye. They were punching each other in the face, and Roman noticed with surprise that he did not feel the blows. Suddenly, Albert jumped back, waited momentarily, and then planted a crushing roundhouse kick to Roman's lower rib cage, right over the liver. Roman bent forward with pain, and at that point he realized he was dealing with a trained fighter. Albert grabbed him by the hair, pushed his head down and crashed a knee into his face with full force. Piercing pain exploded in Roman's nose, radiating all over his head. Blood flowed from his nostrils, quickly coloring his shirt and pants and the asphalt sidewalk.

With his fingers still pulling on Roman's hair, Albert threw him to the ground. Roman lay there for a few seconds before slowly pushing himself up.

Albert chuckled. "You don't look too well right now, foreigner. Next time pick your fights." He turned to Evelyn. "Let's go." She didn't make a sound, she was just staring at Roman, her lips showing a hint of a smile. They both started walking away.

After a few yards, Albert stopped and turned around. "By the way. Do you want to know how much I sold your diploma for? Nine thousand dollars. That's a pretty penny, don't you think? You took care of my financial troubles. And you still can't prove that I did it." He let out a short laugh, and they disappeared from sight.

ROMAN STOOD ON THE PARK PAVEMENT, shell shocked, motionless. The initially soft noise in his ears changed to intense hissing and he began having difficulty seeing. He felt nauseated and lightheaded and he knew that if he didn't quickly lie down on the ground, he was going to pass out. He managed to take a few steps toward the lawn, where he slumped on the grass and rolled over on his back. With the blood now starting to return to his head, the hissing and nausea began to subside, and his vision cleared. He broke out in a sweat, and it felt refreshing. Closing his eyes again, he stayed on the grass for a few minutes. When he sat up, he realized that twilight had set in.

He had to get back to the camp. His first thought was to take the subway or walk to the train station, but when he saw his bloodied clothes, and imagined what his face must look like, he rejected the idea. He was sure his appearance would cause revulsion in some and pity in others, but he was mainly concerned about attracting the attention of the police. He hobbled over to a group of oak trees, sat down, and leaned against a large trunk. His new plan was to wait until complete darkness and then venture to the train station, but he was weak and exhausted, and even though his nose and ribs were badly hurting, his eyes started to close.

He woke with pain and cold shivers. He glanced at his watch. It was past midnight which meant that the last train to Gerstand had already left the station. He might as well stay in the park. He was so drained that, despite his intense discomfort, he was able to fall back to a restless sleep.

When he fully roused, the sun was just coming out. Coils of milky haze were rising from the grass and from the surface of the pond that was covered in yellow leaves. The air was chilly. His whole body ached and he was shaking with cold. When he touched his nose, he screamed out in pain.

He looked around. Except for a young woman pushing a teal-colored stroller toward the oak grove, the park was empty. She was already passing by without having noticed him when he summoned his resolve. "Miss? Do you have a minute?" He spoke as softly as he could.

She turned, and when she caught sight of him, her symmetrical face twisted into a startled, terrified grimace, and she gripped the handle of the stroller and bolted.

"I mean no harm, Miss," he called out. "I really need your help."

With a safe distance between them, she slowed her pace and then stopped. He saw a blond baby sleeping in the carriage.

"What do you want?"

"I got in trouble last night. My clothes are all bloody, and I can't go out in public like this. Could you possibly get me a pair of pants and a shirt? I'll give you ten marks. That's all I have on me. I don't care how the clothes look, as long as they are relatively clean."

The woman opened her mouth in surprise.

"I know it's an unusual request. But do you think you could?"

She studied him carefully. Something must have convinced her that he did not have bad intentions because she smiled hesitantly, and then she relaxed into a quiet laugh.

"Yes, it's an odd request. I've never bought clothes for a bloodied man lying in the park. But there is a first time for everything. There happens to be a consignment store several blocks away. I'm not sure if they are already open, but I'll walk over there and see."

"I appreciate it very much. Also, if you could get a towel or a piece of cloth so that I can clean my face."

"That is not a problem." She took a few wipes out of a plastic box hidden in the pouch of the stroller, moved closer and handed them to him. "They work well for little Sebastian. I am sure they will work for you too." She reached out for the ten-mark bill. "Normally I would not accept this, but I lost my job a few weeks ago and things have gotten a little tight. So, I'll take it. We'll be back."

An hour passed, and Roman lost faith that she would return. *There goes the ten marks.* But in another five minutes there she was, crossing the street and walking back to the park. A paper bag was lying in the storage space of the stroller.

"Here you are." She gave him the bag. "I don't know if they'll fit, but at least they are clean." She looked at Roman's nose. "That must hurt," she said. "How many were they?"

"Just one. Embarrassing, I know. A big guy who knew how to fight. I don't want to bore you with the details."

"That's fine. What brought you to Ostbaum?"

"A need for a change in environment." He briefly told her his story. "How old is your son? I mean, I assume he is your son."

"Yes, he is my son. He is nine months old. A little bundle of joy, especially when he's asleep." She laughed. "Well, I better get going."

"You don't know how much I appreciate what you did for me. Thank you again. My name is Roman."

"I am Andrea. Are you going to be OK?"

"I hope so."

"Alright then. Take care of yourself." She pushed the stroller to the small sandy beach by the pond. Little Sebastian started wailing.

CHAPTER 7

THEY HAD THEIR FAVORITE HANGOUT, a small bar sitting at the end of a long narrow winding street high in the hills of Prague's Lesser Town, so high that, particularly on a foggy day, it seemed like the lane was opening straight into the airy infinite. They liked to take walks in the maize of cobble-stoned streets of The Old Town around the Tyn Cathedral, and further down, close to the river, in the clutters of small, dark alleys lined with derelict buildings where, at dusk, women in brown uniforms, carrying long wooden poles equipped with metal hooks at their ends, came to turn on the gas lamps.

"I've been thinking about you a lot lately," Eva said, a slender young woman with misty gray eyes and long wavy auburn hair, a doctor at the hospital, his partner in crime. In the time working together they had grown close. That night they were sitting in a small Old Town tea house, reclining on chenille throw pillows and sipping Indonesian black tea. Yes, one could find even an exotic brand of tea in that little oasis. "Is it love?" she asked.

Roman held her hand. What is love? Is it the painful vacuum that a person is drowning in when someone close to them has just departed, and the delight they are drenched in when that someone reappears? Is that love, or is it just a powerful flood of hormones and neurotransmitters and other molecules of magic that overwhelm the brain with ephemeral intoxication?

On a late summer afternoon after a long day at work they decided to trek back to town instead of riding the reeking bus. The trail they chose wound through dense woods where multiple shades of green were melding with slivers of the blue hue above. By the time they arrived in the city, the sun was setting and the clouds were hazy pink. "I am hot and thirsty. Let's have a beer," Roman proposed, and they walked into the nearest bar they saw, a hole in the wall right by the railway station.

"I would love to ride in a Porsche convertible in the Sahara Desert. My long hair blowing in the wind, the tires kicking up geysers of white sand against the big blue sky," Eva said after finishing her second mug of Pilsner. "I love wide-open endless spaces."

"How about going to Columbia and party with cocaine-snorting crazy young Americans at a seedy beachside motel. Or going down to Tierra del Fuego and hang out with the Patagonians. Things we'll never be able to do."

"After high school, I went hiking to the Romanian mountains with my paramour at the time. We got lost in the woods and lived on plants and frogs for a week until we ran into a group of fiddle-playing Mountain Gypsies who rescued us. True story." Eva fished out a pack of Virginia Slims from her purse. "A token of appreciation from a patient," she laughed as she took out a cigarette and lit up.

"I would like to go to Kazan," Roman said.

"To Kazan? The Russian city? What's in Kazan?"

"I don't know. I used to have a recurring dream as a kid. In it, I somehow ended up in Kazan, and all that was there were empty, abandoned brown buildings. Surprisingly, it made for an appealing impression. I have no idea why I had dreams about Kazan. Anyway, since then I've always wanted to visit."

"I thought you hated Russians."

"I don't hate Russians. I hate the Soviets."

"Okay. What else would you like to do?"

"I thought about roaming the hills up north on cold winter nights in a long white robe and snowshoes. The yeti has infiltrated Bohemia! Or walking up to people in the street sticking my fingers in their face and screaming at them *not schizophrenic!* or something of that sort. How about that?"

"Not bad." She chuckled. "The sirens are wailing. The closed unit is waiting."

THEY TOOK A TRAM TO ROMAN'S APARTMENT. There, Eva situated herself on the couch, resting her head and arms on the throw pillows. Roman put a couple of spoonfuls of ground coffee into a copper coffee pot, added cold water and a tiny amount of sugar, gently stirred the mixture, boiled it until a froth formed and poured it into small blue-patterned porcelain cups. He enjoyed the ritual of making Turkish coffee almost as much as he relished drinking it.

He put the cups on the low wooden table in front of the couch. Then he walked over to the record player and placed *Blonde on Blonde* on the turntable. He had bought the album at the street market of used records that was held once a month in one of the suburbs, the only place in town where music from the Free World could be had. He slowly lowered the arm so that the stylus settled gently on the revolving black surface. They both lit up a cigarette.

"A glass of wine?" Roman asked. "I have a big bottle of Federweisser in the refrigerator."

"A big bottle of Federweisser? You want to get me really drunk, don't you?"

"The coffee will mitigate the alcohol."

"That wine is so easy to drink because it's so sweet. I could tell you some embarrassing stories about drinking Federweisser," Eva laughed.

Roman took the bottle out of the fridge, opened it, and poured the cloudy white wine into small glasses. They both took a sip. The record was playing "Sad Eyed Lady of the Lowlands". They stopped talking and just listened to the beguiling slow rhythm and Dylan's eleven minutes of raw drawl. They lit another cigarette. Every time Dylan sings *lowlands* in the refrain, marveled Roman, he changes the cadence of the word but he manages to keep the rhythm of the song intact. Somewhere in the middle of the tune he draws out the *looowlands* to a ridiculous length yet the steady flow of the rhythm remains. Whenever Roman heard this part of the song he could not help but smile. Dylan was a magician.

They were just chilling, enjoying the moment. Roman put his arm around Eva's shoulders and gently pulled her closer. They started kissing. Dylan was singing "Leopard-skin Pill-box Hat." The wine bottle was almost empty. Eva extinguished the cigarette and slowly unbuttoned her black silk blouse.

"I WROTE A POEM THE OTHER DAY," she said later, sitting on the edge of the sofa. "Would you like to hear it?"

"Of course."

She recited the poem. It was not long, essentially a children's verse, about two crickets who could not find their way back home in the shrubs. They end up in space and, observing the Earth from above, chirp with admiration about its blue color, hoping that the obtuse humans would not blow it up.

"I love it. The essence of our times captured in just a few rhymes. You should send it to one of the youth journals. They are always on the lookout for new talents, at least that's what they advertise. Little chance of getting it published, though. Not ideologically correct." He laughed and glanced at his watch. "Darn, it's four in the morning. We'll have to leave for work in two hours."

A NOTICE CAME FROM THE CAMP ADMINISTRATION that Roman had to move out in a week. The camp was getting full, and those who did not apply for asylum in Germany were the first ones to have to leave .

"You are lucky," a city social worker told him in her downtown office.

"We own some apartments in town, and a few of them happen to be empty. We can put you up in one."

"Great! How are the apartments? Just wondering. Not that I have a choice."

"It depends. It won't be a four-star hotel. I can tell you that."

"One star?"

She gave him a contemptuous look, and he realized that she was probably thoroughly sick of refugees coming to her every day, demanding stuff, not speaking her language, smelling repulsively, scrounging off the system the best they could. His intent was not to scrounge. He wanted to get out of the country at the earliest, but telling her that would hardly make a difference. Still, he wouldn't have to be homeless in the streets, and he was grateful to her for that.

She wrote down the address on a sheet of paper, signed her name, and handed it to him. "The concierge lives on the second floor. His name is Carlos Seldano. Pick up the keys from him."

"Alright."

"Since you are not allowed to work in Germany, you'll receive one hundred and fifty marks each month for basic expenses."

"Thank you. I truly appreciate it."

She gave him another scornful glance, but this time the expression on her pale, dark-eyed, not unattractive face had an added trace of pity.

ROMAN FINALLY LOCATED THE BUILDING that matched the address. It was in a large apartment project on the north side of the city. A four-story gray structure, flanked by sidewalks with dried up urine and vomit from the night before. The front gate of the building was ajar. There was garbage on the staircase. He knocked on Carlos' door. There was no answer. He knocked again. A hoarse howl came from the inside: "Was [what]!"

"Schlüssel, bitte [the key, please]," Roman answered. In the time he'd been at the camp, he was, slowly but steadily, picking up German.

"Schlüssel? Was zum Teufel [what the hell]!" The door flew open and a short dark man with a black eye and a beer bottle in his hand appeared. He was wearing boxer shorts and a dirty white undershirt. He was very unsteady.

"Carlos? I am Roman Hollander. I was sent by Fräulein Rosenbach from the Sozialamt." He showed him the piece of paper. "Key to the apartment number 44, bitte."

"Mmmh..." Carlos growled and glared at him with his bloodshot eyes. "Zehn mark!"

"I don't have ten marks."

"Flüchtling?"

"Ja."

He waved his hand in disgust. "Aah, ficken flüchtlinge, ficken ausländer [fucking refugees, fucking foreigners]." He had a strong foreign accent. He turned, unlocked, with some difficulty, a key box mounted on the wall and started fumbling through the keys hanging on the hooks. Finally, he picked one and began walking back toward the door while holding on to the wall, but he suddenly lost balance and fell flat on his face with a big thud. The beer from the bottle he was still holding spilled all over the floor. He was motionless for a few seconds, then his whole body sprang up and down in a straight horizontal line like a plastic board and he screamed out so loudly one would have thought he had just taken a kick in the gonads. "Scheisse, ficken scheisse! Ficken flüchtlinge! Ficken ausländer!"

Roman could hear a door open inside the apartment, and a woman emerged in the hallway. She must have been in her fifties, hair dyed black, heavily layered pink and blue eye shadow, purple lipstick. She wore an above-the-knee nightgown revealing thin legs with wrinkled skin.

"Carlos, du scheisskerl [you motherfucker]!" she yelled, "stehst auf [get up]!" She shook him but he didn't move. He just groaned. "Fucking son of a bitch," she said in English. "I know he's faking, but he's not going to get up. Help me carry him, bitte." Roman grabbed the concierge under the shoulders, she held him by the ankles, and they dragged him into the bedroom, lifted him up and threw him on the unmade bed covered with empty beer bottles and torn up bags of potato chips and cigarette butts. Carlos let out a moan, then rolled over on his side looking quite comfortable, and immediately started snoring.

Roman went back to the hallway and picked up a key from the beer puddle. He hoped it was the right one.

"Moving in?" the woman asked.

"That's right. Is he like this all the time?"

"Most of the time. He drinks like a fucking Dane pretty much from Thursday to Sunday. Monday is a hangover day. Not a good day. Then he starts again on Tuesday and gradually picks up speed. So, Tuesday and Wednesday are the two days when you may catch him only partially drunk and still relatively coherent."

"I get the picture. Today is Thursday."

"We should get together once you settle in, young man." She lifted her nightgown a little higher, threw her head back and stuck out the tip of her tongue. "Twenty marks. Much better deal than downtown, trust me on that."

"Not a bad idea, Miss, but I don't have any money to spare right now."

"Yeah, money is hard to come by these days. Tell me about it." She laughed, a rough alcoholic laugh." Maybe later."

"Sure, we'll talk later." He grabbed his suitcase and lugged it up to the fourth floor.

THE KEY WORKED. The door opened into a studio apartment, completely empty save for a small electric stove in the corner next to the sink and a couple of wall-mounted cabinets above it. Thick dust wads covered the gray linoleum floor. There was a chink in one of the window panes, but at least it was not completely cracked. No window treatments, but that wasn't a concern, they could easily be made from wax paper. A single bare lightbulb attached to a wire hung from the ceiling.

He will sleep on the floor tonight, and, in the next few days, he will start scouring the streets for household articles that middle-class

Germans put in front of their apartment buildings and houses once they have worn out their welcome. He had noticed those items, those silent witnesses to the joy and suffering that transpires inside four walls, stacked in neat piles in the streets at certain times of the month, mostly in good condition, waiting to be appropriated by the poor.

He will need a mattress, a pillow, a few blankets and towels, a chair, a small table, basic kitchen ware, a broom, and a dust pan. Not much is required to sustain the fundamentals of daily living. He will make this place inhabitable eventually.

CHAPTER 8

DAYS WERE PASSING BY, getting shorter, colder, darker. No news on his asylum application. Grayness, stagnation. Roman was in a funk. Yes, the apartment was looking better. He had found a sofa bed, its orange corduroy upholstery worn out in places but in relatively good shape overall. A random good man from the street helped him haul it upstairs. Roman even procured a black and white TV, a large heavy box with only one channel coming in, but at least there was a human face on the screen speaking directly to him, or that is how it felt after weeks of barely saying a word to anyone.

Solitude alters reality. Solitude begets more solitude. Disengaged humans in the distance only deepen the loneliness. Turkish housewives chatting in the courtyard glowering at him suspiciously when he walked by. The woman in the apartment next to his, whom he never saw, singing, fiddling, yelling out of the window at her man to come back home and swearing when he did not comply. The couple in the apartment above him having loud sex and playing pinball.

Mad thoughts were getting hold of him, days and nights were fused into one painful coil. Restless sleep and torture to wake up. Any odd sound startled him, crowds of people made his pulse race. He was leaving the apartment less and less; a voluntary solitary confinement.

One late evening, he was coming home from the neighborhood Aldi store, an unavoidable trip, carrying plastic bags filled with groceries. The hallway and the staircase were black, either the electricity was out or all the lightbulbs died in unison. Just as his vision was beginning to adjust to the darkness, and he started scaling the stairs, a ghastly face with bulging bloodshot eyes and bared teeth suddenly popped up next to him, a flashlight under the chin. Roman jumped, stumbled on the steps and landed on his stomach, bags falling out of his hands, groceries rolling down the staircase. "Flüchtling!" Carlos screeched and aimed the light beam at him.

Roman pulled himself up and felt the stifled tension inside him suddenly release like a geyser. "You fucking drunk, I'll beat the shit out of you, fucking asshole!" He tried to grab Carlos but the janitor turned off the flashlight and instantly disappeared into the darkness. Roman sat down on the stairs. Less than a minute later the lights came back on, and he began to gather the groceries. He dragged himself the rest of the way upstairs, and, once inside the apartment, he bolted the door and put away the provisions. He took a can of beer out of the refrigerator and slowly lifted the tab, listening to the crackling noise produced by the scored part of the lid folding, and watching the off-white beer bubbles push up through the hole. This small ritual of opening a can of beer or soda, with its sound-and visual effects and gustatory anticipation had a soothing effect on him. He sat down on the couch.

He could have run into his singing neighbor on the dark staircase. He could have run into someone else. He could have run into no one, but he had to run into crazy Carlos. In a warped, uncanny way, the grotesque encounter, the twisted hollering face illuminated by a narrow beam of light surrounded by darkness, was the expression of the state he was in, of the loneliness screaming for help, of the painful existence wanting to burst out of the imprisoning isolation. This graphic, detached realization of his plight slowly induced, surprisingly to him, a tranquil, unencumbered state of mind. He walked to the kitchen area, turned on the burner, filled a third of the volume of a small pot with water and put it on the stove. It will be rice and beans for dinner tonight.

THE TOP OF THE SCRATCHED UP COFFEE TABLE in Roman's Prague apartment was covered with beer bottles, ashtrays full of cigarette butts, and news magazines. Roman sat down on the sofa, picked up one of the journals and started mindlessly turning the pages until the photograph of a painting caught his attention, a young woman with her eyes closed, long bluish hair covering the shoulders, the gentle outline of her naked arms and torso blending with the honey-colored background of the canvas. "His paintings reflect mature realism and are an indelible testament to a life of toil and bleakness in the Moravian Highlands during the interwar period," the caption below the picture read. "For his work, he was awarded one of the highest state distinctions, The Medal of Labor." *The absurdity of socialist journalism*, Roman sighed, closed the magazine and put it back on the table.

Eva had left an hour earlier, after a long difficult conversation. She cannot run away with him. She couldn't leave her parents behind. Can he? She is a patriot at heart. Life is good everywhere but it's the best at home, the adage goes. No matter what the circumstances? No matter that the princes of darkness will rule forever? Roman countered. No, this was something she just was not able to commit to. Did he realize the momentousness of this move? she asked. But he hadn't made a decision yet. And if he resolved to escape, he wanted her to join him.

For Roman, leaving the country was, at first, a recurrent but fleeting thought, a wish that with years gradually acquired a more concrete contour. It was increasingly difficult for him to accept the oppressive, omnipresent hegemony of the state. He could not abide with the mendacious media and with the fake, farcical elections in which every adult was forced to participate. He was fed up with the inability to travel to the west of the border without hindrance. He was incensed with the state-sponsored Jew-hatred.

The whole nation was indoctrinated in Marxism-Leninism. Students had to take state examinations in the risibly absurd, pseudo-science fields of Marxist philosophy, Marxist economy, scientific communism. Severe censorship and intimidation gutted the cultural scene. The demagogues clamored for the defeat of the West. The Soviets placed nuclear warheads in the countryside, with the servile blessing of the local puppet-politicians. Naturally, freedom of speech was non-existent, and those few who still thought that it was their moral duty to practice it, faced harassment, loss of job, or prison. Roman knew some of that from his own experience. And, because it was not possible for the regime to completely choke off travel abroad and to totally stifle the universal flow of information, he and many others also knew that a mere two hundred kilometers to the west was a system that allowed its citizens to live in dignity. The presence of that system, so near him, yet so far away, was not lost on Roman.

"YOU NEED SOME TIME ALONE," Eva said to him, a trace of annoyance in her voice, while she ran her long, pale fingers through her curls. "I'm on call tomorrow," she frowned. "It's going to be another fucking killer night. I can feel it my gut." She put on her coat and left, and Roman listened to the echoes of her high heels hitting the cold stone stairs, first clear and resonant and then gradually fading until there was silence, and he unwound their six months-long relationship in his mind like a slow film projection. He realized with shame and embarrassment that he was not even sure if he was honest with her and with himself when he asked her to come with him. He knew he loved her, but perhaps not enough, and he tried to console himself with the thought that she might feel the same about him. He rose from the sofa and started pitching the beer bottles in the trash can one by one. After he threw in the first bottle, each subsequent one made a loud clink when it landed in the bin.

It was very late, and he was getting sleepy. *Sleep is deliverance*, he thought. He turned off the lights and lay down fully dressed on the creaking couch.

*   *   *

A NOTIFICATION FROM THE POST OFFICE arrived in the mail. It was bitingly cold outside that day, minus twenty. He put on several layers of shirts and sweaters and forced the light quilted coat from the thrift store over all that bulk, and he trudged to the post office. A dark-haired lady behind the counter took the slip and, after an attempt at conversation in German, asked if he was Czech.

"How did you know?"

"Just the way you sound. I am Czech. You have a certified letter from Munich waiting for you here. Did you just recently come to Ostbaum?"

"A few months ago."

"With family?"

"Alone."

"That's how I came sixteen years ago."

Roman leaned on the counter. "Right after the Russians rode in?"

"Yes. My friend was leaving with her whole family in their car so I bummed a ride with them. I ended up in Gerstand and I just stayed in the area."

"I was recently kicked out of Gerstand. Not the funnest place to be. How was it in sixty-eight?"

She handed his mail over. "Jam-packed. We had to sleep on mattresses on the floor. The camp management couldn't keep up with the demand for food. But the atmosphere was kind of heady. Most of us there were Czechs and Slovaks. We were upset about our situation, and enraged about the invasion, but we were also looking forward to a new beginning in the West. After some time, reality set in. That it's not going to be a cakewalk. Anyway, do you know anybody here? Have you made any friends yet?"

"Not really. It would be nice to meet some people." His brain was shouting, *yes, yes, I want to meet people, I have to meet people, I am going crazy!* But he maintained his composure.

"We have a small group of ten, fifteen people who occasionally get together. Mostly Czech immigrants from sixty-eight and after, so a middle aged and younger crowd." She pulled out a small calendar from her purse. "In fact, we have a party planned in a week. Very informal. Would you like to join us?"

"I'd be delighted."

"Good. Here is the address. Come around six o'clock. My name is Milena."

"Great talking with you, Milena. Thank you for the invitation. See you then."

Outside the building, he opened the letter. It contained the date of his interview at the American Consulate in Frankfurt, the outcome of which would determine if he would be granted asylum in the States. The interview was scheduled to take place in three months. Things were finally moving forward. Notwithstanding the cloud of the diploma theft looming over him, he was, to his own surprise, sanguine about the future.

WHEN HE ARRIVED at the address Milena had given him, about a dozen people were already sitting on a long gray sofa and in black vinyl chairs arranged around a large heavy-appearing rectangular wooden table. The room was dimly lit and well heated, a welcome change after coming from the bitter cold outside.

Milena waved from the sofa. "This is Roman. A recent arrival," she said.

"Hi Roman," multiple voices answered.

He glanced around and sat down on the couch next to Milena.

"Are you staying in Gerstand?" a bearded man in blue denim overalls, appearing to be in his early thirties, asked him. He was balding but his remaining straight blond hair was shoulder length.

"I was. Now I'm in an apartment."

"Same here," a young woman sitting next to the bearded man said. "We couldn't wait to get out of there. Our pad is in the attic, and the ceilings are so low that we have to walk bent over, but we learned to live with it."

"Do you both work?"

"Franta hauls milk, and I am a student at the business school."

"You haul milk? My great-grandfather was a milkman. Those were different times then."

"Yeah, I work for the Gelhausen dairy. It's at the outskirts of town. I get up at two thirty in the morning, I drive to the surrounding milk farms in the country, pump the milk, and then I unload it at the dairy. The tank can hold twenty tons of milk."

"How long does that all take?"

"Fourteen-hour days, man. Cows are milked twice a day, seven days a week so it is pretty much the whole week with a day off here and there."

"That's rough. I hope at least the paycheck is decent."

"The money's not bad. Jiřina is almost done with school, about half a year left. Then I expect a pay back." He smiled at his lady.

"We'll see." Jiřina let out a raspy laugh. She was a shapely woman with small upward slanting blue eyes. "Maybe I'll give you a little break."

"I've worked for them for almost a year, so I should be getting a week of vacation pretty soon," said Franta. "Those trucks, man, they don't maintain them very well. A few months ago, one of the wheels fell off. I was going slowly up a hill when it happened. Luckily, the truck didn't turn over or slide or whatever. I got out and I started chasing the wheel. Those wheels are big fucking monsters. The cars on the road were trying to dodge the wheel, and I was dodging the cars. The wheel was gradually packing speed, and, in the end, it was literally flying down the hill, and I was flying right behind it, but I couldn't keep up." Franta stubbed out his cigarette. "Eventually, the wheel rolled off the road into the ditch. Then I had to push it all the way back up. Since that happened I've been having tightness in my chest and difficulty breathing during my runs. I smoke a lot, so I thought it was bronchitis, but my doctor told me it could be panic attacks. I don't know. I'm thinking about quitting and buying a food stand to be my own boss. But that can be a lot of pressure too, and the income is unpredictable, so I guess I'll just have to stick it out for a while longer, in spite of the panic attacks."

Franta surveyed the room. "Anyone else here on a budget?"

Most people raised their hands.

"It's good to know the priest is on a budget too," Franta said laughing. That was when Roman noticed that one of the guests wore a black suit and white collar. The man sat in a chair next to the far end of the couch. He must have been in his fifties, with healthy rosy cheeks and silver hair. He smiled shyly.

"So. For those of you on a budget, I have a good suggestion for a meal. Dandelion soup," continued Franta. "It's actually an old French recipe. Last spring, I went to the city park and collected dandelions. The good citizens of Ostbaum gave me stares, but I didn't let it bother me. You have to pick the dandelions early, before they bloom, then they taste sweet. The soup was alright, wasn't it, Jiřina?" he turned to his girlfriend.

"Well, I don't know. You are the breadwinner for now so I have to conform to your choice of meals," Jiřina said somewhat dismissively. The sound of her voice was surprisingly gruff.

CANS OF COLD BEER, several bottles of wine, and two pitchers filled with water appeared on the table, and the conversation was getting louder.

"Who brought the stuff today?" the priest asked.

"I've got it," said a lanky young man sitting in a chair across the table from Roman. "Should be good shit this time. Not like the last batch. At least that's what the dealer told me. He brought it from the Caribbean."

Milena turned to Roman: "Have you ever smoked pot?"

"I'm embarrassed to say. But no, I haven't."

"Don't be embarrassed. I'll walk you through it," she smiled.

The young man skillfully rolled four joints and distributed them among the party attendees. "There's more," he laughed and lifted a ziploc bag that still contained a considerable amount of greenish particles.

"Each doobie will be shared between several people," Milena explained. She lit her joint, inhaled deeply, held her breath, let out the smoke slowly, and passed it to Roman.

"See, no biggie," Milena reassured him. "Your throat will be dry so have a sip of water after each toke. And just one at a time, then give it to the next person."

Roman inhaled and held his breath. There was a scratchy feeling in his throat, and he had to drink nearly a full glass of water to extinguish the spasmodic coughing spell that followed. This unpleasantness diminished with each ensuing inhalation, and he was getting more comfortable.

People around him were smiling. Warmth and excitability settled in his lap. He pressed his leg against Milena's, and she did not pull away. The tape was playing "Stumblin' In," the Chris Norman - Suzi Quatro duet, the rhythm was much crisper than what he remembered it to be, the guitar edgier; he could identify new tones and harmonies that he had not been able to discern before. Was this the true sound of the song, the true baseline? Should people always be high when they listen to music?

The voices around Roman started to fuse together, creating a drawn-out, loud, jumbled sound. He was still relaxed, but his senses were high-strung. Then, a diffuse heaviness found room insidiously in his throat. He lay down on the couch, closed his eyes and stretched his neck on a pillow to ease the discomfort, but the scattered pressure congealed into a large, stifling lump, and his breathing became labored. He was hungry for air.

His heart was pounding, and the tips of his fingers were so cold they ached. Suddenly he became convinced that he would not make it out of the room alive, that he would choke to death. He thought about asking Milena to take him to the emergency room, but he was sure she would refuse. He was certain she would rather let him die than risk getting in trouble. *This may be the end.*

Milena must have noticed something was not right because he heard her ask if he was okay. He felt her hand on his chest.

"Your heart is about to burst through your rib cage!"

"No, I'm not OK. I am scared shitless," Roman groaned.

"Panic attack," Franta said, nodding his head gravely.

"Listen to me." Milena squeezed Roman's hand. "Take long, deep breaths. Do it with me. One...two...three..."

It worked. After about ten deep breaths, the choking sensation and the fear started to subside. It felt like salvation, like coming out of the death's grip. His pulse slowed, and his hands were turning warm.

He sat up. "That was very scary. It was like I was knocking on heaven's door."

"I am sorry," Milena said. "This was supposed to be fun."

"You had a panic attack from the marijuana," the priest said, then he turned to the fellow who'd brought the cannabis. "Jarda, what strain is this?"

"It's mainly sativa."

"Cannabis comes in two strains, sativa and indica, and their properties differ somewhat," the priest explained pedantically to Roman. "Some flowers contain predominantly sativa, some indica, and some are hybrids. If you smoke pot again, you should probably stay away from sativas. And smoke less of it next time." With this, the priest took a toke so substantial that the tip of the joint lit up with a small flame, and he let out a thick cloud of smoke.

"Thank you, Father," Roman said, "you sure know a lot about weed."

HE WAS RECLINING ON THE COUCH, a large pillow under his head, oblivious to his surroundings, appreciating his regained ability to breathe effortlessly. Small red and blue dots were pleasantly flickering in slow motion in front of his closed eyes, and he felt happy and weightless. He gradually drifted into a soft, undulating slumber. He dreamed about giggling children playing with enormous fluffy rabbits on a pink meadow. It was enjoyable. Nothing mattered.

CHAPTER 9

ROMAN WAS JUST ABOUT TO ENTER THE HOSPITAL lobby when a silver Mercedes sedan with diplomatic license plates pulled up quietly. A middle-aged woman with carefully arranged dark-brown hair, wearing a black rain coat and high heels, climbed out of the front passenger seat and walked up to him.

"Could you direct me to Dr. Stránský's office?" she asked in English.

"That's in another building. But he's probably here in the conference room getting ready for rounds. I can let him know you are looking for him. Follow me. It stinks inside, be prepared."

Predictably, her head jerked backward and she gagged when he opened the door. "Oh, that hit me like a flying dirty rag," she said in a muffled voice after she'd pulled a handkerchief from her purse and pressed it against her face. "That is something. That's your greeting every morning?"

"Yes. Like an invisible guard lurking behind the entrance that punches you in the nose as the penalty for crossing the threshold— sorry, you asked for it."

"Horrific."

"It is. But what we lack in air freshness, we make up with peerless care."

*   *   *

"You had an unusual visitor this morning, Milan," he told deputy chief Stránský later in the day. They were walking on a path that connected the main hospital building with a smaller structure where Stránský's office was. Roman had a patient in the smaller building that he needed to check on.

"Oh yeah. I used to have quite a few foreign diplomats and their families as patients at Pinnacle Health. Most of them have left for their home countries, but those who replaced them still somehow find out about me. Word of mouth, I guess. Some of them follow me here."

"How do they cope with the smell?"

"They learn to accept it. I think they probably like me because I believe in a holistic approach. I don't just look at a symptom. I look at the whole person. I talk to them, not at them. I examine them. I listen to them. That goes a long way to creating a good relationship."

"Talking and listening is nice if you have the luxury to do it. After I'm finished with the morning injections and with chart reviews, I barely have time to check these poor people's pulse, and I have to move on to the next person. At least I feel their pulse. The window into health and disease, as Svoboda likes to say."

"Yes, I know. Wait a few more years for some level of seniority. But back to the visitor. She is the wife of the Belgian ambassador. Funny lady."

"I noticed. We had a good conversation. So, you are getting an occasional vicarious contact with the outside world. That's good."

"It's good, and it's not. It makes you wish for what you can't have. And that can get you in trouble. Trust me, I know. But it does keep you thinking."

Roman finished dinner in his Ostbaum apartment; beef with dumplings and gravy. It was tasty. Satisfied with his self-learned, and improving, culinary abilities, he turned on the news and lay down on the couch, but two loud knocks on the door interrupted his evening siesta. Roman was not expecting anyone, and the door did not have a peep hole. "Who is it?" he called out.

"I am a friend," a deep male voice responded in what sounded like an American accent.

"Whose friend? I am sorry. I am not expecting anyone. Just leave."

"You are Roman Hollander, right?"

Roman did not answer.

"Do you remember Alfred Guntherschön?"

"No."

"The undercover cop who interviewed you at the camp. He told me about you."

Now Roman remembered. He was the fellow who attempted to convince him to become a spy.

"I am with the CIA," the man said in a low voice, almost whispering.

"You are? How do I know you are not a Czech or a Russian agent?"

"If you open the door, I will show you my ID."

"I am asking you to leave."

"Listen Roman. I suggest you open the door and let me talk to you. I know you have an interview scheduled in Frankfurt. I know you want to get to the United States. We have ways to influence that."

He still could be a communist spy. But then again, why would a communist spy waste his energy on an insignificant defector like himself. Roman opened the door. The man standing in the hallway was middle-aged, of medium height, with rounded shoulders and a thick, graying moustache. He was wearing a beige raincoat. He immediately stuck an identification badge in front of Roman, but all he was able to discern was the name on it: Stanley Goldfarb.

"I am Stanley. Are you going to let me in? Or we could go to a bar. Whatever you'd like."

Roman stood in the doorway, thinking about the man's question. If he had nefarious intentions, he would be capable of hurting him both in private and in public, but being in public felt safer. "Let's go to a bar."

There was a below-the-street-level bar a block away from the apartment building. It was almost empty, and they sat down at a small table in the far corner of the room. "Order whatever you'd like. Uncle Sam is paying."

"Uncle Sam?"

"Yes, Uncle Sam. That's what we call our government. The American government."

"I will not cost Uncle Sam much. I'll just have a glass of beer."

The waiter came to the table and Goldfarb ordered a pint of Andechser Hell for both of them. He glanced at Roman, then he turned his attention to a large photograph that hung on the wall, showing a group of beaming young women in dirndls, standing on an alpine meadow, each holding a humongous beer mug. "Fräulein," he chuckled. Then he looked at Roman again. "Alfred spoke to me. Obviously, we cooperate closely with German intelligence agencies. He described you as a smart, educated young man who could help us. A brave man who does not get easily intimidated by the comrades. He said you declined his offer to work with us. I simply came to ask you to reconsider."

"As I told Guntherschön, I don't think I would be a good spy."

"What makes you believe that?"

"I am not a particularly adventurous type. Continuing my career in medicine is a much better fit for me."

Goldfarb laughed. "You are underestimating yourself. The fact that you left your country the way you did already makes you adventurous. The fact that you were in the State Security's crosshairs proves that you are adventurous. You don't have to be a James Bond. Look at me, I'm not one. Roman, there is an existential struggle between the Free World and communism, the force of evil. I don't have to say that to you, do I?"

Goldfarb paused and stared intently at Roman. "Tell me," he resumed, "why did you leave Czechoslovakia? I know, it's a rhetorical question. But if you answer it out loud, I think you'll better understand why we are asking for your assistance and why you should help us, and help yourself."

Roman took several moments to scrutinize the American. He saw a sincere face, a tired face at the end of a long work day. "I left to be free," he said.

"See, as simple as that. But freedom has a price. It's your obligation to help us. Your moral obligation. And you may need our help too. I know about your little mishap."

"What are you talking about?"

"Your stolen diploma."

"What? How on earth would you know about that?" Roman almost yelled.

Stanley put his hand on Roman's arm. "Calm down. We just know about it. We know about a lot of stuff. I do want you to realize you may need more assistance than you think."

"Are you blackmailing me?" Roman pulled away. "America is a free country. I will decide about my fate and my future."

"Yes, it is a free country. But you are not yet in it." Goldfarb wiped the beer foam off his moustache. "You are still sitting here in Bavaria, somewhere where you don't want to be. For a Jew, the history here is loaded with some nasty shit. I understand that. I'm a Jew, too."

"I thought so, based on your name, if that's your real name. So why don't you let your Jewish brother live in peace?"

"It's my job not to leave people in peace. Listen, I need to get going." Goldfarb stood up and handed Roman a business card. "Call me if you change your mind. I am sure we'll be in touch."

Roman walked slowly back to his apartment. Either Goldfarb was bluffing or the CIA intended to exert power over him. Did the avuncular Stanley simply know about the diploma's disappearance, or was the CIA involved in the theft? Was Albert on the agency's payroll? Was Marie and her whole family? But then again, why spend so much effort on an insignificant man like himself? On the other hand, if they needed people like him, why not? He had an uneasy feeling he was being ensnared.

*　　*　　*

His path, already gnarled, just grew more complicated. But life's vicissitudes were unavoidable, he thought in an attempt to assuage his frustration and self-pity. His mind wandered to his old friend Adam Nedoma and the disaster that had befallen him in a not-so-distant past. He and Adam went back a long way. They had first bonded in high school owing to guitar strumming and long hair and the music of The Beatles. During summer vacations, they hitchhiked and trekked together across the country, and in the winter, if there was snow in Prague, they would put on lace-up rubber ski boots and take their wooden skis with Kandahar cable bindings for some shredding in the hills on the outskirts of town. After high school, Adam went to college to study photography.

Spending time with Adam had never been dull. Roman remembered with particular fondness their summer hiking trip to Slovakia during which they crossed perilous mountain passes in hail storms, skied with borrowed equipment on patches of old snow right under an alpine summit, ate the delectably greasy potato dumplings with cheese in mountainside chalets, making acquaintance with the hill-folk. On a cold early morning they ran into a black bear feasting on raspberries in a thicket by a glacial lake. When the bear took notice of them it flattened its ears, huffed, and pounded its paws on the ground. "Peace, boss," Adam spoke quietly. "Raspberries taste much better than we do." They slowly backed away and came through unscathed.

One episode from this trip made Roman laugh whenever he recalled it; they were planning to traverse a mountain creek that they expected, based on word given to them, to be shallow and slow-flowing. However, with a heavy downpour earlier in the day, the peaceful brook transformed itself into a fast-moving, churning water mass.

"We can't cross it," Roman declared when they arrived at the creek. He dropped his backpack on the bank in a sign of resignation.

"Oh, come on," Adam said as he stepped into the current. A few seconds later, he slipped on the smooth wet rocks, fell backward, and was rapidly carried downstream, rolling and spinning and intermittently submerging. Running through the wooded area alongside the creek to catch up with him, Roman lifted two strong sticks from the ground, got ahead of Adam and, balancing himself with the sticks, waded into the water. When Adam came close, screaming and sputtering, Roman reached out with one of the sticks, and Adam was able to get a hold of it and wedge it between two rocks and pull himself up. "That was fun," Adam guffawed.

"Yeah, you could have fun drowning," Roman said as they were carefully treading toward the shore.

One time in Prague, after leaving a bar, Adam climbed up the wall of a building, holding on to the lightning rod wire, he reached at least twenty feet above ground before realizing that it would be wiser to descend. Roman, drunk himself, was standing on the concrete sidewalk ready to catch him, or so he thought, if Adam came gliding down.

Once at a house party, after chugging five quarts of beer and swallowing ten aspirin tablets, Adam decided to jump out a third-floor window. "Goodbye, boys," he uttered serenely, straddling the windowsill. Roman and two other fellows pulled him back inside before he could leap into the air.

A couple of weeks after Adam's near self-defenestration, on a sunny summer day, he and Roman were ambling through downtown streets of Prague without a particular aim, and they sat down to relax on a bench in a circular plaza that provided an exquisite view of the glistening river. There was a fountain in the middle of the circle and a young woman, barefoot, in a tank top and shorts, was running back and forth under the fountain. The water, golden-colored by the sun rays, was streaming through her long, flowing hair, and her fast-moving feet kicked up crystal-like cascades jetting along the back of her tanned, sculpted legs. Adam was fascinated by the sight. He pulled the camera out of his bag, attached to it a long lens and started taking multiple shots in rapid succession. "Fantastic," he shouted when he was finished. "If the pics come out right, I'll send them to a photography magazine.

I have to talk to her though to make sure she'd be in agreement."

"So?" Roman asked when Adam came back.

"She was fine with it." Adam smiled. "And we'll be going on a date."

"You're a babe magnet, dude," Roman laughed.

"Yeah," concurred Adam and proceeded to detach the lens from the camera.

Roman took advantage of a brief pause in the conversation. "Listen Adam, this is not easy to bring up," he began, "especially since I, too, enjoy alcohol. But I am still able to stop before hurting myself or killing myself. I think you are past that point. I think you need to start keeping it in check."

"Don't preach Roman. I hate preachers. Are you suggesting I have an alcohol problem?"

"No, I'm making no conclusions of any kind. I am just reacting to what I see, out of concern for you."

"I think I can take care of myself." Adam frowned. "Let's go. I need to get home to develop these photos."

They took off walking to the subway station. Neither of them was saying much. "Your train is coming," Roman told him on the crowded platform. "We'll be in touch soon, right?"

AND IT SO HAPPENED, a few months later, that on a very early morning after an all-night bar-hopping session with random friends, Adam was walking home and tripped over the tram tracks and fell just when a tram was fast approaching, one of the rare trams in the city that provided a twenty-four-hour service. Adam was trying to get out of the way, but his brain was floating high on alcoholic vapors, so he was not able to, and the conductor was frantically ringing the bell and trying to stop the metal behemoth he thought he had under control, but he was not able to, and when the sharp wheels of the tram rolled through, Adam's body was outside the tracks and his legs were inside, both cut off symmetrically at mid-thigh level, and Adam was rapidly running out of blood and out of life.

An ambulance arrived and the paramedic and the driver placed tourniquets around his leg stumps as tightly as they could. They bent the vestiges of his thighs at the hips and secured them against his abdomen. They stacked layers of bandages and gauze on the bleeding wounds, and they connected a bag of fluids to a vein in his arm, rolling the flow control clamp wide open. "I don't think he'll make it," the paramedic said to the driver after they loaded him into the van, and the driver nodded and turned on the siren and pushed the gas pedal down to the floor.

SEVERAL DAYS BEFORE HIS ULTIMATE DEPARTURE, Roman went to see Adam at the hospital where he was languishing in a small dark stuffy room, its walls painted grass-green. Green is the color of freshness and rebirth, but in these environs, it was the color of infectious diarrhea, of blemished skin, of soiled sheets, of repulsive food. Adam was waiting for prosthetic legs to arrive. His pale, sullen face brightened when he saw Roman open the door. "Did you bring a hip flask of rum? Or at least a bottle of beer? Just kidding."

"I brought you some photography journals and a couple of books. And I brought kolaches."

"You brought kolaches? I love you. How many?"

"Ten."

Adam opened the paper bag with the pastries, deeply smelled the contents, then took out a poppy seed kolache and devoured it in seconds. "That was a sublime experience. Thank you. The chow here is horrid. They will murder me with their chow."

Roman smiled. "Other than that, how are you doing?"

"Down. Depressed. What can I tell you? I think I'd rather be dead. That damned tram should have killed me."

"You'll get your prosthetic legs, and you'll be back to walking."

"Some life that will be. Full of success, and a bunch of women on each arm. Speaking of women, have you seen Lenka lately?"

Roman shook his head.

"Would you get in touch with her and ask her to stop by? She used to profess her love to me on a daily basis before my accident, but she hasn't come to see me here at all."

"I don't know if you can blame her. She was really into you all the while you were shtupping multiple other women. So, what did you expect?"

"Payback time, huh? Still, ask her to come by."

Roman chose not to react to Adam's request. He changed the subject instead. "Just so you know. Things are getting crazy at work. They are putting us on call several times a week. I may not be able to visit you for a while."

Adam's smile faded and his jaw dropped slightly, but he didn't say anything. Noticing his friend's disappointed look, Roman was embarrassed. Was he leaving Adam in the lurch? Suddenly feeling awkward, he put his hand on Adam's forearm. "Best of luck with rehab if I don't see you before you get your new legs. Hang in there, buddy. Don't be surprised if it gets worse before it gets better, but it will get better eventually." Roman gave him a big hug.

CHAPTER 10

THE YOUNG BRUNETTE IN BLUE JEANS and a red spring jacket who was walking on the other side of the street looked familiar. It was a surprisingly warm March day, and after months of bitter cold temperatures and dark days, people acted giddy, drunk with the sun.

"Andrea," he shouted as he was crossing the street.

She stopped and looked at Roman. So it was her. "Do I know you?" she asked, taking a deep draw from her cigarette.

"I am Roman. Remember? Last fall? The park. The bloody face. The clothes from the consignment store?"

"Oh yeah. I remember now. How could I not? I would not recognize you, though." She laughed. "You look much better. How have you been?"

"Pretty well. I don't want to hold you up. Can I walk with you a little bit?"

She hesitated briefly. "That's fine. I have some errands to do. I just dropped my son at my girlfriend's house for the night. We are both single moms, and we occasionally watch each other's kids to get a break."

AS THEY AMBLED, they talked about everything. East and West, German beer, Ostbaum, Roman's big leap westward, growing up. Andrea was from a small town in Hesse. "I was very bored when I lived there. There wasn't much to do." She chuckled. "Except drugs, and I did plenty of those. Well-behaved kids were ordered by their parents to stay away from me to avoid getting into trouble. I had only a few friends, all dopeheads like me."

Andrea's home situation was part of the problem. Her father was a truck driver, bringing Mom gifts of rashes and discharges from the road. Mom was a constant nervous wreck. They divorced when Andrea was twelve. By the time she was seventeen, she somehow managed to clean up. She finished secondary school and then enrolled in college in Ostbaum. Mom committed suicide while Andrea was in college, but, despite that calamity, she was still able to complete school and get a degree in art. Sebastian was born during her time in college; his dad did not stay around, but at least he was paying child support.

THEY WERE STROLLING through an area of the city Roman had never been to, a residential neighborhood with tree-lined streets and modest apartment buildings. "After college, I found a job with a small publishing company," continued Andrea. "I loved the work. But after a year, they decided to downsize, and I was the first one to be let go. Then I worked as a waitress, a secretary, a tattooist. In the end, I just got tired of job-hopping and I chose to take a few months' break."

"How do you manage?"

"You mean financially? We have a cushy social support system, almost too cushy. I know I need to start searching again, but it's easy to get lazy." She stopped in front of a pink-colored building. "This is where I live." The facade was cracking and peeling off, but the setting sun rays enveloped the damaged walls in an elegant purple hue, and for a moment, Roman imagined that he was looking at a long-abandoned derelict grand palace somewhere in Italy or Greece.

He turned to Andrea. "I had a great time. May I see you again?"

"Why don't you come up for a few minutes."

They climbed up to her fifth-floor apartment and sat down in the kitchen. It was rather small, with a beige cloth-covered rectangular table in the middle of the floor. Andrea took a bag of tobacco and a box of papers out of a wall-mounted particle board cabinet, and she rolled two cigarettes in a rolling machine. "Would you like a beer? I hope I still have some." She opened a tiny refrigerator. "Last two bottles."

WHEN ROMAN WOKE NEXT MORNING, Andrea was lying next to him, her cheeks flushed, gazing at him with her large amber eyes. "I typically don't sleep with someone I barely know," she said, "but involuntary celibacy was getting difficult to handle. I haven't had sex in four months, if you can believe it."

Roman let out a hearty laugh. "Even longer for me. It was a wonderful night." He put the palm of his hand softly on her nape.

She looked at her watch. "We have to get up. I need to go to town to pick up Sebastian."

They got out of bed and quickly dressed. Before she left, Andrea took him to the basement and wheeled a bicycle, one of several, from her storage space. "It's old, and it may need some fixing but it's generally usable. Would you like to take it? It's a convenient way to move from place to place, especially if you want to save a few pfennigs."

Five minutes later, Roman was on his way to the apartment on his newly acquired fixed-gear steel horse. He used to bike quite a bit back in Bohemia, and it felt good to be pedaling again.

ROMAN BOARDED THE TRAIN to Frankfurt. It was seven in the morning, and the interview was scheduled for noon. The ride would take around three hours, but he wanted to have enough temporal reserve for unforeseen circumstances and for gathering his thoughts. The time of judgement was approaching.

It seemed like only yesterday when chief Svoboda had asked him to come to his office for a private conversation. "So going on vacation to Paris. Not bad, Roman. You'll be back, I assume?" It appeared Svoboda was getting right down to business.

"Yes, I will return, of course. No intention to stay outside."

"You know," the chief said, looking beyond Roman wistfully into the distance. "My sister defected in sixty-eight. She settled in England, and I went to visit her about ten years ago. They let me out to see her. She introduced me to the director of one of the hospitals in the city where she lived. The director liked me. He said he would give me a job if I wanted to stay. I thought about it but in the end, I decided against it."

"Why did you? Just curious."

"Multiple reasons. A big fish in a small pond, versus a small fish in a big pond. Family. Language. Ability to make new friends in a foreign country. Ability to ever feel at home in a strange land. Being looked on as less worthy because I am from somewhere else, and being queried about where I came from every time I open my mouth. That alone would assure that I would feel forever different. See, my sister told me all about that. She told me she acquiesced to the status of the odd person out. I don't think that I would have been able to accept that. Deep down, humans are still tribal in nature, and everyone has a need to feel allegiance to a tribe. I don't think I would be allowed by the outside world there to have that allegiance. But maybe," he shrugged and raised his eyebrows, "maybe I just wasn't confident enough. Maybe I chickened out. I am not sure. The immediate attraction was intense. The life they have in the West is unbelievable. I thought about all the aspects. I lined up the positives and the negatives on a sheet of paper and assigned points to each and compared the scores. I returned, as you can see."

He paused and stared at Roman with a concerned gaze. "You strike me as a sensitive guy. Like me."

Like him? That quarter of an ounce of sensitivity, if it was there at all, must have been assiduously camouflaged in the years Roman had known him. Was he now attempting to create a bond?

"Emigration can be hard," Svoboda continued. "Especially for certain people. I've heard of quite a few folks who would gladly reverse their decision to stay out if they could. Come back home. Keep building your career here."

Roman listened to him carefully. He was not certain what the purpose of Svoboda's exhortation was, but he presumed that the chief was concerned about how the defection of a subordinate would reflect on him. Roman knew that, notwithstanding his resolute comportment in his fiefdom, Svoboda desperately desired to remain on safe terms with the authorities. He did not want to forfeit the golden goose.

At the same time, someone less skeptical than Roman may have felt that the man was speaking from the heart.

THE AMERICAN CONSULATE was about thirty minutes from the train station on foot. He sat down in the waiting room. There were a few other people there, mostly couples, some in chairs, some restlessly pacing. Two American women, with ID badges clipped to the collars of their blouses, were walking across the hallway, and a little girl in a white ruffled dress pursued them from behind, imitating their accents, sounding like having a hot potato rolling around in her mouth. After about an hour, a striking young woman with a dark complexion and long, straight black hair entered the waiting area from a side door and called his name.

"I am Alexandra. I will be the interpreter during the interview," she said in Czech. They shook hands. "Are you nervous?"

"A little bit." Then he had to add: "Your Czech is perfect, but I can detect a lilt."

"Yes. I am Bulgarian."

"How did you learn Czech?"

"I spent some time in Czechoslovakia in my earlier years."

"Under what circumstances?"

"I am afraid I don't have enough time to explain," she said. His imagination took over. *A communist spy? A femme fatale who uses her looks and charm to infiltrate Western governments?*

"Let's go inside. They are waiting," she nudged him.

THE CONSULAR OFFICER was the opposite of the interpreter. Short and stocky, with a dour countenance, her tawny hair wrapped in a severe bun crowning the top of her head, she nodded without looking him in the eyes, swore him in, and pointed to a chair across the desk. They all took a seat. She opened a dossier bearing his name and turned several pages, then she closed it. "Why are you asking for asylum in the United States?"

"I want to live in freedom."

"How did the lack of freedom affect you directly?"

How did it? The consular officer was now staring at him, with a pen in her hand and a writing pad in front of her, ready to take notes. The interpreter was also looking at Roman, with a smile that he felt was supportive.

Roman still had a vivid recollection of an encounter he would now relate to his questioner. One week after the party to which he brought the samizdats was interrupted by the State Security, he was the involuntary guest in a bare-bones, white-walled room at The Tiled Cage. "Who gave you the samizdats?" asked the pink-faced State Security officer called Nesvadba, his straight black hair swept across the forehead in one greasy layer. The plastic rocking chair he sat in produced an irritating high-pitched squeak each time he leaned backward, leaving Roman wondering if the noise was an intended sensory component of the interrogation.

"What are you talking about?"

"Don't fuck with me. You got rid of them at the party. You flushed them down the toilet. We have evidence. Who gave them to you?"

Roman was convinced that it was a ruse. "I had no samizdats in my possession at the party."

The cop rummaged through his pockets. "Shit, where is my lighter," he mumbled. "I must have left it on the shelf."

He rose from behind his empty desk and headed toward a wall shelf by the window. As he passed by Roman, he staggered and bumped into his wobbly chair, making it tip over, and Roman fell heavily to the floor. *This was intentional.*

"Sorry, punk." Nesvadba laughed, grabbed his lighter, and ignited a Laika. "So, who gave you the samizdats?"

Roman pulled himself up. "No one."

"Sit back down, sport, don't be scared to sit down. We'll be contacting the dean to have you expelled from the med school."

Was he still bluffing? Perhaps. Perhaps not. Roman didn't respond, but, internally, panic set in.

"Unless," Nesvadba said slowly, raising his eyebrows and lifting up his index finger, "unless you decide to lend us a hand. We need informants. We *always* need informants. You have friends among the dissidents. You know some of those deluded bourgeois writers and poets, those purveyors of degenerate art. Yeah, you could help us quite a bit. What do you say?"

Having heard his acquaintances give accounts of their experiences with the State Security, Roman was not surprised that it came to this. He knew that the demand to collaborate was almost always coupled with a threat of some kind. The threat he had just received was very tangible. He could tell him he would think about his coercive request, or take a gamble and refuse it outright. Or he could be indirect, he could digress, obfuscate.

"I am not sure why you surmised that I knew any dissidents, or that I have associated with bourgeois writers and poets. None of this is true. I keep too busy to be involved in pursuits of this sort. You said you'd have me kicked out of medical school. I'm in my fourth year. By this time the state has invested a small fortune into my education. Do you realize all those funds would be squandered if I was not able to finish university? That would not be the best use of governmental resources."

Nesvadba was still glowering at him, but perhaps with slightly less confidence, less determination. "You think you're smart, eh? We'll be keeping tabs on you, tough guy," he snarled. "You'll be hearing from the dean. Now get out of here, bum."

"FOR SEVERAL WEEKS AFTER THIS CONFAB with Nesvadba," Roman said, attempting to penetrate the consular officer's deadpan countenance, "I expected that each single day at the school would be my last. But I received no summons to meet with the dean. No registered letter came announcing my expulsion. Life continued as usual."

"Anything else?" she asked.

"Nothing for a few years," said Roman, watching the officer's pen move along the lines of the note pad. He had still been distributing samizdats and still kept in touch with a limited number of dissidents, but he was making an effort to be very careful. Then one day, it was soon after he finished his military service, he was sitting in a bar, by himself, having a few drinks. He had recently started working at the hospital, having graduated from medical school before his involuntary army stint.

He just wanted to relax that evening. A couple of strangers joined him at the table, and they struck up a conversation which, with the alcohol on board, rapidly veered in the wrong direction. He declared, among other things, that if the Czech nation was to ever restore its pride and dignity, it had no choice but to fight the occupation. After hearing this, the men discreetly vanished.

Roman did not think anything of their disappearance and continued drinking, until an hour later two uniformed cops arrived and arrested him for sedition. He was interrogated for three days. Nesvadba was glad to see him again. They beat him. They did not let him sleep. They barely gave him any food and water. After concluding that he didn't plan to incite an insurrection, they let him go, but not before the prosecutor decided that his case of one drunken subversive sentence warranted a trial. He had one, and the judge gave him one-year probation.

"Did you lose your job?" the consular officer asked.

"No. I was prepared to become a digger or a night watchman, but it never came to it. I still don't know how to explain that. I must have had a guardian angel watching over me," Roman laughed.

"Why do you think they let you out of the country?"

"My theory is that they want to get rid of Jews and other undesirables.

And rabble-rousers in general."

"What do you plan to do if you get to the States?"

She did not inquire about the diploma. Did she know about the theft? The CIA did. But if she knew, she would have addressed it.

"Practice medicine again," he answered.

"Your sponsor lives in Georgia, but you have a sister in Vermont. Where are you planning to go?"

"Probably to my sister. She's family, after all. And I like the mountains, too."

"Yes, Vermont is pretty." She softened up at last. "Make sure to dive into a swim hole when you're there. Incidentally, your English is excellent. You did not keep our interpreter busy at all." Her stern face mellowed with a slight smile. "I have no more questions for you. We will notify you with our decision within a month."

CHAPTER 11

"**I**MPRESSIVE," ALEXANDRA SAID as she led him back to the vestibule. "I didn't have to translate a single sentence. That almost never happens."

"Thank you. Maybe now you could share the story of your proficiency in Czech? My interest is piqued."

"I can't. Not while I'm at work. But if you insist on hearing it, I have time in the evening."

The train to Ostbaum was leaving in a couple of hours, and he had already paid for the return leg of the trip. He had thirty-five marks in his pocket, which was barely enough for a modest dinner and another ticket if he let the existing one lapse. He would not be able to afford a hotel for the night, but sleeping on a bench at the train station, if necessary, was an option. "Yes, I would like to hear it. What time can we get together?"

"I assume you don't know Frankfurt at all, true?"

"True."

"There is a restaurant on this street, two blocks from here. When you leave the consulate, it will be on your left. It is called Der Grüner Jäger. Let's meet there around seven."

"See you there. I'm looking forward to it."

* * *

THE DINING AREA OF THE TAVERN was a spacious, softly lit hall with long mahogany-colored tables and heavy ornamental chairs, and murals depicting hunting scenes, each painting featuring the identical young nimrod with a thin moustache and a blue jay feather in his cap; a romantic lone huntsman with a smile of innocence, felling big game in idyllic landscapes.

They took a seat at one of the tables. A waitress soon approached with the menus, and Alexandra ordered a schnitzel with potato salad, Roman went with bratwurst and sauerkraut. They each had a glass of Riesling.

"Are you sure you want to hear the whole account? It's long, and it's not pretty." Alexandra scrutinized Roman's face.

"I'm sure."

"Alright then. The story starts in nineteen sixty-eight," she said, taking a sip of the wine. "My mom was a nurse in the Bulgarian army. She was called up to join the units that participated in the Soviet-led invasion of Czechoslovakia. Her company was stationed in a small village about thirty kilometers west of Prague. Even though the Bulgarians stayed in the country for only six months, during that time she managed to fall in love with and marry a man from the village. My parents had long been divorced, and when she left for Czechoslovakia, I lived with my grandparents. My father was not involved in my life at all. So, mom married this Czech man and moved into his house. Several months later I joined them. I was thirteen at that time."

"Is it something you wanted to do?"

"Yes. I missed my mother. Miloš, my step dad, was a mason. He had a regular job with a construction company, and he took side jobs on the weekends and sometimes even after hours during the week, building or fixing people's homes."

"I know about that," Roman said. "An illegal but accepted, and, in fact, sought after enterprise under socialism. The Communist bosses depended on these guys as much as regular folks did," he laughed.

"We lived in a large house. Just the three of us. Miloš had a big yard, and he kept sheep. The sheep cleared the grass on his lawn so perfectly he never had to mow it. He loved that. He also had chickens that laid blue eggs. That was the first time in my life I saw blue chicken eggs."

"I've never seen blue chicken eggs. Have I missed anything?"

"Yes. For a kid, they are exciting. So, my mom got a job at the local grocery store, and I was going to school. Miloš was a jovial man to the outside world. He was well-liked in the village. He was good with the clarinet, and in his spare time he played in the local band. At home, Miloš was tolerable at first. He was demanding and controlling, and that led to frequent arguments with my mom, but nothing worse than that.

"Then one night, Mom showed me a bruise on her calf. She told me that he'd thrown her against the bed. I'm not sure why she shared that with me. I guess she had no one else to tell. Things got worse from there, and, eventually, he beat her for everything he considered an infraction, even in my presence. It was gradually becoming a desperate situation. Mom felt completely trapped. There were no women's shelters. She was a foreigner in a small, tight-knit village. She was afraid to talk to anybody about the abuse or go to the police. I wanted to defend her, and when he beat her in front of me, I jumped between them and I tried to push him away. He was a big bear of a man, so not only did that not work but before long he started hitting me too. This went on for almost a year."

"That must have been a terrible predicament."

"Yes, it was. I thought about running away, just to get as far from that place as possible. But I loved my mom, and I wanted to protect her. So, instead of bolting, I began thinking about killing him. Initially, it was a fleeting idea, but it gradually developed into an obsession. I came to the conclusion that doing him in was the only solution to our situation. In my teenage mind I didn't consider other options or the consequences."

Alexandra paused and concentrated on her meal.

"Teenagers can think very impulsively," Roman remarked.

"He had hunting rifles in the house," she resumed. "But I had no experience with shooting guns. Another thought I had was to poison him, but eventually I settled on using a knife. I started practicing. I would sneak out to the barn at night with a kitchen knife and plunge it into tightly packed straw. I could see my speed and strength improving. I was terrified of this whole business. I was scared of myself. But I still pushed ahead with the plan. One evening, when mom worked the late shift at the store, and I knew he would get home before she did, I hid behind the front door. When he opened it, I stabbed him twice in the back with as much force as I could. He keeled over, moaning, gasping for air. I tried to stab him again, but the knife went in so deep the second time that I couldn't pull it out. Then I ran. Next morning, the villagers and the police found me in the woods not far from town."

Roman was watching her face and her hands as she talked. Her fingers were slender and delicately shaped, but twine-like veins protruding from under the skin of the back of her elongated hands betrayed their strength. She had an aquiline nose, full lips, large pale-blue eyes that stood out sharply against her olive complexion, and the combination of these features made for an arrestingly attractive, untamed face that contrasted with the even and quiet voice with which she was relaying her disturbing tale.

"I know you warned me it's not a pretty story," he said. "But this... you barely know me. Isn't it difficult to talk about this?" *You are sitting across the table from a woman who is capable of extreme violence. But aren't most humans, under desperate circumstances?*

"Of course it is. But I had a feeling from the interview that you were considerate and open-minded. You grew up in that country. I thought you would listen."

Roman nodded. "What happened with the man and with you?"

"He survived. I was sent to juvenile detention. I had a trial. The judge was a young woman, and I had the impression that she carefully listened to Mom's account, even though Mom's Czech was hard to understand, and she was bawling all through her testimony. Miloš flatly denied that any abuse had existed. He said we were two Balkan witches who conspired to kill him. I had already spent six months in detention before the trial was over, and the judge sentenced me to another six months. A very lenient verdict considering what I had done. In the meantime, Mom moved to Prague and changed her name to hide from Miloš. I was sixteen when I got out. I was empty. Nothing really mattered. I lived with my mom in a one-bedroom apartment in Potůčky. You know Potůčky, I am sure."

"Of course. I avoided that neighborhood when I could."

"Mom worked in a factory, and I enrolled in trade school, but I became a truant. My future didn't look good. Now that I was back with Mom, she started planning our return to Bulgaria but in the meantime, I met two young West German truck drivers. After finding out where I was with my life, they offered to take me across the border. I asked them what I would do in Germany, and they laughed and said that I would not have to do much at all. That in Germany money grew on trees. They put me in a big box with bubble wrap all around me and smuggled me out. So that's the story."

"How are you doing now? Were you able to recover, if there is ever a possibility to recover from something like that?"

"It's been getting better lately. When I first came here, I quickly found out that money didn't grow on trees. I became a dancer. I drank and I did drugs. Then one night a patron was shot dead in the parking lot of the nightclub where I worked. I witnessed the murder, and I was afraid that the killers would go after me. My life sucked, but I was not ready to croak yet. I needed to get out. There was an American Air Force officer who was a regular at the club. A decent man, a single guy who came every couple of weeks to, how should I say this, relieve himself of his sexual frustration. I asked him to help me out and he did. He found me an office job at his base. For the first time in as far as I could remember, I had some normalcy in my life. I was making an effort to stay away from too much excitement. I was quickly learning English. I worked at the base for about a year when the American Consul General came to visit. He needed an impromptu German interpreter, so my supervisor asked me to assist. The Consul found out that I spoke several languages, and he offered me the position of an interpreter at the Consulate. I've been here for the past three years. In the end, my life has turned around."

"If anybody deserves a better life, it's you. One day you should write your story."

"I've been thinking about it. I'll need to wait a few more years for all the memories to settle and then maybe. Well, enough about me," she laughed, for the first time since they met. "I learned bits and pieces about you from the interview, but I want to know more. Tell me about your life back there. Whatever comes to your mind."

CHILDHOOD IS A HAVEN for evocative reminiscences. Family vacations every summer, always in unassuming locations, mountain cabins with leaky roofs, the pungent odor of burning kerosene lamps and the long shadows they cast. Picking blueberries and raspberries in the morning haze. Making tea from pine needles and breathing in its sharp aroma. Trekking. Swimming in streams and teal-colored lakes.

Walks in the city with Mom and Dad on the weekends at least once a month, reading inscriptions on buildings, on statues, Dad pointing out which ones were accurate, which ones mendacious. "When you are passing by a building, always lift your head and look at the whole of it. You'll miss a great deal if you only register what's at eye level. See that beautiful balcony, that relief sculpture, that mosaic?" Dad used to tell Roman and his sister during these strolls, and Roman heeds his advice to this day.

Kicking the soccer ball in the park after school with the neighborhood ragamuffins, and playing marbles, glass marbles in an infinite variety of sizes and colors, magical tones of azure and emerald and amber and ruby. Some marbles had multiple hues, some were transparent. Those with the most enchanting coloration were prized the highest, and fights would break out over them, children's fists can be merciless, noses were bloodied, teeth were knocked out for the most ravishing marble.

Frequenting the nearby film theater to watch movies for the nominal price of one crown, "The General," "City Lights," "Laurel and Hardy," "High Noon," "The Big Country." Standing on river banks and bridges with Dad and feeding ducks and sea gulls, while talking about Egyptian Pharaohs and Napoleon.

"Those are wonderful memories," Alexandra said. "You had a happy childhood."

"Relatively happy and uneventful. Life took a different turn when the Soviets arrived. I was twelve when they showed up unannounced. But it's clear from your story that the invasion impacted your life in a much more drastic way than mine."

"Isn't it a coincidence? We are from different countries, but we've been both seriously affected by the same event."

The waitress came to take away their empty plates, and she refilled the carafe with water. Alexandra gazed at Roman. "I'll change the subject for a moment. I was wondering what will happen if you don't pass your medical exams once you are in the U.S.? What will you do? Do you have a backup plan?"

"I hope that won't be the case." Objectively, Roman knew he would not even get to the point of taking the tests without the diploma unless some miracle occurred. Yet, perhaps due to a subconscious effort to protect his emotional sanity, he did not allow himself to accept this reality. *Let's get to the States first. Then we'll see.* He did not have a backup plan.

"I hope so, too, but you can't be certain. Have you ever considered the option of working for the government? They need people like you."

Hold on. He heard this before. Gunterschön in the camp. And of course Goldfarb, the CIA man. But Roman was not about to ruin the rest of the evening he was spending with this alluring woman. This dangerous alluring woman? He did not respond.

Alexandra looked at her watch. "It is late. Already eleven thirty.

The restaurant will be closing soon. Where's your hotel?"

"I don't have a room booked. I'll spend the night at the train station. I doubt there are any more trains departing for Ostbaum at this hour."

She looked amused. "At the train station? With drug pushers and thieves? Not a good idea." She shook her head and thought for a moment. "You can stay at my digs for the night."

SHE LIVED IN A SMALL CHIC APARTMENT near the financial district, with a view of the Main River. The living room had black leather furniture and an art-deco table. After showing him where the bathroom was, she went to a hall closet, took out a pillow and a couple of blankets and laid them on the divan. "You must be tired. Thank you for listening to my story. See you in the morning."

ROMAN TOOK OFF HIS JACKET and his tie, lay down, and stretched his limbs. What a day. The image of the short, stocky consular officer swearing him in jumped in front of his closed eyes. Then Alexandra holding a big kitchen knife, ready to kill. Then Alexandra naked. He pushed off the covers, stood up and walked over to the window. The street lights were casting their long white reflections on the smooth surface of the river. There was a light touch on his shoulder, and he turned his head. Alexandra was standing behind him, holding a shiny object in her hand. He froze, and felt the blood draining from his face. Then he realized the glistening item was a small hairbrush with a silver-colored top. He hoped Alexandra had not noticed his reaction.

"You can't sleep?" she asked.

"No. Since you're awake, too, maybe we can stay up together."

"That view," she said, pointing to the window. "Like flickering damned souls in the darkness. Or like angels of salvation." She motioned with her head toward the bedroom. "Come."

CHAPTER 12

HOW WAS THE INTERVIEW?" Andrea asked. It was a sunny Saturday afternoon, and they were biking to the Friedländer brewery which was located about fifteen miles south of the city. Earlier in the day, Andrea had dropped Sebastian off at her girlfriend's apartment.

"I feel good about it. I should know about their decision within a month."

"If they granted you asylum, when would you leave Germany?"

"Probably two to three months after I've received it. At least that is what the guys from the immigration agency told me. The agency groups refugees together and organizes flights to the States several times a year."

They left their bikes in the parking lot and took a tour of the brewery, its two levels of stainless-steel pipes and vats and historical photographs. The brewery was on a hill, surrounded by a large garden overlooking the village below and the Bavarian countryside, with patches of fields, meadows, and oak groves stretching into the distance. Wooden tables with benches, big rocks, and stylized ruins made of dark-red brick, were randomly strewn about the grounds. Adjacent to the garden was a plot of hop bines, twisting and climbing high along taut wires. Roman and Andrea sat down with pint-sized mugs of ice-cold Yellow

Unicorn, a pale ale to be found only in Bavaria. The beer had a crisp, fruity taste. Several tanned farmers in lederhosen were sitting at the table next to theirs, drinking, smoking pipes, talking in hushed voices. It was a splendid afternoon, a time to loosen up. They finished the beer, rode down to the village, and the sky was so blue and the breeze so gentle that they had to stop at a garden pub for a couple more glasses.

On their way back, they chose a slightly different route. Another magnificent sunset was on the display, a huge fireball slowly disappearing behind the bluish hills. Cars with their headlights on were humming by. Roman and Andrea turned onto a wide road paved with large rectangular granite slabs, with weeds heavily sprouting from the slits between the blocks.

"Unusual road," Roman remarked.

"It is indeed. Built during the Nazi times. It leads there." Andrea pointed to the dark silhouette of a partially ruined colossal structure reminiscent of a Roman amphitheater. Roman realized that he had seen this edifice before, on photographs and in documentaries.

"So, this is where those massive Nazi rallies took place? Moms, dads, children, all with their arms raised, crazed look in their eyes, screaming 'Sieg Heil'?"

"That's right. Now it's a venue for rock concerts."

A LETTER ARRIVED FROM DÜSSELDORF. "It took me a while to track you down, but I finally did," Roman was reading. "I received my artificial legs a few weeks after I last saw you and five months later, I was able to take a few steps. I was like a toddler at first, but it's been getting better ever since. About three months ago they let us take a trip to Düsseldorf to see an orthopedic surgeon who is an expert in prosthetics, and we decided not to return to Czechoslovakia. Things have been good so far. We already have a place to stay and Lenka is looking for a job. I think I'll take up painting; photography may be problematic in my circumstances. So, watch for Mr. Artist Adam Nedoma!

Lenka saved me. She pulled me out of a deep funk. I wouldn't be here if it was not for her. You need to know that because you convinced her to come back to me. I owe you. I really do. And I am sober. I haven't had a drink since I got out of the hospital. Düsseldorf seems like a very hip city, full of art – "

Roman paused for a moment. He wasn't sure if he could be happy for Adam, but he presumed he could be happy for Lenka. He finished reading the letter, pondering about cause and effect, purpose and destiny. He wished for a wise man to get the answers.

ROMAN BECAME FRIENDS with milkman Franta and his girlfriend Jiřina whom he had met at the marijuana party. They were staying in a modestly furnished one-bedroom apartment, with a worn out gray couch, an easy chair, a TV set, and a small round plywood table in the living room. Tonight, the table was set for a two-course dinner.

"I used to work in an electronics parts store back in Prague," Franta told Roman after taking a gulp of beer. Roman was visiting on Franta's day off, and, surprisingly, this was the first time they were reminiscing about the past in some detail. "Typical socialist enterprise. I scratch your back, you scratch mine. Many parts were perpetually in short supply so a regular guy who just walked in and wanted something that was in high demand didn't have a chance. Either a little financial encouragement was offered discreetly on the side, or something else that the customer could provide that we needed or wanted. Kind of a barter system. Otherwise, sorry, we can't help you. Unless they asked just for a few screws, or something banal like that, they were out of luck. So, understandably, the atmosphere was always tense, and many people were leaving the place very pissed off. One time, a customer slapped me in the face when I told him we were sold out of an item that a dude who was just in front of him in line was still able to get. The irony was that in this particular instance, I was actually telling the truth."

"That's what telling the truth gets you. A whack in the face." Jiřina laughed.

"How did you two meet?"

"In the store," Franta said.

"So she wanted to buy something and she could offer something you wanted?"

"It sort of worked out that way."

"Oh don't listen to him, he is full of shit!" Jiřina chuckled, her face mildly flushed.

"Why did you decide to leave?"

"It was getting a little dicey in the store," Franta explained. "Not that I was afraid I would get busted. The way we were operating was no different from how most of the other so-called businesses were operating. It was more the relationship among the guys in the store. Everybody was getting greedier and greedier. It developed into this cutthroat jealous competition. Who can steal more? Who can make more under the table?"

"In the end, he was constantly upset and mad and stressed," Jiřina added. "He couldn't sleep. He was insufferable to be around, poor guy. He was thinking about switching jobs. But, in the meantime, we were able to go on vacation to the West, and we said fuck it, we are not coming back."

"Here it's different," Franta said. "No corruption. Only hard work. And you know what? I complain about it, but I really don't mind. It's purifying. A little purgatory. I can sleep at night. I am happier. Except for those panic attacks I'm having from time to time."

Franta stood up. "OK, dinner should be ready." He left for the kitchen area and came back a minute later with a big pot that he set in the center of the table. "Leek soup. I hope it turned out well. Dig in."

"Excellent, Franta", Roman said after tasting the soup. "It reminds me of those smoky Czech pubs and eateries with dirty tables and rude waiters but honest, no bullshit food."

"Leave room for the second course. Roast beef and potatoes with dill sauce. I had some time to play in the kitchen today."

"Wonderful dinner," Roman said after carefully getting the last drop of the dill sauce off the plate and into his mouth. Then he turned to Jiřina. "What's next for you? You should be close to finishing school."

"Yeah. Only a month or so to the graduation. I am already looking around for jobs in the business sector. It seems like there are some options to choose from. So, life should become much easier in a little while."

"Oh yes, once she finds a job, I'm done with milk trucking. I'll take a few months off, and then I'll look for something easier."

"You deserve a break, Franta," Roman said.

"Yes, he does." Jiřina gave Franta a caring look and gently rubbed his shoulders.

ABOUT SIX WEEKS LATER, in the morning, just when Roman was getting ready to run to the store for weekly supplies, there was a loud bang on the door. "Roman, are you there?" he heard Franta's voice.

Franta stood in the door, haggard, pale, with purple bags under his eyes, his blond hair matted, a limp cigarette dangling from his dry lips, his hands shaking.

"Franta! What the hell happened? Come in, sit down."

Franta walked in and sank onto the sofa. Roman quickly opened a bottle of beer and carefully put it in Franta's hands. "Have a sip of the lifesaver, buddy." He patted him on the shoulder.

Franta took a swig, leaned his head back and closed his eyes. He was silent for a few seconds and then he started to talk, slowly, with a trembling voice.

"So. You know Jiřina graduated?"

"About two weeks ago. Right?"

"Yes. Even before her graduation, what started happening occasionally was that she wouldn't come home for the night. One time, it was a night of studying with the girlfriends, preparing for finals. Another time, it was a party with the girlfriends that lasted until next morning. There was always an excuse, and even though I was getting pissed off, I believed her. Other than that, everything was as usual. Yesterday again, she didn't come home in the evening. I went to bed around midnight, but I couldn't sleep because I was mad. Several hours later, at about three, I hear the door being unlocked. It's Jiřina, I thought. I was glad that she was back, but I was still furious, so I closed my eyes and turned to the wall pretending I was asleep so that I didn't have to talk to her. Then, about thirty seconds later, I feel a painful jab in my ribs. I jump up completely startled, my heart pumping in my throat, and I am staring at the barrel of a sawed-off shot gun.

"Holy shit!"

"You said it. That was easily the scariest moment of my life, I can tell you that. The guy who is holding the gun is all in black, with a mask covering his whole head except for a slit for the eyes. 'Get up,' he says, 'open the safe or you're dead'."

Franta lit another cigarette. "There is a safe in the corner of the bedroom, fastened to the wall. There was money in it because I don't trust banks. I deposit only part of my salary. The rest of it I keep in the safe. I was the only one who knew the code. Jiřina did not like that at all. She accused me of being controlling and suspicious, and I probably was. Now it looks like for a good reason. So, I do what the dude says. I open the safe, he empties it. Then he takes my phone, rips the cord out of the wall, and tells me to stay inside for thirty minutes after he leaves. Otherwise, his buddies who are watching outside would smoke me. Then he points his gun at me one more time and darts out of the pad."

"This is crazy," Roman said. "How much was in the safe?"

"About thirteen thousand."

"Holy fuck. That's a big chunk of change."

"Yeah. Then I'm thinking; this guy opened the door without any problems. He probably had a key. He knew I had a safe, and he clearly knew there was money in it. And he seemed to know his way around the place very well, like someone who had been there before. That's when I am sure he had an accomplice on the inside."

"Are you saying...Jiřina?"

There was quiet in the room. The two men were staring at each other, motionless. The story was so wild that it was almost unbelievable. But Franta's appearance and his demeanor and body language convinced Roman that he should trust him.

"What did you do next?"

"I waited thirty minutes. Then I ran out. I went to the phone booth that's on the street corner, and I called the police."

"Did Jiřina ever show up?"

"No. I suspect she is long gone, with the guy. They may be out of the country by now. The money is one thing, but that's not the worst. The worst is the betrayal. I supported her. I worked my ass off so she could go to school full time. I loved her." Franta put his face in his hands and started to weep. Roman stood up, not sure what to do. He paced for a few seconds, then he sat down beside Franta and hugged him.

"It's still possible that she was not part of it. Maybe it's just a weird coincidence," he said to Franta. "It's hard to understand why she would do something like that. She just finished school. She was about to land a good-paying job."

"I am sure she and the robber are lovers," Franta said, staring at the floor. "That explains all those nights when she was not home. One of them, or both, needed quick money for something. She used me."

"What are you going to do now?"

"I don't know. If I don't go back to work tomorrow, I'll get fired. I don't think I'll have enough strength to go back. I can't think straight. I thought things were on the right track, but they really were not, probably not for a long time. That woman. How could she have done that to me?" He shook his head. "I don't know. I may just pack my bags and go back to Prague."

"Why?"

"I need security. I need safety. I need to get away."

He is irrational. "You'll have safety and security in prison if you go back. The best thing you can do is to go to work tomorrow. That will keep you occupied during the day. Your judgement is clouded right now. In fact, it is completely off, and that's understandable. So, don't make any big decisions now that you'll be sorry for later. The first step is to go back to work tomorrow morning."

Franta just sat on the couch with a blank expression.

"This must hurt tremendously," Roman said. "And it will hurt for days, probably weeks. That's natural. Don't fight it. Let it settle. I suspect that after a few weeks, things will start improving. In the meantime, I'll help you."

Franta slowly rose, his shoulders stooped, his head hanging down to his chest. "I'm going back to the apartment," he said in a hollow voice.

"I'll go with you."

They clambered into Franta's old jeep. "Are you sure you are up to driving?" Roman asked.

"I drove here, didn't I?" Franta snapped back.

On the way to his place, they stopped at a department store where Franta bought a new phone. They also grabbed a few frozen meals, a twelve-pack of beer, a carton of cigarettes, and some juice and water.

"Franta, do you want me to stay with you until tomorrow?" Roman asked when they got to the apartment.

"I don't think so."

"You'll have to go to work tomorrow morning, alright? I'll stop by here in the evening. And if you need anything, you come to me in the meantime."

Next day in the early evening, Roman rode the tram to Franta's apartment. He rang the bell but there was no answer. He walked around the neighborhood for a half an hour, then went back and tried the bell again. Still no answer.

The following day, around noon, Roman called Franta's employer, the Gelhausen dairy. "He hasn't been here for three days," the voice on the other end of the line answered. That evening, Roman went to Franta's digs one more time. No one was home. There are two possibilities, thought Roman. Either Franta killed himself or he left the area. And if he left the area, he most likely went back to Czechoslovakia.

Roman called the police.

Two policemen came and worked their way into the flat. Roman followed them. No dead Franta was found inside, and Roman sighed with relief. There was a dresser and a closet in the bedroom. In the dresser were Jiřina's outfits. In the closet were more of her garments, and Franta's winter coat and winter boots. There were no other clothes of his.

Roman's heart sank. He should have stayed with Franta for a few days, and this might not have happened.

"I think he's gone," Roman said after he got hold of himself. "He's most likely back in Prague. Did you know he's the same man who was robbed at gun point several days ago? He suspected his girlfriend was an accomplice."

"Yes, we are aware," answered one of the cops.

"Have you got any leads yet?"

"No. But when we do, we'll let you know."

To Roman, those words sounded painfully familiar.

CHAPTER 13

ROMAN WAS STARING at the short note with his mouth open. "After a careful review of your application, it has been decided that your request for asylum in the United States of America will not be granted. This decision is final."

He slapped the paper with the backside of his hand in exasperation. This was not right. He had given them valid reasons to let him in the country. He had a good profession, a solid sponsor. His English was fluent. He had a close relative already living in the United States. He must have been at the top of the list of qualified candidates, yet they turned him down. Something else must be at play here. He threw the letter on the floor, wanting to tear it up with his feet, but he held back.

For a moment, he sat down, his elbows on his knees, his face in his hands. Then he rose and started pacing around the apartment. Goldfarb. There is no other possible reason. The CIA must have intervened. He sat down again and tried to put his thoughts together. Now he had no doubt that if he wanted to get to the States, going through Goldfarb was the only way. And going through Goldfarb meant joining the CIA.

*　　*　　*

"MY ASYLUM APPLICATION was turned down. Do you want to tell me more about that?" Roman's voice vibrated with tension. He was exhausted; he had been awake the whole night.

They were sitting on a bench by the river. Goldfarb was smoking a cigar and feeding the pigeons, throwing them small pieces of a baguette and enjoying himself watching the birds pecking at each other over the crumbs. "I am afraid I have no knowledge of that, but I am very sorry to hear it. What are you going to do now?"

"Don't give me this shit. You, or rather your organization, is behind this. Did you inform the consulate about the stolen diploma, knowing that any doubts on their part about my ability to practice medicine in America would make me a much less attractive asylum candidate? Or did you come up with something else to tell them?"

"You didn't answer my question," Goldfarb said. "What are you going to do? You didn't call me just to have a diatribe, did you?"

"I want you to tell me what is going on. I see no reason for having been rejected other than on account of some intervention coming from you."

"I can still help you. Be realistic. With your diploma stolen, you will have difficulties continuing as a physician. You could do other things but as it stands now, your main problem is they are not letting you in the country. You could stay in Germany, but I know you don't want to."

"You are blackmailing me."

Goldfarb threw more bread to the birds. "Call it whatever you want. If you decide to contract with the agency, we'll be able to get you to the US within several weeks."

"And then what."

"We sorely need translators right now. You know three of the languages that are spoken behind the iron curtain. So, my assumption, which I think is a safe one, is that you would go to Langley to join one of the translator teams to start with. You have a great potential. I wouldn't be surprised if you eventually made it to an analyst."

"What is in Langley?"

"The CIA headquarters."

*　　*　　*

Roman recalled their last meeting before his departure from Prague; they were strolling toward the city center after having had a few drinks in their favorite bar in The Lesser Town. "You won't miss it?" Eva asked. "The city? The river and the bridges? The smell of the lilacs in the spring? The taste of the bread? The sound of the language? Have you considered it? The sentimentality aspect?"

Their relationship had changed over the past few months. They still had feelings for each other, but they were both making an effort to keep their emotions in check, they were on guard, they were holding back. "What if it doesn't work out for you the way you imagined?" Eva continued. "If you come back, you would be looking at prison."

"I won't come back." A wave of intense melancholy pressure gripped his chest. "But I will miss you, Eva."

"No one's making you leave. It's your choice," she said, keeping her gaze straight ahead.

It started to rain, first a few large hesitant drops splashed on the cobblestones, but soon thick piercing perpendicular sheets of water were whipping the sidewalks, drainpipes on nearby buildings shook with the load, and the street emptied. Drenched, they hid under an awning, they hugged and kissed on the spur-of-the-moment, and they pulled apart just as quickly.

He hated himself.

"So, no asylum in the U.S. Does that mean you are staying in Germany?" Andrea was in the kitchen making an omelet with green peppers and onions. Her budget was very limited and her meals were simple, yet they tasted delicious.

"That's just it. I am not sure."

"What other options do you have?"

"One other. Working for the US government. If I sign up to work for them, I suspect they would override the denial. That would be the whole point of signing up."

"Government? That's a broad term. Which part of the government?"

"The CIA."

She turned from the stove to look at him. "The CIA? Do you know what you would be getting yourself into?"

"Not really. Spy business can be dangerous and unsavory. That's common knowledge. I guess it depends on what the assignment would be. The CIA officer who is stationed here in town, the one that's been working hard to trap me in his web, says they need translators. The way it looks to me, it is either joining or staying here."

"I would like you to stay."

They embraced. "It would hurt to leave you, Andrea. It would hurt a lot. But I just don't know. America has a huge allure. And there are other aspects. Germany is too close to the Soviets. I was hoping to get as far away as I could. And staying in Germany as a Jew...I am not sure how I feel about that."

Andrea finished the omelet, cut it in half, and served it on two plates. "You know what they say. 'Short term gains can be long term pains.' This idea, this plan, may backfire on you. And once you are in, it will be too late to change your mind."

"I am trying to picture the worst-case scenario. The riskiest CIA assignment that I could get."

"What would that be?"

"An undercover mission back in Czechoslovakia."

"If you went, what do you think would happen to you if your cover was blown?"

"Being a Czechoslovak citizen who defected, and is then sent back by an enemy power to spy on the Czech government? I would be probably tried for treason, and that might mean the death penalty." Seeing her alarmed expression, he quickly added; "But I really doubt the CIA would dispatch me back across the border." He took a deep breath. "I want to ask you something. If I decided to join the CIA, would you come with me to America?" She studied his face.

"I didn't expect you would ever ask me that. You mean my little boy and me coming with you?"

"Yes."

"Would I move across the ocean with a man who just joined the CIA?"

She paused, and, with a flick of her head, moved a lock of hair that was covering her eye. She smiled. "I would."

"WHAT HAVE YOU DECIDED?" Goldfarb inquired. This time, they were convening in a beer garden. Delectable catfish filet and fried vegetables went well with the suds. Once again the Americano was footing the bill.

"First level with me," Roman said "Were you behind my asylum rejection?"

"I have no idea what happened. Apparently, you did fine at the interview."

"Ah, see, you know all about it. You are not a very good spy, Stan. You just told on yourself. Is Alexandra, the Bulgarian translator, on your payroll too? Is that how she can afford that nicely furnished apartment in downtown Frankfurt? Working two jobs?"

"I don't know what you're talking about." Goldfarb raised his mug of ale to his lips. "Let's get to the point. Are you with us?"

"I have some conditions."

"What are they?"

"The main one; I cannot be sent on a mission to any communist country."

"That is not up to me to decide."

"Then there is no deal. I am willing to take risks, but not to accept the risk of a death sentence."

"As I said, I cannot guarantee anything. But, between you and me, your chances of being ordered to a communist country are absolutely minimal to none."

It was a weak assurance, but Roman effectively resigned himself to the outcome that he came to believe was inevitable. "Another thing. I met a person here, a fine young woman. She has a child. They would have to be allowed to come with me."

"German citizens?"

"Yes."

"That should not be a problem"

"I will need it in writing."

"You'll have it in writing. Anything else?"

Roman thought for a moment, then shook his head, pushing his empty plate away. "I guess not. I hope I won't be sorry for doing this."

"I don't think you will be. You will be on the side of freedom. That's a reason to be proud. I am not bullshitting you. I mean it."

Roman looked at Goldfarb. He disliked him intensely but he also understood him.

"I'll bring you a contract to sign within a week." Goldfarb stretched out his hand.

"I can't shake your hand. You trapped me. I know you were doing your job, but I am very angry with you."

"Fair enough."

IT TOOK ONLY SIX WEEKS to get the paperwork arranged. They will enter America on work visas. Once in the United States, the agency will help them secure permanent residency status, said Goldfarb.

Roman and Andrea were able to fit all the possessions that were important to them, and small enough to transport, into three large suitcases; not owning much proved to be beneficial. Roman's luggage did not lock well, and he had to secure it with twine. They took the few pieces of furniture, and the other items that they decided to leave behind, to the sidewalk to make them available for folks who might find them useful. Among the objects that they carried down were still some that Roman had picked up from the street a year earlier.

A week before the departure, Roman paid a visit to the social worker, Fräulein Rosenbach, for one last time. When he informed her that he will be gone for good, her eyebrows rose and her eyes widened. "Are you serious? Most of my clients never leave." She opened the safe and gave him his full monthly allowance.

THE PLANE TOOK OFF THE TARMAC and the high-rises of Frankfurt quickly disappeared under the cover of clouds. This was the first flight ever for both of them, for all three of them, but, luckily, Sebastian was already asleep in his toddler seat.

The destination was Washington, DC, and then Langley, Virginia.

CHAPTER 14

IN A SMALL WINDOWLESS OFFICE, Roman translated military, economic, and political documents, and agents' notes and letters. Ponderous Czech and English word-definition lexicons and a Czech-English dictionary occupied half of his desk. Because of the profusion of technical terms in the documents, it sometimes took him a whole day to get through only two or three pages. Jirka Čep, a veteran Czech translator with whom he shared the room, could not lend him a hand because they were not allowed to communicate about the content of the materials assigned to them. Roman had never been prone to headaches, but now he started having them daily, dull and oppressive frontal pains.

During breaks he and Jirka usually shared a cafeteria table with two Hungarian brothers, Jancsi and Józsi, also translators. The brothers had escaped a few years earlier by making their way from Yugoslavia to Italy on a small boat.

"In the Rome refugee camp, we were approached by two heavies. They were the emissaries of the Hungarian mafia based in Los Angeles," Józsi recounted one day. "They were trying hard to recruit us. They painted a wonderful picture of a legitimate business opportunity, but we had heard about the Hungarian mafia before we left the country so we knew better. They said they would smuggle us out across the ocean to Mexico, and from there to the US. We kept brushing them off, and we eventually signed up with the CIA."

The brothers did not miss Hungary much, only Hungarian food. "Hungarian crepes are so deliciously thin," Jancsi and Józsi were taking turns reminiscing and reading each other's mind, "no one else in the world is able to reproduce that ultra-skinny crepe dimension. There was a crepe shop on Ferenc Boulevard in Budapest, down by the Danube. Watching the girls cook the crepes and flip them by artfully jerking the frying pan was a mouth-watering overture to the experience. The assortment of fillings they had – peach, raspberry, strawberry, ground walnuts, poppy seeds, cocoa, farmer cheese, and always with plenty of sugar on top and a hot chocolate topping, we could easily annihilate ten crepes each when we went there, our taste buds are going crazy right now," the brothers sighed wistfully in unison.

"And other foods, like buttered noodles with ground poppy seeds and sugar, nothing complicated to make, but it tasted heavenly, or stuffed peppers, you can find those here, too, but they don't even compare. How about cold gooseberry and sour cherry soups," and now the brothers' faces lit up with a connoisseurial smile and they both nodded knowingly, "the sour cherries are actually sweet, and the soups are made with cream and served in the heat of the summer to cool off.

"Don't forget chestnut puree," continued the brothers, "that pungent flavor, that pale-brown color, it goes well with whipped cream topping, and corn on the cob covered with layers of butter and salt, they sold it in the streets and underpasses in the winter. And the cheap underground wine caves on every corner, so dense with cigarette smoke you could carve it with a knife, stopping there after work and downing a couple of tall chilled wine spritzers always helped dull the frustrations and stupidities that had piled up during the day."

It was lovely when the brothers embarked on one of their voluble nostalgia trips, and Roman and Jirka were careful not to interrupt too often, they just kicked back and enjoyed another chapter in the series of the siblings' gustatory recollections.

* * *

THEY LIVED IN A ONE-BEDROOM APARTMENT in Langley. Andrea worked at the CIA daycare where Sebastian was enrolled. They were adjusting—rapidly and slowly. They were drinking loads of dark-brown chemical soda pop, but they still had difficulty merging on the freeway. Andrea was pregnant.

After four months at the headquarters, Roman took a Friday off —his first vacation day. Jirka Čep and his wife had agreed to watch Sebastian, and Roman and Andrea took off for the capital. They stayed in a small hotel above Dupont Circle, and they explored the city on foot. They strolled up Connecticut Avenue, past the Zoo, miles up, all the way to the genteel Chevy Chase, then back down south, stopping at The Politics and Prose bookstore to look for some Beat paperbacks, Roman's fascination. They had a cup of doppio there on the basement floor at a grungy wooden table, then on to the Phillips Gallery with Rothko's blacks and Picasso's blues. In the evening, they had dinner at a small Italian restaurant on Dupont Circle, and, after a brief walk in the warm night, they sat down on a stone bench by the white marble fountain in the center of the Circle, where a duo of gray-haired street musicians were playing "Hallelujah."

The next morning they strolled to Rock Creek Park that was filled with an amalgam of auburn, pink, and crimson fall colors. Then on to Georgetown, and to the White House and the Mall, along broad leafy boulevards with large sedans quietly rolling on blacktop roads. They sat down at the Reflecting Pool, feet in the water, waiting for nightfall when the dome of the Capitol would light up, a soft yellow against the dark sky. They did not talk about the near future, which they sensed was unpredictable. They talked about the beauty of the moment and about other beauties that were sure to come.

WHY WAS HE MUSING about Milan Stránský right now, his former colleague? Sometimes Roman thought that he had an uncanny and trouble-some ability to evoke the memory of a person just before something disastrous, like death, befell them, or before the individual was about to resurface in Roman's life, often under unpropitious circumstances.

When Roman had gone to say goodbye to him, Stránský was sitting at his desk that was almost completely smothered in charts stacked up in several tall columns. Stránský appeared overwhelmed. "Can we talk tomorrow morning?" he pointed to the charts, assuming Roman wanted professional advice from him, as was often the case.

"No, it's not what you think. I am going on vacation tomorrow. To France. Just wanted to say goodbye. I'll see you in two weeks."

"Oh yeah, vacation. I forgot. Where to? Paris?"

"Yeah."

"Well, enjoy it. Mesmerizing city."

"Have you been?"

"Years ago. In the sixties. Aside from the incredible sites and views, what I remember most from that trip was that I almost passed out in a music store when I saw the huge record selection they had. I think the name of the store was Fnac. It was cruel to come back to the gray reality, let me tell you."

Stránský stood up and walked around his desk to Roman. They gave each other a backslap and Roman turned to leave.

"Roman," Stránský called out to him.

"Yes?"

"Don't hesitate."

He's encouraging me to go AWOL. "I'll be back in two weeks, Milan."

Stránský just laughed.

IT WAS LATE FRIDAY AFTERNOON, and Roman locked the documents in the safe, picked up his bag and walked out of the room. He had almost reached the main door leading to the lobby, when his case officer Mike Corsi came up to him from a side hallway.

"Roman, I need to talk to you before you leave. Let's go to my office." Corsi was a large rumpled man with a thick dirty-blond mane swept back in a ponytail.

He sat down behind his desk, and Roman pulled up a chair to face him. "You are probably wondering what this is about," Corsi said, looking at Roman with a fixed gaze. "I may as well make it short. I just received a communication from the Chief of the East European Division. You are being sent on an assignment to Czechoslovakia. I wanted to notify you as soon as I could."

A flood of icy sweat ran across Roman's body, and his heart took off racing. His stomach twisted with a piercing pain that made him bend forward. Here was the worst-case scenario that he had talked to Andrea about. He had worried about it at first when they came to Langley, but after months of translating and settling into a routine, he had gradually started feeling safer, and all but stopped entertaining that possibility. And now...

"Why am I being sent there?" he asked, breathing heavily.

"We received a cable from the Prague station two weeks ago. One of the Czech agents was arrested. Arrests like this are always bad news. He was a careful man. At least we thought he was. Married, two kids. About a week before his arrest, something unfortunate had happened. Do you remember doctor Stránský?"

Sixth sense? "Of course. What about him?"

"He's our agent. In fact, he's a double agent."

What? Stránský, the consummate physician staying at the hospital until late, working on charts? That scholarly appearance. That devotion to his work. Roman was flabbergasted. But then again, Stránský's past had been checkered. And all those Western patients of his. Well, anything is possible.

"You know Stránský was in prison?" Mike asked after giving Roman a few moments to recover.

"Yeah. He didn't want to talk about it."

"He was selling prescription drugs on the black market. Not narcotics or any other mind-altering drugs. Nothing like that. Mainly anti-inflammatories like ibuprofen, naproxen, diclofenac. There's a huge demand for those on the black market in communist countries."

"I know. I used to live there."

"It began as a one-man operation," Corsi continued. "First he started lifting meds from the hospital pharmacy and giving them to patients in return for bribes. But then he thought of putting a price tag on the drugs. He teamed up with the pharmacy manager and another physician. They were writing fake prescriptions. The operation grew; they had to hire people on the outside to distribute the drugs. Eventually it branched out into a big enterprise with multiple parties involved, and that was their ultimate downfall. When one of the middlemen was arrested on an unrelated charge, he spilled the beans about the drug racket."

Roman was silent. The revelation about Stránský was astonishing, but, at this point, he was much more interested in learning why he was being dispatched back to Czechoslovakia.

"Stránský, as the ringleader, was hit the hardest," said Corsi. "He was tried and sentenced to twelve years in prison, which is an unusually long time for a white-collar crime. They may have held him to a different standard because he was a physician. An excellent physician in a top hospital where he treated high-ranking Western diplomats. He was able to establish close patient-physician relationships and friendships with many of them. That didn't go unnoticed by the State Security. A trusted physician would be an ideal confidant. They recruited him in the prison with the intent to make him maintain ties with his prized patients after his release, get useful information from them, and pass it on. In return, he only had to serve two years in the slammer."

"Obviously things were working out. I remember the Mercedes Benzes and Jags with diplomatic plates pulling up in front of our obscure dinky hospital."

Mike nodded. "It was going very well. That's how our Prague guys caught sight of him. We hoped he would give us information he gained from communist diplomats whom he was meeting casually through his Western contacts. We knew that he was greedy, and we made him an offer he couldn't refuse. He's been our agent for several years now."

Mike took a sip of weak lukewarm coffee from a polystyrene cup. "Now back to what happened most recently. Let me explain. First you should know that our agents are not supposed to know each other. We want it that way to limit further damage if one of them is uncovered and interrogated. So, about a week or so before the arrest, our officers were scheduling car passes with Stránský, as well as with the man who was later arrested. A car pass is a quick exchange of material between an officer and an agent done through a car window. The car passes were planned for the same time, same place, but three days apart. There was a mistake made, however, probably on our end, when the dates were communicated to the agents, and Stránský and the other man both showed up on the same day. When Adam, one of our officers, drove up, he saw both of them there, getting ready for the exchange. He realized the error and just rode through, aborting the operation. Soon after, we contacted the two men to find out what they thought had happened. They gave us an identical impression of the encounter. They had noticed each other and made the conclusion that the other person was most likely also an agent. But they didn't talk and went their separate ways. A week later, the arrest came. What bothers us is the temporal relationship between the botched exchange and the arrest. It may very well have been coincidental, but we have to put Stránský under surveillance. He has been a valuable agent to us. At least that's what we thought. We hope that he has nothing to do with what had occured."

"Why would Stránský report him?" Roman asked. "You were paying him well. Everything was going fine up until then, correct?"

"Why would he do that? That's the question. As I said, he may not have done it. But let's say he did it. One possibility could be that he was never serious about betraying the Czech secret services.

"He still works at that same old hospital you were at before you left. We need you to keep track of him for a while." Corsi must have noted the startled, puzzled look on Roman's face because he added; "You will discuss all the details with Johnny Jones, the Prague station chief.

You'll meet him in Ostbaum before you cross back to Czechoslovakia."

"Stránský was my friend. He was kind to me. You're asking me to spy on him. I don't want to do that."

"Roman, I understand how you feel. But on the other hand, you must understand the reality. You signed a contract with the CIA. This is what we do."

"Stránský sensed that I would not be coming back from my vacation. If he still worked for the Czechs, he would have reported me."

"Not necessarily," Corsi replied. "Defection here, defection there. I am not sure that they are extremely worried about that."

"Am I going to have any type of immunity?"

"Only members of the diplomatic corps have immunity. All of our officers are also members of the diplomatic corps, which is why they have immunity. And, in addition, you are still a Czechoslovak citizen. Unfortunately," Corsi shook his head, "you will not have immunity."

"So, if I get arrested, they could try me for treason."

"They could. But we would do everything in our power to help you get out of that predicament if it ever happened."

"Your power behind the iron curtain is very limited."

"You are right, it is."

Roman closed his eyes. The memory of an episode from his childhood emerged. It had happened when he was about ten years old, on vacation with his parents in the mountains. He and his father went on a hike, and, as they were on their way back, a severe lightning storm hit. They had to cross a narrow ledge with sheer cliffs on each side. The rocks forming the ledge were very smooth, polished by thousands of boots that had trodden on them over the years. That day the stones were also wet, and Roman had already enough experience with hiking to know that to step on them was dangerous. "Dad, I don't want to walk over the ledge. We'll slip and fall and die," he said, close to crying.

"We have to get down, son. We have no other options. There are no trees around us. We are the tallest ones here. That makes us easy targets for a lightning strike. Let's get going. We will not slip." His dad put his arm around Roman's shoulders. The truth was, and they both knew it, that if they lost their footing, they would almost certainly be falling down hundreds of feet to their deaths. "We'll have to scramble," his dad said. They dropped down to crawl on all fours, carefully crossed the ridge and made it down safely.

"What are you thinking?" Corsi asked.

The question brought Roman back to the present. "Andrea is pregnant," he said. His voice sounded strange, distant.

"That's great news, but not great timing, I have to admit. I don't think there is anything we can do, Roman. You'll have to go there."

Roman's mind wandered away again. He remembered the conversation he had had with Eva before he left, and her subtle warning that things might not work out to his expectations. He thought about Andrea and the baby. He thought about Mom and Dad. He thought about Stan Goldfarb's assurances.

"Roman?" he heard Mike's voice and he raised his head.

"You'll need to relocate to Camp Peary. That's where we provide training for clandestine tradecraft. It will be more or less a crash course, a few weeks. Once you're done at Camp Peary, you will fly to Europe."

Roman stood up and walked to the window. It was dark outside, and sparse snowflakes, large and fluffy, were slowly falling. "Good night," he said, and headed for the hallway.

CHAPTER 15

FIRST A PHYSICIAN, then a refugee, then a CIA translator, now a spy in training. The fleeting moments of a car pass or a brush pass, best spots for a dead drop, obsessive attention to every detail in the course of any, even the simplest, operation that is undertaken, self-defense, resistance to interrogation; during the time at Camp Peary, Roman mostly felt like he was in a dream, in a hazy, convoluted, disturbing dream, he felt like this was not him, like he was a detached observer looking with indifference at someone else's daily absurd staggerings through a house of mirrors.

The inevitable realization that followed, that this was his life, always left him in a momentary state of paralyzing surprise. But then he had to admit to himself that it was his choice to come to America, on the terms that were offered to him. No matter how trapped he may have felt, this was his choice. Hesitatingly, a little thread of thought started carving inroads into his frontal lobes, the thought of accepting the reality and going along with it, even identifying with it. After all, it was about fighting the Bolshevik, wasn't it? A higher calling.

AIRPORT GATE. Time to board. Roman and Andrea were hugging and neither of them was willing to let go. That strange, unexplainable, forlorn feeling that grips us when we have to leave someone we love, for a long time or forever, that feeling clutched Roman, it permeated his chest, his guts, it glued his legs to the carpeted floor. "I'll turn to God for you," he heard Andrea say. "I'll pray every day that He keep you safe. You will come back to me, my love. I know you will."

And then he was in his assigned seat, he didn't know how he wound up there but there he was by the small round window, the flight attendant demanding that he straighten the backrest and fasten the seatbelt.

ROMAN UNPACKED THE SMALL LUGGAGE at his new residence, a damp studio apartment on the second floor of a building with a green facade, on a narrow and twisty street in the hills of Prague's Lesser Town. He had arrived earlier in the day. Crossing the border from Germany was as smooth as wine; he had been calm and cool and jovial with the guards, but now he felt on edge. It had to be the city making him nervous, his presence in it. He used to live here, then he left, and he was not supposed to be back. But he did come back, with an eerie mission, and it felt very odd to be here, it felt surreal, fateful.

He knew he had to pull himself together if he wanted to make it through in one piece. Desensitization, exposure, that is the way to defeat fears, the good psychologists say. He put his warm coat and hat back on and went out into the streets. He noticed his reflection in a storefront windowpane. He was not yet sure how to reconcile his new looks; glasses with thick, tinted lenses, shoulder-length auburn hair, a neatly trimmed brown beard.

Mounds of blackish snow lined the sidewalks, and the sky was low and heavy. The green domes of St. Nicholas' church, one large and round with a small cupola, the other one tall and narrow, dominated the cityscape, rising above a sea of dark-red Spanish tile roofs. He took a left before Charles Bridge and walked toward Valdštejnská street with its embassies and terraced gardens, and he continued up the hill to the Castle, a long, steady climb, until a magnificent panorama opened before him, multiple domes and steeples scattered over the valley and the hills, bridges spanning the winding river, a beautiful city under a heavy boot, breathing but not living.

It was freezing inside the apartment when he returned. He went down to the dank dark basement, loaded a coal scuttle with briquettes, and back in the pad he made fire in the small metal stove.

Tomorrow will be his first car exchange.

HE HAD RECEIVED THE KEYS to the studio two days earlier from Johnny Jones, the Prague station chief. "We are renting it from a very secure source," Jones told him when he handed him the keys. They were in Ostbaum, in a CIA safe-house apartment, where they huddled over sandwiches and a bottle of coke. The small windowless room they were sitting in had a concrete floor, completely bare gray walls, and a sink in the corner. The door was equipped with a hefty latch.

Jones must have been in his forties, trim and athletic, short dark hair slightly graying on the temples. His official role at the American Embassy was assistant cultural attaché.

"I have two deputies, Gina Roberts and Adam Norlund," Jones continued in a slow bass-baritone. "They've been in Prague for a little over a year. As I am sure you know, the Czech secret police closely tracks American diplomats. We've developed ways to get away from them for brief periods of time so that we can accomplish things we need to. In Prague, with a bunch of narrow tortuous streets and abundant passageways, it's actually easier to elude surveillance than in most other East European capitals. But the State Security is still on our asses most of the time. We will give you an electronic transmitting device to send and receive encrypted messages. But when it comes to providing and exchanging material, it will have to be through car passes or brush passes or, less preferably, through dead drops. Our direct contact will need to be limited to only seconds at a time and to instances when we are not being followed, otherwise they would quickly detect you through us."

"We practiced all this at Camp Peary," Roman said. Soon he may be assessing familiar Prague streets for car pass suitability. It felt bizarre.

Jones opened his briefcase. "Here is your fake passport and identity card."

Roman carefully examined the documents. They were in the name of a Jan Paleček.

"Don't ask me how we came into their possession," Jones said with a short laugh. "Other than changing the photographs, we just had to tweak a few data. The guys who worked on this are experts, so have no worries. Here is an exit visa permit and a train ticket for tomorrow morning. Border crossing stamps and the exit visa permit indicate that you left Prague two weeks ago for a tourist trip to France and Germany. I wrote up a little sightseeing itinerary for you in case they ask where you've been. So you may want to glance at it this evening. I assumed it would be easier if I put it together rather than you having to cobble up a vacation plan tonight. Here are a thousand crowns. We'll supply you with more once you're in Prague. You shouldn't carry too much across the border." He reached under the desk and pulled out a shopping bag. "I bought you some gift items so that you are a convincing tourist."

Roman emptied the bag. "Nice beer mug, John. It'll come handy. If there is one thing I'm looking forward to, it's a pint of cold crisp Gambrinus[2]." There was also a jar of Ostbaum mustard and a box of lebkuchen[3].

"How are you feeling?" Jones asked.

"If I told you I was completely at ease, I would be lying."

"Understandable and expected." Jones looked at Roman intently; "You need to know that we will do all that's in our power to keep you safe. This can be a dangerous business, but rest assured that we will have your back."

A warm, relaxing wave spread through Roman's body. This was the first time during their conversation that Jones showed concern and perhaps even a hint of emotion. Whether he meant it or not, was secondary. Roman just needed to hear it.

"If you are asked about what you do for a living, tell them you're a paralegal in a law office. This is the office address, and here is the name of one of the lawyers. You may want to memorize this information."

Roman chuckled. "The darkest place is under the lantern. That's how the saying goes. Let's hope it's true."

"We'll have to execute a car exchange soon after you arrive in Prague," Jones said. "I checked out some potential sites we haven't used yet. One suitable area for this seems to be Bronzová Street. It has four sharp curves, and, within a two hundred yard stretch, there are three side streets and three pedestrian passageways branching off of it. That provides enough opportunities to shake off surveillance."

Roman used to ride his bike on that street, and he remembered the switchbacks with fondness.

"We'll put a package together for you. The transmitter, some invisible ink, water-soluble paper, a few other things. And more funds, of course. How about if we plan the exchange for the day after tomorrow? One day after you arrive in Prague. Let's do it after dark. At about seven. Will you be up to it?"

"We may as well get it done."

"If you approach Bronzová from Národní Avenue, the first passageway is located right after the second curve. We will come in front of the passageway in a small Fiat with diplomatic license plates. If either you or we sense that it's not safe to proceed, the missions will be immediately aborted. In that case, we would try again the following day. An hour later."

"Will the passageway be open at those times of day? Some of them close after six."

"It's open. I checked yesterday to make sure," Jones answered and paused briefly, refilling the plastic cups with Coca Cola.

"Now let's get down to real business," the station chief resumed. "It's my understanding that Mike Corsi informed you about the arrest of one of our agents and about the possible connection to Milan Stránský."

"Yes, he gave me a detailed briefing."

"Okay. We'll need your help getting information on Stránský. As much information as we can get. What is the layout of the hospital?"

The plain nature of Jones' demand and question made Roman shudder inside. He knew all along what his general task would be, but now, facing the stark reality of having to spy on Milan, he was filled with revulsion, frustration, and shame. "There are two buildings, about three hundred yards apart," he said after a tense pause. "They are connected by an asphalt walkway. There are rather dense woods surrounding the campus, including the walkway. Most of the foot traffic is in the larger building. The smaller building has some hospital beds for stable patients. Stránský's office is in the smaller building."

"Are the buildings locked at night?"

Roman nodded. "The main doors. But both buildings have a service elevator. The elevator can be entered from the outside, and you can then get into the building using the door on the other side of the elevator."

"That sounds auspicious." The hitherto stone-faced Jones showed a reserved smile. "One way to get information from Stránský would be to bug his office. Planting the equipment should be feasible based on what you just told me. We could place a bug in his office, but we would then need a radio transmitter with a built-in tape recorder somewhere in the vicinity to record the conversations, and we'd have to collect the full tapes and exchange them for empty ones at regular intervals. Going back repeatedly to do this may be our only option, but the risk of eventually getting uncovered will increase with each retrieval. Can you think of any other way to handle the recordings? Anybody there you could completely trust to help?"

Roman took his time to answer. "Whom can you completely trust?" he laughed. "You know as well as I do, or even better, that the country is saturated with the State Security and their informers. I'll give it a consideration, though."

CHAPTER 16

THE CAR PASS WAS ACCOMPLISHED within seconds and without a hitch, at least that was his impression. A young woman, it must have been Gina Roberts, drove up with the passenger window already rolled down. Roman got a glimpse of the short curly red hair and an open, smiling face. She gave him the package and was gone.

He quickly blended into the passageway. Stepping into a nook in the wall where a storefront of a now closed shop was located, he slipped the package inside his backpack and resumed the brisk pace. He walked around the National Theater building and, instead of taking the closest bridge across the river, he chose a longer route, making sure he only walked for a short distance on a particular street before switching to a different one. He was grateful for the confusing dense web of narrow intersecting roads in the Old Town.

After about a mile, he concluded that he was not being followed but continued with the precautions nonetheless. He started having severe hunger pangs, a sensation that he would often develop when a tense situation he had been exposed to, abated. Once in the apartment he ravenously attacked the small fridge, taking out whatever food he could lay his hands on and shoving it in his mouth. Twenty minutes later, with his hunger subsiding, he opened the package. There was the electronic transmitter, along with all the other items that Jones had talked about. Roman found the cash in a separate small plastic bag, and he unpacked several items to be used for disguises: glasses, fake beards and moustaches, wigs. There was also a tiny iron that he put to use right away to bring out the text of the note that Jones had written in invisible ink. In it, he encouraged Roman to familiarize himself with the transmitter and asked him to send a message once he was ready to begin surveillance on Stránský. It was clear that Jones wanted to get things moving as soon as possible.

ROMAN STOOD ON THE STREET CORNER, his hat pulled so far down on his forehead that it almost covered his eyes. It was five o'clock, and his parents just left their apartment building. He was glad to see that they still adhered to their daily routine—a stroll before dinner in every season. They turned toward their destination, a small park about half a mile away. He watched them from behind. Dad, tall and erect, wearing his favorite black fedora with a wide brim and a long black wool coat, Mom without a head cover, in a beige down jacket, their silhouettes diminishing. He so much wanted to run to them and hug them, to tell them the whole story, or just parts of it, to sit down with them at the kitchen table with that familiar patterned laminated top, like they used to. He turned around and, fighting tears, started walking away, first slowly and then with increasing speed, blending with other moving figures into a dark continuous mass rolling through the city streets.

ROMAN TOOK THE LAST BUS RIDE of the day to the hospital. It was Tuesday. Hospital visiting hours were limited to Tuesdays and Saturdays, and the physician on call on Tuesdays was always chief Svoboda. This way he was able to apprise the families of their relatives' condition and graciously accept their incentives. Roman could only hope that this arrangement still continued. It was nine in the evening when he exited the bus. Visiting hours should be over by now. Nursing shift change would be taking place at eleven. He expected the traffic on the road leading to the hospital to be minimal, but there could still be an occasional ambulance riding by, so he chose to walk in the wooded area adjacent to the driveway.

After five minutes of treading carefully so as to minimize the noise made by his footsteps, he was able to see the small hospital building in the clearing, its gray facade illuminated by a lonely neon light above the main entrance. He waited in the woods, observing. He located the window of Stránský's second floor office. There was no light emanating from it, and Roman thought it safe to assume that Stránský had left for the day.

There was dead silence around him, so complete that it was noisy; ringing and sibilant sounds enveloped in blackness. The nurse must have already finished dispensing the evening medications, and she is probably sitting comfortably on the couch in the nurses' station, legs crossed, door closed, sipping a cup of coffee or a glass of wine, smoking, watching the tube.

After taking one more look, he dashed to the service elevator at the back side of the building. He stepped in and waited for a few seconds. All was quiet. Carefully opening the inside door, he saw the dark hallway of the first floor. He advanced, slowly, gingerly, moving noiselessly by the closed door of the nurses' station. No patients were wandering the halls. He reached the stairs and started going up. Stránský's door was closed but not locked. This was what Roman anticipated.

He quickly slipped into the office and shut the door behind him. He collapsed into the rolling chair at the desk and sat there motionless, chin on his chest, arms hanging over the armrests, legs stretched. A few minutes later, with his heartbeat and breathing calming down, he felt his mental strength coming back. *Let's get to work*, he prodded himself.

He moved to the floor and opened his backpack. He pulled out a flashlight, put his handkerchief over it to dim the glow, and surveyed the walls. He located two electrical sockets and removed the covers with a small screwdriver, and he placed a tiny microphone bug in each socket hole. The devices were sound-activated, with a battery life of up to eight weeks and a signal range of five hundred yards. State of the art, according to Jones. They had debated about tapping the phone too, but bugs were easily detectable in phones, so they had decided against it. Roman screwed the outlet covers back on and carefully checked the white paint around them. It was intact. There was a light dusting of plaster on the carpet under the sockets, and he meticulously removed all of it with a piece of cloth.

Roman stood up and briefly shone the light at the desk. It was almost completely covered with charts, except for one corner that was taken up by two framed photographs. One was a headshot of a smiling woman with a tanned face, eyes the color of periwinkles, and short, curly, mahogany hair. The other photo showed Stránský with two teenage girls, standing on a lake's sandy shore, Stránský in the middle, holding both girls' hands.

ROMAN LOOKED AT HIS WATCH. It was ten o'clock. He had to leave right away. Nurses would usually come about half an hour before the start of their shift to have enough time for the sign out and for some chatting and exchanging gossip with the outgoing team. He opened the door. All was peaceful. The elevator was still on the first floor. Soon he was outside and, under the cover of the woods, he put on his head lamp. After some searching, he located the trail that he had occasionally taken to the city, alone or with Eva, when he still worked at the hospital. He opened a thermos bottle, took a big drink of warm, sweet tea, and set out on his way.

CHAPTER 17

IT WAS THE EVENING RUSH HOUR in Prague, and Eva Kubová emerged from the subway, clutching her bag tightly in her hand. She was being thrown and knocked around from all sides, until the throng released her in the underpass outside the entrance where, sighing with relief, she stepped on the escalator that carried her to a tram stop in the street above. There was a mass of people there too, waiting, inert for the moment, but ready to unleash its entropic kinetic power once a tram was in sight. Eva was not ready to face another human press, choosing instead to walk to the next tram stop that she knew would be less crowded. In front of her, the sharp black steeples of a neo-gothic church towered over other buildings like a giant two-armed candelabra. It was late winter, dirty snow remnants had melted away, and days were becoming longer, heralding the season of renewal.

"How are you, Eva?" she heard a male voice. She turned her head, startled. The voice was familiar but the person it belonged to was not.

"Who are you? How do you know my name?"

"You know me, Eva. How was the hospital today?"

She looked again at the man who was speaking, and her eyes widened. Now she knew. "Ro..." He grabbed her wrist and put his finger across his lips, stopping her from saying his whole name.

"What are you doing here? And this new appearance? What is going on?" she asked in a hushed, tense voice.

"I'm back. Can I walk with you?"

"You are here, and they didn't throw you in jail?"

"No. Tell me Eva, how have you been? How's work? Still toiling in our precious little hospital?"

"Yes. Nothing much has changed."

"Stránský and Svoboda still competing with each other?"

"More than ever." She shook her head and raised her eyebrows. "Roman, I don't understand. Tell me—"

"How are you otherwise?" he interrupted her. "Still single?"

"Still single. What about you?"

"Likewise."

"So, what country did you end up in?" she asked after a brief pause.

"Somewhere out there."

"Are you going to tell me why you came back?"

"It's a little complicated. I will try to explain. Where are you headed?"

"The tram stop in The Peace Square, but we are almost there. I can skip it. We can walk a little longer and talk," Eva said.

They were at an intersection, and Roman turned onto a quiet narrow street to their right. Eva followed. Roman looked around. He could not see anyone tracking them. They resumed walking.

"Eva, I've been often thinking about the time when I left. I hurt you. I am sorry."

"Don't be sorry. Let's not hark back to it. Let's just remember the good times we had together." She slowed her pace. "Are you going to tell me what is happening? You didn't just run into me by chance, did you?"

"Fortuity is an occasional necessity, Eva. So, you're not angry with me?"

"No. I admit, I was angry and hurt for a while after you left, but emotions tend to fade as time goes by."

They walked in silence. He wanted to get to the point, but he hesitated. The day before, he was still certain that he could trust Eva. But tonight, a thread of doubt crept in. They had not seen each other in months. They used to be very close, but he had ended their relationship by leaving the country. It would be natural for Eva to resent him, notwithstanding her reassurance to the contrary. And how could he be sure that he ever truly knew her?

He still had time to back out. He could say goodbye to her and vanish into the darkness and tell Jones that he got cold feet. But in the end, his faith in her prevailed.

"Eva," he said, breaking his stride. "I trusted you back then. Can I still trust you?"

She gave him a puzzled look. "Trust me with what?"

"With everything."

"Roman, what are you up to?"

"Can you first answer my question?"

They were passing by a strong neon light. She gazed at him with her dreamy gray eyes and smiled. "Of course you can."

WHEN JONES HAD ASKED Roman in Ostbaum if there was someone in the hospital he could count on, he had thought of Eva right away. But this would not be asking someone to watch their house or a piece of luggage or a dog. This would be asking someone to get involved in a very risky enterprise. Eva was no sworn enemy of the regime. She was no Mata Hari. Why would she agree to work with Western spies? And to hell with the mission goals trumping conscience, why should he be putting her in peril? He had brooded over the bizarre prospect of contacting her for several days, and, in the end, he'd rationalized that it would be her free choice to get involved. He notified Jones that he intended to approach her, and, after exchanging several communications, Jones gave his approval.

"Eva, I am working for a Western government," Roman said, after glancing around to make sure no one was nearby. "I need your help."

Eva's alarmed expression was of no surprise to Roman, nor was the long silence that she finally broke. "Did you come back as a spy?

And why on earth are you talking to me about this?"

She was going to bolt. He shouldn't have contacted her. It was a mistake. But to his astonishment, she continued to walk next to him; she didn't run away. They took a shortcut through a deserted park. Dark silhouettes of dense tree branches illumined by a pale moonlight were violently swaying in the wind like a portent, a foreboding.

"So you became a Western spy. You are not a doctor any more. Oh my gosh, Roman." She sighed. Then she asked: "Help with what?"

Roman looked at her, surprised by how easily, how naturally the question came out. "Placing a device in a certain location and checking on the device. There would be a financial incentive associated with this."

She took a few steps away from him, then turned to face him. "This is crazy. I am heading home from work minding my own business, and a former boyfriend ambushes me with the proposition that I become an agent." She shook her head. "I wish I was still in love with you. It would be an easier decision."

He did not respond.

"How did you get involved in this?" she asked. "A higher purpose, higher than curing people? Or something else?"

"Initially something else, but later a higher purpose became part of it." He touched her arm lightly. "Eva, are you considering helping us?"

"I don't know. Why should I? Because I hate the communists? Wanting to be part of something bigger? Because I may still like you? Because I am crazy enough to put my life in danger? Money? I don't know. Why don't you give me some more details about what you would want me to do. What kind of device we are talking about? Who, or what, you're asking me to surveil because I assume that's your objective? Knowing more would help."

"Eva, I don't think the details would help you make a decision. The job related to the device itself has a low risk. It's really deciding about the big picture of getting involved with a hostile agency. Think about it. Let it sink in. How about if we set up a time and place to meet. Maybe a week from now? You would come only if you chose to join us. If you turn up, I will give you a packet with some items and instructions. If, after looking at what's in it, you change your mind and conclude you do not want to do this after all, you would just need to let me know. I will leave you information on how to notify me about both a positive and a negative decision."

"This is a spy film." Eva forced out a laugh. "I am telling myself this is a spy film."

"Not a bad way to think about it." He paused, then asked; "Would meeting a week from now, next Thursday, work for you? At seven p.m.?"

"Let me see. I am post-call that day so I will be able to leave the hospital on time. That should be fine. Where?"

"The corner of Karlova and Jilská Street, in front of the Matryoshka store. It's a pedestrian zone full of people any time of day, but that's to our advantage. The more tumult the better. I'll stick around until seven thirty. If you are not there by then, I will assume you opted against working with us."

"Fair."

"Eva, if you come, it will have to be a very short encounter. I will hand you the packet, and you will need to hide it fast. I will quickly disappear. I don't think I am being followed as of now but that may change."

She looked at him intently for a moment, then glanced away. "This is all so unreal."

"I used to feel like that, but the longer I do this, the more real it seems."

"Which country do you work for? Germany?"

"I prefer not to go into that. I trust you completely but it's better for both of us if I share less information with you for now."

"Where are you staying? Do you have a stable roof over your head, or are you just hiding in the dreary streets of Prague?"

"I am kind of everywhere. I'm getting to know my native city from a different perspective. From a creepy, surreptitious perspective."

They turned onto a busy, well-lit street with a nearby tram stop. They both came to a halt. Roman felt guilt-ridden; he'd just bushwhacked his friend and erstwhile lover and made the craziest request she had probably ever received. That must have left her very confused and upset.

"Eva, you listened to me. You didn't run. You are a beautiful woman inside and out. I so wish that the circumstances could be different."

"Life follows a twisted path sometimes, Roman. I may bump into you in a week at seven p.m., right?"

JOHNNY JONES SET UP AN URGENT CAR PASS to provide Roman with a radio receiver and a supply of tapes. If Eva did not come to their arranged meeting location, Roman would be ready to place the device himself.

HE MADE A FIRE IN THE RICKETY STOVE and sat down next to it to absorb the soothing heat. When he could not see the steam of his breath any longer, he moved to the small rectangular desk, its worn plywood surface covered with carvings of dagger-pierced hearts, skulls and bones, misshapen faces, sex acts, a trail left behind by its successive, nameless users. What were their life stories? Roman wondered. He started composing a note to Eva. He let her know that Stránský was the person under surveillance but he did not specify the reason why. He explained that the tape in the receiver was set to automatically start rolling at five p.m. and to stop two hours later to capture the time that Stránský was most likely spending in his office after finishing the afternoon rounds. The tapes could hold four hours of recording, so a new tape would need to be inserted every other day. The start and the stoppage of the tape was noiseless. Eva could hide the radio receiver in the wardrobe in her office, which was in the larger hospital building, about three hundred yards from Stránský's location, still within the range of the reception signal of the listening devices.

Roman directed Eva to make one chalk mark on the electrical box standing on the corner of Vodní Street and Fiala Street if, after having gone over the contents of the packet, she resolved to collaborate, and two marks if she decided not to. He asked her to burn the items from the package if she made the decision not to work with them, and to bury what could not be burnt. He also set up a date and location for a quick exchange of full and empty tapes and any other material in a month, in order to have the exchange already planned if Eva was to join them. He put the instructions and the radio receiver and fifteen recording tapes in a small cardboard box and carefully sealed it.

Tomorrow was Thursday. He was thinking about Eva. He was hoping she would be there. He wanted to see her again.

CHAPTER 18

EVA CAME FIVE MINUTES AFTER SEVEN, wearing a long narrow black coat that made her look even taller than she was, blue jeans, knee-high leather boots, and a red beret. She carried a turquoise patterned bag. She scanned the surroundings, turned to the shop window full of dolls, then she pivoted toward the street again. Roman watched her for a few seconds from across the road. She could have made herself appear a little less conspicuous, he thought. He surveyed the area one more time. About twenty yards from the store was a passageway. People were ambling and milling around, a large group of boisterous tourists was approaching, likely East Germans. Auspicious conditions. He was holding the parcel in his right hand, covered with a wide scarf. He quickly crossed the street and walked up to Eva. Their eyes met. He moved the scarf to his left forearm for distraction, handed her the box, and she slipped it into the bag. They smiled at each other, and he took off for the passageway in a brisk walk. The German tourists were strolling by him, laughing, singing.

He almost reached the passage when the revelry abruptly changed into screams and curses. He turned his head and saw several men in gray coats and black hats pushing through the dense crowd, shoving people out of the way. They were moving in his direction.

Fuck. He darted into the passage, took a right after a few yards, then a quick left. He glanced back. He didn't see the men but heard their shouts and the sound of boots thumping the ground. There was an open metal door on his right, probably a back entrance to a business, he ran inside, slammed the door shut and locked it. He looked around, disoriented. A young woman in a white apron and a chef's hat was standing in the middle of a dimly lit room. "What do you think you're doing here? Get out, now!" She pointed at the door.

There are moments in life to take a risk and hope that it will pay off. This was that moment. "I am running from the State Security. I need to hide. They will be here any second." Just as he finished, the door started echoing with a barrage of bangs, and bellowing voices demanded to be let in. There was a massive refrigerator standing against the wall. The woman strode to it, unlocked the wheels, and moved it by a few feet with surprising ease.

A recess in the wall, previously masked by the behemoth, appeared. The banging continued. Roman ran to the alcove and crawled in. He barely fit, but he squeezed in as tight as he could. The woman moved the refrigerator back into its original position. Roman heard a clicking noise; he presumed she locked the wheels in. Then the sound of the door opening.

"What took you so long? This is State Security!"

"I was in the kitchen flipping steaks. This is a restaurant."

"Did you see a man run in? Medium height, thick glasses, beard, long hair?"

"No, I did not."

"Let's scope the place, boys. Let's make sure."

He heard the cops opening and shutting the fridge door. Then the huge cuboid started to shake and rock, but its base stayed in place. "The bitch doesn't want to budge, dammit," Roman heard a thick voice say. "Let's move on."

They must not have noticed the wheels. Their voices grew gradually distant, they probably advanced to the kitchen and on to the dining area. Roman was taking shallow breaths. His temples were pounding. He hoped Eva got away. The hand off had been as fast as lightning, the package was concealed by the scarf until the last moment. There had been crowds of people in the street, but nobody close to Eva and Roman. The security goons hadn't seen the exchange, they couldn't have, he was trying to convince himself. He was not able to explain what had happened. He had taken multiple detours to get to the meeting place. He was certain no one tracked him. Those brutes were lying in wait. They knew he would be there. Someone had alerted them.

IT FELT LIKE HE WAS IN HIS NARROW HIDING PLACE for eternity. Then, at last, he heard the woman's voice. "They've been gone for over an hour. I even checked outside, and I didn't see them." He heard the clicking sound again, and the fridge moved. He stepped out of the nook, stretched, and took several deep breaths. He looked at the woman. Only now did he notice her large brown eyes and light complexion, with a multitude of small freckles sprayed on her cheeks and over the bridge of her upturned nose. She wore a subtle, sympathetic smile.

"You did something very few people would do. You are brave. I don't know how to thank you," Roman said to her.

"You better get going before someone walks in here on us. Good luck. I hope I won't see you on the evening news."

"I'll do my best to avoid that. I'm not very telegenic. Where's the bathroom?"

"There is a hallway right outside of this room. Turn left into the hallway. You'll see the bathroom door on your left."

Once he locked himself in the bathroom, Roman removed the glasses, the fake beard, the wig, and placed them all in his backpack. Suddenly, his cold hands turned warm. He felt relaxed. He was hungry, and he was thirsty. He walked into the restaurant. It was full of people, and he saw only one empty seat, across from a middle-aged man who was working on his meat and dumplings.

Roman strode to the table and pulled out the chair. The waiter happened to be right there, balancing a large circular sheet metal tray on his shoulder and the palm of his hand. The tray was loaded with dewy glass mugs overflowing with beer. Without asking, the waiter put a pint in front of Roman on the table with a big thud, as if making a point. Roman took a swig and wiped the foam off his lips.

The beer had a sharp, bitter bite. It hit the spot. The server was still nearby, offloading the mugs, and Roman placed an order for beef liver. Just then he noticed that his neighbor at the table was smiling at him. Roman smiled back.

"Thirsty, huh?" the man said.

"Yeah. I had a busy day."

"What do you do?"

"I'm a grave digger," Roman replied.

"Then you should not be afraid of dying, with so much death around you."

"Good point."

"Think about death five times a day, and you won't be scared of it. That's what some people say." The man laughed. "But they don't tell me this. Why do most people die in the early morning?"

"Maybe it's the mercy of the higher powers. If you die in the early morning, you usually die in your sleep. Isn't it a beautiful death?" He should have come up with some other idea for an occupation.

"Where do you dig graves?"

"Up in the Olšanské cemetery."

"Your hands are not rough enough for a grave digger."

"I put lotion on them, and I wear gloves. I want my hands soft when I caress my wife."

"How thoughtful of you. You sound like a decent fellow." He turned serious. "I see death too, sometimes. I'm a cop. I work in the criminal division. Today's my day off."

Roman dug into the liver smothered in roasted onions. It was bloody and delicious.

"Pretty hungry, too," the cop said. "Looks like you haven't eaten the whole day."

Roman nodded. The man leaned a little closer. "Did you just shave off a beard? The lower part of your face is much lighter than the rest."

"This morning, in fact. I got tired of it. Have you ever grown a beard?"

"Nope, I like a clean shave."

"It's hard to sleep with a beard. The pillow pulls on the hairs. But my wife enjoyed it when I tickled her belly with it." Roman finished the liver. The beer was already gone. He put twenty crowns on the table. "Gotta go. It's getting late."

"Good grave-digging!" the cop chuckled, showing yellow teeth.

It was nine thirty. There were still plenty of people in the streets. Roman walked at a rapid pace, with his face down. The apartment could be under surveillance, the police could be waiting for him there. But he had to alert the team about the unexpected turn of events, and he didn't have the electronic transmitter with him. Almost subconsciously, he started heading in the direction of his digs.

Once on his quiet lane, he scaled down his speed, now inching ahead cautiously, watching the surroundings. Enough light was emanating from the street lamps to tell him that the few cars parked along the curb were empty, unless someone was hiding in them lying on the floor. The building gate was open, and the hallway light was on. A good sign. He crept inside and started going up the stairs slowly, quietly. The door to his apartment, as well as the lock, didn't look damaged. He took a deep breath, turned the key, and stepped inside. No one ambushed him, and the pad appeared untouched. He closed the door behind him and locked it.

He walked to the bed, lifted the transmitter from underneath it, put it on the desk, typed in his message and labeled it urgent. He lit a cigarette and started pacing around the small room in rapid circles until he felt dizzy. He stirred the embers in the stove, added a few briquettes, and he filled the kettle with water for tea and placed it on the stove top. He put a couple of sugar cubes and a tea bag in a slightly chipped porcelain cup, and once the water was hot, he poured it in the mug and resumed pacing, at a lower speed than before, the tea cup in his hand.

He glanced at his watch; he had sent the message half an hour earlier, and still no answer. He picked up his copy of *The Three Musketeers*, the only book he had in the apartment; he forced himself to sit down, and he opened the novel on a random page. *"Count de la Fère,"* *whispered Milady, turning pale and retreating until she was stopped by* *the wall. "Yes Milady," said Athos. "Count de la Fère is coming from the* *underworld to enjoy the pleasure of your company."*

The transmitter beeped and he lunged toward it.

The message was from Adam, Jones' junior partner, and Roman hoped that Adam had been able to communicate with Jones before he sent it.

"You need to get out of the country," he started reading. "The State Security and the uniformed police are looking for you. If you try at an official border crossing, you will be identified. Taking you across in a van is out of question; vehicles are searched. Your only choice is the border fence. The risk is huge, but there are no good options right now. I contacted Jan Soukup, a lieutenant with the Border Patrol and also our agent. He'll wait for you in Knížecí Pláně between six and seven p.m., starting tomorrow, then daily for seven days. Coming into town from the East, take the second road on your right from the main street. You will see a wooded park on your right. In the middle of it is The Memorial of The Heroes of The Revolution. Look for Soukup around there. He will be in a green parka and a black scarf. When you see him, say this in English: *Steal a little and they throw you in* *jail*[4]. He will respond, also in English: *Steal a lot and they make you* *king.*[5] He will provide you with items and instructions to help you get across the border.

The transmitter will not be of much use to you during the escape. In fact, it would implicate you if the police found it on you," the message concluded. "Burn it, together with any other incriminating items, before you leave. Best of luck."

He was tapping the desktop with his fingertips. Could it get worse? Yes, it could. But this was bad enough. If he is arrested, he is doomed. The worst imaginable outcome, the trial for treason that he had talked about with Andrea before he made the decision to join the CIA, was becoming a distinct possibility. His chances of pulling through were extremely tenuous.

He was sinking into despair. Should he give himself up to expedite the inevitable? He thought about his parents. They lived so close. Less than two miles away. He wished he could just walk over to them and confide in them and get their advice. He laughed at the absurdity of that notion.

His parents escaped almost certain death during the war. They fought for their lives. They did not capitulate.

Roman sat down on the bed, leaned forward and closed his eyes. He evoked the image of his parents as fighters. He pictured them with machine guns in their hands. Or placing explosives next to the railroad tracks.

He rose and lit another cigarette. *I am their son*, he said to himself, crisscrossing the room. *I am their son. I will not surrender.*

Back at the desk, he unfolded a map of Czechoslovakia. Knížecí Pláně was smack on the Southwestern border with West Germany. He was barely able locate it; the name was typed in the smallest print. The distance between Prague and this one dog town was one hundred and sixty kilometers. Two hours by car. His journey there will take much longer.

He made himself concentrate on his escape. It may take him several days to get to the border. He will likely have to spend the nights outdoors, and navigate in the wilderness. He should avoid going to stores to shop for supplies. He has to be ready for hostile encounters.

He took a notepad and wrote down a list of things he needed for the road. About ten days earlier he had gone to the supermarket and bought some items that he thought would be important to have in an emergency situation. The CIA team had also supplied him with a few items for that purpose. He walked over to the small particle board dresser and opened the drawers. He was relieved to see that he had most of the articles that he had written on his list.

He picked up his rucksack, sat it on a chair and unzipped it. He packed some supplemental clothes—a woolen pullover, a knitted hat, a scarf, and ski gloves. He added a head lamp, extra batteries, a compass, several pieces of rope, each about one and a half yards long, a roll of duct tape, an emergency blanket, a first aid kit, toilet paper. He will carry a Winchester folding knife in his pants pocket.

He opened the refrigerator and took out three bottles of water, several buns and rolls, a few apples, and a bag of walnuts. The backpack was getting full, and he had to use the remaining space artfully to fit all the food in. He still had a couple of hard-boiled eggs in the fridge that he would pack in the morning before leaving.

It was past midnight when he finished his preparations. He was getting sleepy. He planned to take off between five and six in the morning, unless the Security boys got to him first.

CHAPTER 19

A NINE-YEAR-OLD GIRL sat in a wicker chair on the back porch of a weekend house, drinking a glass of carrot juice, a tabby kitten curled up in her lap. Her mom and dad were leaning against the wooden balustrade, looking at her with adoration. Behind them, into the distance, a multitude of tall orange sandstone rocks protruded from the dense, dark-green vegetation. "I love the cottage." The girl's singsong voice made her parents smile. "It's so much nicer to spend the weekends here than in Prague."

The child's father sat down beside her. He was a solid man with a ruddy complexion, a large furrowed forehead, and a sharp, determined gaze. "Yes, it's wonderful here," he said and he patted her gently on the head with his rough, meaty hand. "You know, Eva," he continued after a short pause, "your mom and dad didn't have a childhood like this."

"I know. Grandma told me. Sometimes you went hungry."

"Yes. Your grandparents were workers, at the mercy of the factory owners. When they didn't have work, which happened often, they could not provide for their children, they could not put food on the table. That all changed after the war."

"Yeah. Because we have socialism now," the girl said.

"That's right. Our communist leaders are making sure it will stay that way. And the Soviet Union is standing behind us. They are our most faithful friends. Our everlasting friends. You know, these days everyone has a job. You don't see beggars in the streets, do you?"

"No, never." The youngster indignantly shook her head.

"Children don't go hungry. People are healthier because it doesn't cost them any money to go to the doctor. Schools are free. You can be whatever you want to be as long as you do all your homework."

"I want to be a cook when I grow up. Or a gardener."

Her father smiled, then his face turned focused again. "There are people, some of them rule whole countries, who've been trying to take our system away from us. To change it back to how it was before."

"Those are bad people."

"Very bad people. And we need to protect our country from them."

"Yes Dad, I will protect it." She saw Mom nodding with pride from the railing.

"Evička, I am telling you all this because you are now big enough to know and understand. And you should always remember what we just talked about."

Eva did not forget. But as she grew older, as she became a teenager, she discovered that quite a few of her friends and classmates had views, albeit expressed carefully and quietly, that were not hers. They ridiculed the obtuse leaders with rudimentary vocabularies, they mocked the five-year economic plans that were putting the country more and more behind; and some, admittedly not too many, even dared say that there was no freedom in the land. Eva wanted to fit in, she wanted to be a cool kid, and she learned not to show her views, to listen, not to disagree.

Later on, she even adopted some of the contrarian opinions and criticisms of the system, but her basic conviction, that the communist rule was fundamentally right and just and worth defending, did not change. And when she received a call, in the first year of medical school, from a captain Kohout with the State Security, she agreed to meet him without hesitation. Kohout informed Eva that her father had worked for the State Security for decades and only recently had asked to be relieved of his responsibilities because of his age.

The captain knew that she was not aware of her father's involvement, but he had her dad's permission to tell her about it. Kohout imparted to Eva that the State Security needed young people from all walks of life, explaining that the communist regime was still facing threats, internal and external, and it had to be protected by citizens like her.

"I will protect it," she remembered telling her dad on that balmy sunlit afternoon more than ten years before, with a tabby kitten purring in her lap. "I will protect it," she said to captain Kohout in his office in The Tiled Cage, the feared national headquarters of the State Security.

EVA THREW HER COAT over the backrest of the chair in her kitchenette, poured a tall shot of Pernod and gulped it down. She could not get the image of the secret police chasing after Roman out of her head. She fixed herself another drink, opened the package Roman had handed to her, and started reading the note. So, it was Stránský they were after. *Huh, interesting.* She always suspected he was a fellow State Security agent, she had run into him once or twice in the dark corridors of The Tiled Cage, they barely acknowledged each other there. Why would he be on the radar of a Western intelligence service? She knew the Westerners did not have enough manpower in the country to spy on State Security agents. There must be something more to it. She will let Kohout and his men figure it out.

She turned on the TV. Late night news was on, the anchor announcing a critical shortage of coal. She snickered. *Classrooms won't be heated. Children will have a coal vacation.* She started thinking about the last week, about her work, the other work. She wasn't a small-time informer. She believed people should be free to say whatever they wanted unless they were plotting against the system. She did not report Roman when he told her he planned to defect, not only because she loved him, but because she did not think it was important.

Occasionally, she crashed diplomatic functions and parties at embassies, she did not truly crash them, Kohout always procured an invitation, these were fertile grounds for spies and counter-spies, and her charms proved invaluable; but most of the time she just kept her eyes and ears open and she let people come her way. She believed in coincidences, in chance encounters, in fate.

A couple of months earlier she had met a fellow in a bar, an affable man, very handsome, his face looked vaguely familiar but she couldn't place him. He told her he was a journalist, two children, marriage on the rocks, they quickly hit it off, and when they were riding on the subway train on the way to her apartment, she suddenly remembered where she had seen him.

About two years before, she had been running some errands in the suburbs. It had been a steamy day, and she had to sit down on a bench to take a rest. She saw a man come out of the wooded area of a neighborhood park the bench was facing. He had a bag over his shoulder. He briefly stopped at a lamppost, moving his hand as if he was drawing something on it, and then he started walking in her direction. Strange.

She quickly rose and slipped behind a large oak tree that was standing near the bench. She carefully observed the man as he was passing by. He was tall, tanned, with light-brown hair and striking blue eyes, wearing a khaki tee shirt and tight black jeans. He soon turned into a side street, and she went back to look at the lamppost. There were two vertical lines, with a horizontal line through them, all drawn with pink chalk.

Holy cow. Were these chalk marks a sign that he had successfully picked up a dead drop, or was she just paranoid? She was not sure what else could explain them. She did believe in chance encounters and coincidences.

She called Kohout and described the circumstances and the man. A tall guy with brown hair and blue eyes, Kohout laughed, there are thousands of those roaming the streets of Prague. Nonetheless, he praised her for a potentially good pick up and said he would station someone in the area for a while.

IT WAS HIM, she was certain. They had an hour of wild sex in her apartment. He kept telling her that he couldn't get enough of her velvet-smooth thighs, of her ravishing ass, she asked him to stay for the night, but he said he had to leave, he asked her to take a shower with him, but she told him she just wanted to lie in bed and enjoy the nirvana, and when he closed the bathroom door and turned on the water, she jumped up, knowing that she had a few minutes to look for information, for evidence, for something incriminating.

She tried to open his briefcase, but it was locked with a code. She went through the pockets of his coat, his jacket, his shirt. All empty. Then, in the back pocket of his pants, she found a crumpled piece of paper. She smoothed it out. It was a copy of a receipt from a vacuum cleaner repair store. It was dated for today, so he may have been there just a few hours earlier. There was a name on the receipt, different from the one he'd given her when he introduced himself, and there was an address, too. He was careful, but not careful enough. Assuming, that is, that the name or the address on the slip were real. Perhaps he was momentarily distracted in the store, and he put the receipt in his pocket instead of the briefcase, a fateful mistake for an agent, if he was one.

The next morning, she called Kohout. "Hey Eva, what's new?" he said when he lifted up the phone receiver. He always smiled when he heard her pleasant, slightly husky voice.

"Something you may be interested in," she answered. "Remember the guy in the park from two years ago? I ran into him again."

A week later, she received a callback. "We arrested him, and he confessed during interrogation," Kohout said. "He is a CIA agent. Comrade Kubová, you deserve a medal."

"WHERE IS HOLLANDER NOW?" Eva asked Kohout after she told him about Stránský. The contents of the package that Roman had given her—the note, the radio receiver, the tapes, were spread on her kitchen table.

"My men haven't called me yet," he answered after a brief hesitation." They're probably processing him as we speak. I'll let you know tomorrow morning. Great work, Eva. Sleep well."

Eva hung up. *They are processing him as we speak.* Soon he will be in the torture chambers of The Little House[6], his fingernails being pulled out with special small pliers, a nifty Czech tool made just for this purpose. She shuddered and ran her fingers through her hair.

Two people had been arrested over the last several months and a third one soon may be, due to her tradecraft. The two will most likely be eligible for the rope. Stránský could be too, depending on what the interrogators learn. Nevertheless, she's doing it for the good of the country. For a system that, in its essence, is fair and just. She'd had pangs of conscience before, and this reasoning usually helped her get rid of them, but not so today. Had she been fooling herself all these years? Was she covering her eyes with a pink blindfold?

Another shot of Pernod. She still had feelings for Roman, she still cared about him. Stránský was a good colleague. But these men knew the risks when they decided to become spies; they knew what could be coming to them. This is what she did, this was her second job. She can't let emotions and doubts get the better of her.

Heavy tension was building up behind her eyes, and she had to clear her head. Even though it was past midnight, she put on her coat and left the apartment to get some air, but outside she was ambushed by a howling, freezing wind, darkness, a starless sky, emptiness. There was no relief.

Back in her living room she lit a cigarette and sat down in front of the mirror. An oblong face, pale complexion, high cheekbones, a straight nose filling just the right amount of space between the smoky gray eyes and the soft full lips, white teeth, a beautiful face by definition, but tonight she saw a monster staring back at her.

They will hang, death will be deliverance for them after all the suffering, but dying will be torture, the executioner knows how to handle the rope so that it doesn't kill right away, a few minutes of choking before dying, she felt her stomach twist, she ran to the bathroom and vomited, painfully, violently, a catharsis but no liberation.

She dragged herself to the bedroom and sat down on the edge of the bed. People had to die because of her, people had to die for an experiment that will one day fall like a house of cards. What was happening with her, why these sudden revelations now when it's too late, when the damage has already been done many times over? The image of Roman being tortured with electrical shocks, having his head held in the sink under water, invaded her mind. She screamed and writhed on the comforter.

And then there was clarity. She opened the drawer of her nightstand. Her revolver was lying there, a handsome piece with a handle inlaid with ivory, a gift from Kohout. It was a solid gun, she could shoot bullseyes with it from twenty-five yards, simple mechanism, destruction guaranteed. She took it out of the drawer and put it on the nightstand. She raised her hands. They were steady. She stared at the gun for a long time, at the barrel, at the trigger. What were the choices if forgiveness and atonement were impossible?

She reached for the revolver. The smoothness of the ivory handle was suddenly soothing. She turned the gun from side to side and cocked the hammer.

CHAPTER 20

U SING MULTIPLE TRAM AND SUBWAY CONNECTIONS, Roman made his way to a small bus station at the outskirts of the capital. He was wary of leaving Prague from the main bus terminal in the city center because it was possible that the agents would be waiting for him there. He boarded a bus going north, in the direction of communist East Germany, a safer way to get out of the capital than riding west, since it was more likely that the State Security would be monitoring the westbound bus lines. It was early afternoon when he disembarked somewhere in the northern part of Bohemia, in a forsaken city covered in black soot drifting in from the surface coal mines located in its periphery, with scrawny dead trees lining the deserted streets. He consulted the timetable at the bus stop. A bus would be leaving from there in about an hour, heading southwest. Across the road was a devastated city park, and Roman plodded through it, surrounded by its bleakness, until it was time to return to the bus stop.

When the vehicle arrived, he boarded, and sat down in the last row by a grimy window, his nerves taut with tension. He had a walrus moustache in place of a beard, the glasses were gone, and the hair of his wig was dark-brown and shorter, only covering his nape. A woman took the seat next to him. At least a dozen peeping chicks were sticking their ruffled yellow heads out from a bag that was in her lap. She noticed Roman looking at them. "Would you like to buy a few?" she asked. "I don't know what to do with all of them." Roman shook his head. She alighted a few stops later.

They arrived at the terminal in three hours. People were standing up to leave. Roman looked out the window; outside the door, under a dusky sky, a policeman was checking the passengers' identity cards as they stepped off the bus.

Up until now, his journey from Prague had been astoundingly smooth, but a snag like this was bound to arise sooner or later. He was not surprised and not yet ready to give up. Disembarking and using his false papers might prove fateful. To his left, he noticed a large tarp that was lying on the floor behind the seats. He rose, crouching, and lifted the edge of the sheet. It was covering some cardboard boxes. He lay down next to them and pulled the tarp over himself. It was big enough to conceal his whole body.

"Everyone's out?" he heard, and then the door closed and the bus took off, his body being thrashed around, he was barely able to hold on to the legs of the seat in order to avoid rolling into the aisle. Then at last the vehicle came to a halt and the engine stopped.

Rapid steps came near, and the edge of the tarp moved up. A startled face was gazing at him. "What the fuck!" the driver yelled, and Roman jumped up to his feet. The man was retreating, shouting about calling the cops. Roman grabbed him by the shirt with his left hand and punched him in the stomach with a hammer-fist strike with his right. The driver doubled over, groaning. Roman hit him in the ear with an elbow, and the man sank to the floor. Roman quickly pulled a rope from his backpack, dropped his full weight on the driver's legs, tied his ankles, and sealed his mouth with several pieces of duct tape. The fellow was still dazed. Roman rolled him over on his stomach and tied his wrists behind his back. "Sorry, buddy, you'll have to give me a head start," he said to the man, stood up, threw the backpack over his shoulders, pushed the bus doors open, jumped out and shut the doors behind him.

He was in a covered parking lot, and he saw that other buses were stationed there for the night. He darted out of the structure into a large, open space strewn with mounds of trash. Huge electrical transformers buzzed nearby. He assumed he must be at the edge of a town, and he knew he had to get out of here very fast.

He set out toward those few neon lights he saw glimmering in the distance, and, after a few minutes of brisk walking, he noticed a sign to the railway station. *Hallelujah.* Soon he arrived there, in front of a low, poorly lit brick building, its entrance adorned with a Czechoslovak and a Soviet flag. Several drunks stepped out of the train station bar, arguing loudly. In the hall, Roman looked at the schedules. A train was leaving in thirty minutes, going south. With luck, the bus driver would not be found before the train pulled out. Roman bought a ticket and strode to the platform. On his way out of the station building he passed by the waiting room. Through its glass door he saw several peasant women in long black dresses, with colorful patterned scarves covering their hair, sitting on a wooden bench. A familiar face stared at him from the TV screen they were watching, it was him, his true visage, then another picture in his bearded disguise flashed on the screen, he had made his TV debut, the hunt was on in earnest, he was the prize.

He boarded the train and took a seat by the window in a dark, empty compartment. After what seemed like an endless wait, he heard the piercing sound of the whistle, and the locomotive started to rumble out of the station. The conductor would come shortly to check his ticket. The backpack was on the seat next to him, and when the sliding compartment door slowly opened, Roman was ready to attack if he had to.

The conductor's sallow, tired profile emerged at the compartment entrance. He took a couple of steps toward Roman, not looking at him, and held out his hand for the ticket. He punched it with a small hole-puncher and left.

Roman let out a deep sigh of momentary relief. He shut the door, locked it, and closed the curtains. He will need to disembark soon, before there are police at each stop along the route. And when, an hour later, the train was approaching the town of Sušice, he knew that he was approximately twenty miles away from Knížecí Pláně, the last stop before the ultimate part of his journey. He put his backpack on, slipped out of the compartment, and moved about ten yards to the exit. When the train stopped, he opened the door that was opposite the platform, facing multiple railroad tracks and the woods behind them. He stepped off, sprinted to the ditch that ran alongside the tracks, and dropped into it.

The train started moving again, and once all the coaches passed, he had a clear view of the station. Three men in civilian clothes stood on the platform, hands in coat pockets, no bags, no suitcases. They huddled together briefly, and then they separated and started making their way across the tracks in Roman's direction. He didn't think they had noticed him. They will run a cursory check of the area and go back to the warmth and blue smoke of the train station dive for a glass of grog or mulled wine spiced with cloves and cinnamon sticks.

He vanished into the woods. He waited until he was far enough away for the railway platform lights to disappear before putting on the head lamp. He checked the compass. He was headed in the right direction.

The air was keen, and he put on his warm hat, scarf, and ski gloves. After an hour of slow winding among the trees, circumventing boughs and twigs on the ground to make as little noise as possible, he arrived at the far edge of the woods. In front of him, barren fields, lit by a full moon, stretched into the distance. If he walks across, he will be glaringly noticeable, but no farmers would be up in March at three in the morning, they would all be asleep in their stuffy thick-walled brick houses. He just had to do his best not to wake up the dogs. He stepped out of the protective cover of the trees and into the open, into complete silence and solitude. After walking about a mile, he found himself on an asphalt road, heading where he wanted to go, southwest. He set a rapid pace and trekked for another hour or so before realizing that the sky was changing, the midnight-blue color tapering into azure, with an off-white rim along the horizon. The sun would be up soon.

The twisting road cut through a wooded area, and Roman re-entered the refuge of the trees. He found a spot where the ground was covered with large heaps of wet leaves from last autumn and took off his backpack. He devoured two buns and swallowed a few sips of water. He wrapped himself in the emergency blanket, lay down, and buried himself under a mound of leaves, thinning out the pile above his face a bit in order to be able to breathe. He had been in more comfortable arrangements in his lifetime, but exhaustion is a strong hypnotic, and, before long, he was asleep.

He woke up soaking wet, shivering and sweating at the same time, a heavy downpour washing away his cover. He had to burrow deeper under the foliage, and when the clouds finally moved on and the sun rays began drying out the leaves and a tinge of warmth started spreading through his body, he heard distant male voices and dogs barking, this was the end, the dogs have his scent, he does not have enough time and strength to outrun them, he may as well just give himself up and get it over with.

The voices and the barks drew closer, and he was about to emerge from the brown pile with his hands raised; but then he heard the men yelling at the dogs to keep searching, and complaining that the animals must have lost the scent, probably because of the heavy rain, and the voices and the baying started to fade until they fused with the ambient sounds of the woods and of the far-off road. He had another lease on freedom and life. He will wait until dark to start the final push to meet up with Jan Soukup in Knížecí Pláně.

What had happened with Eva? He still couldn't comprehend what had led to the fiasco on that disastrous night. He wouldn't be able to live with himself if she was harmed in any way as a result of having been drawn into this imbroglio.

He could hear the call of a cuckoo, the harbinger of spring or doom. It must be perched on a tree branch close by. Was the bird's song an omen? If he makes it to the border, he will do his best to cross it. He had heard the harrowing accounts of the people who tried to breach that fateful divide; those stories were always told by someone other than the would-be emigrants. Did any of the daring souls who ventured to get across make it to the other side?

Soon, he will have his own experience at the electrical fence. Will he live to tell the tale? How did it come to this? *Decisions you've made led to this*, he answered to himself. Suddenly the specter of a German Shepherd along the border fence, baring its fangs, ready to attack, violently sprung up in front of his eyes. He almost let out a scream. Getting torn up by the dogs at the border, a real possibility. He shook his head. No, it can't happen. It won't happen. He will make it. He has to see Andrea again. The baby will be born soon. He will live.

ROMAN CHECKED HIS WATCH. It was ten minutes after six in the evening, and he crawled out from under the pile of leaves where he had been hiding for most of the day. He has been here, in the park with The Memorial of The Heroes of The Revolution in the ghost-town of Knížecí Pláně, since the early morning. He had not encountered any police search parties during the night. They must have assumed he went in a different direction, perhaps straight down south to the Austrian border.

He cautiously moved toward the memorial, staying behind the bushes. A man wearing a green parka and a black scarf was standing a few yards from the granite plaque, his back turned to Roman. "Steal a little and they throw you in jail," Roman said, still hiding in the shrubs.

The man pivoted toward his voice and answered, "Steal a lot and they make you king."

Roman stepped out onto the path. Lieutenant Soukup must have been in his thirties, with a shaved skull, grayish complexion, deep set dark eyes, sharp nose and hollow cheeks, a phantom-like appearance mollified by a pleasant smile.

"So you made it. I am glad to see you," Soukup said.

"I made it...barely, but I am here. Now the grand finale. I hope it will not be in Verdi's style."

Soukup did not react. Likely not an opera fan.

CHAPTER 21

THEY SAT DOWN IN THE BACK SEAT of the lieutenant's black Škoda with tinted windows. The car was parked among the trees and bushes, invisible from the road. "First things first." Soukup handed Roman a big sandwich and a thermos with warm tea. "When was the last time you ate?" he asked, observing Roman's ravenous appetite.

"I had a half an apple this morning. That was the end of my food supplies." Roman gave him a brief account of his journey. The lieutenant didn't say anything, but his face showed a barely discernible hint of respect.

Soukup unfolded a topographical map. "We are three miles from the West German border," he said. "How much do you know about the Western border?"

"I've heard about people attempting to reach the other side, only to end up getting killed by guns, mines, electricity, dogs. Has anyone ever successfully crossed?"

"Yes, some have. There are no more mines or high voltage electrical fences. They got rid of them some years ago. Not for humanitarian reasons, but because of random explosions causing injuries to guards and damaging the fences and other structures. Currently, there's a pair of barbed-wire fences running in parallel lines along the border, with a strip of ploughed barren soil several yards-wide between the two fences for tracking purposes. An additional ploughed strip runs on the outer side of each fence. Before you get to the fences, you will encounter anti-tank obstacles, called Czech hedgehogs."

"Czech hedgehogs?"

"Yes. It is a Czech invention. Large metal contraptions made from I-beams that are all connected with steel cables. Their purpose is to stop any vehicle that would try to ram through the fences. It should not be too difficult for you to negotiate your way around them. The fence closer to the Czech side of the border is charged with a low-voltage electrical current. Not enough to kill, but when the fence is disturbed by cutting or touching, or in any other mechanical way, a short develops in the circuit. That generates a signal that is sent to the patrolling border guards with the exact location of the trouble spot so that they can go investigate that specific area right away." Soukup paused to clear his throat. "In addition, an alarm lamp lights up in the area where the electrical short was generated, also indicating where the breach has occurred. In some areas along the border, there are metal cages housing German Shepherds that have been specifically trained to kill. They are called 'independently attacking dogs'. When the electrical short creates a signal, the doors of these cages automatically open, and the dogs run out and attack anything that's moving. Cool, ay?"

Very. Roman was forcing himself to accept Soukup's merciless, morbid sarcasm.

"The closest one of these dog cages is thirty kilometers away, so this will not be your problem."

So why did he have to tell me about it? Roman was exasperated yet grateful for the clarification.

"Border patrolmen still have dogs with them. That brings me to two rather important details. The timing, and the area where you should cross. The patrolmen have the border fence divided into sections. Typically, a pair of soldiers and a dog guard a section. One of the dogs in our garrison fell ill earlier today, and he had to be taken to the animal infirmary in Pilsen. It so happens that the two guards who are his handlers will be on patrol tonight. But without a dog. Crossing their section this evening will increase your chances of making it."

"How long are the sections they are patrolling?"

"About one and a half kilometers. The best way to deal with the fences is to dig a hole under them." Soukup removed his feet from a duffel bag that lay on the car floor, lifted it up and opened it. He pulled out a sharp-edged, pointed shovel with a folding handle and handed it to Roman. It was surprisingly light. "We've had several unseasonably warm weeks so the ground shouldn't be frozen any more. When you dig, be careful not to disturb the first fence to avoid triggering a short. Here, a pair of wire cutters you can use on the second fence if the digging takes too long." More items were coming out of the bag. Night vision goggles, a pair of work gloves, a long rigid knife, and a handgun. Roman recognized the CZ-75, a reliable and accurate Czech-made fighting pistol. He held the weapon. "This is a great gun, but what's its utility against an AK-47?"

"Take it. It may save your life."

"If I shoot at them and I miss, which I very likely may, they'll finish me off right there."

"Let's face it," Soukup said. "If they capture you alive, you're finished, too, only later." *His frankness is disarming.* Roman felt his chest tightening. Old anxiety, old enemy. He shut his eyes and started breathing, deeply, with concentration, that maneuver never fails, he felt Soukup's hand on his shoulder, it was a firm, supportive touch, and he heard the lieutenant telling him to start getting ready.

"I will leave the gun here," Roman said while they were studying the map one last time and aligning it with the compass.

"Your choice." Soukup put the pistol back in the bag. "Once you get through the second barbed-wire fence, you will still be about a hundred yards away from German soil. That hundred yards of no man's land is an open space, and you'll need to get out of there as quickly as you can; our golden boys will run after you and shoot at you in that space. In fact, they don't hesitate to violate the German territory itself to go after fugitives."

THERE WAS COMPLETE DARKNESS, a starless, moonless sky, a favorable sky. It was time to go. "Best wishes, Roman. Be strong. You are better than them." They embraced. "Before you leave," Soukup said, "I have a message for you from Johnny Jones. First of all, Godspeed. Secondly, they want you to be aware that Stránský was arrested."

Stránský was arrested? Why? How come? But this was not something to try to make sense of now.

The final chapter was about to begin.

CHAPTER 22

ROMAN WEAVED HIS WAY THROUGH rows of anti-tank obstacles until he was just a few yards from the barbed wire. He ran across the smooth brown strip of land, knelt down at the fence and started digging. As Soukup had told him, the ground was not frozen. He worked rapidly but carefully, and the hole was quickly getting larger. He pushed the backpack to the other side of the fence. More digging. No border guards in sight. Should he try to crawl through? Not yet.

More shoveling. He lost track of the time. Then at last he decided the space was large enough. He lowered himself into the hole, flattened his body, and slithered under the fence. Just as he was pulling himself up, a strong white light began flashing a few feet away. *Damn!* His best efforts notwithstanding, he managed to trigger the alarm system after all. *The guards are taking off, machine guns ready, they may be here at any second.* He grabbed the wire cutters, made a jagged opening in the second fence, pushed through the gap, badly scratching his face, and started sprinting to the wooded area in front of him, to Germany.

"Stop or we shoot," he heard someone call out. Then there was one single pop, probably a warning shot. Roman crouched and kept running, zigzagging for his life. About fifty more yards to cross, the longest fifty yards ever. A burst of machine gun fire came from the fence, and he felt a sharp pain in his right shoulder and lower chest. Then a volley of shots rang out from the woods on the German side, and the gunfire behind him stopped. Ahead, he saw several dark figures with rifles in their hands coming out from behind the trees, running toward him, one of the men was a few feet ahead of the others, he seemed familiar, it's Stanley Goldfarb, "Roman!" Stanley yelled, and then they were hugging, and Roman sank to his knees, and several men picked him up and carried him to a van that was waiting in a small clearing in the woods.

"He's bleeding," Goldfarb shouted. Two men bandaged the wounds the best they could and loaded Roman into the van. He was short of breath, and they put some blankets and pillows under his head and chest to prop him up. "He may have a pneumothorax," one of the men said in English with a strong German accent. "Step on it, Guenther, and drive straight to the emergency room."

"You saved me," Roman uttered, barely able to speak. "How did you—"

"Don't talk, Roman," Goldfarb interrupted him. "I received a cable from Johnny Jones that you would be coming, assuming everything went according to the plan. I asked my good friends here from the Bundeswehr[7] to be on hand with some off-the-record firepower, you know, a side job, if and when the time comes. Then, about four hours ago, Jan Soukup confirmed that you would be crossing the border, and we were ready. Yes, we may have saved you, but our impact was limited to the range of our guns. You made it across half the country, evading the State Security and the police. That's some bravery, Roman. That's true grit."

The van stopped at the emergency room entrance. One of the Germans ran inside, and soon a small crowd of nurses and orderlies formed around the vehicle, transferring Roman to a gurney, placing a needle in his arm, and securing an oxygen mask to his face.

"Andrea, this is Stanley Goldfarb with the CIA. You may have heard about me from Roman." "Oh no," Andrea responded, the phone handset almost falling out of her hand. "You have bad news, don't you?"

"No, not at all. In fact, I have good news. You'll be seeing Roman soon."

"Where is he? Is he safe?"

"He is in Germany. He is safe. He had to escape from Czechoslovakia, and he was shot while crossing the border, but he is fine now. Just got out of surgery."

"Oh my God. When can I talk to him?"

"He'll call you as soon as he feels better. I promised him I would contact you right away once he was out of the operating room. When he recovers, he'll be flying back to the States. He can't wait to see you."

Andrea slumped into a chair, shaking and sobbing, releasing the fear, worry and uncertainty of the past months. Then the laughter came on, the uncontrollable tense laugh that can easily turn into a cry. She opened the front door of the apartment and walked out into the street, along the flowerbeds with blooming daffodils and down to the shimmering river where cherry trees lining the banks were just starting to open their faintly fragranced pink blossoms.

ROMAN WAS STARING AT THE WHITE WALL of the hospital room. *Stránský was arrested.* That would mean that the CIA was wrong, that Stránský was not the one who had informed on the Czech agent who was subsequently captured. Stránský was probably loyal to the Americans.

He wiped his sweaty forehead. Stránský must have been busted shortly after Roman had been pursued by the State Security. After Eva had been handed all the information.

That can't be. That beautiful person whom he trusted, whom he confided in, she couldn't have betrayed him. That would have been a masterful deception on her part. But sometimes inconceivable can be plausible. Humans are the same everywhere, in a police state they just act differently, molded by the circumstances. Now Stránský is in prison, most likely facing execution because the agency made the wrong assumption and because he, Roman, contacted the wrong person. And because he contacted the wrong person, he himself had to escape the country with his life.

Abruptly, Roman sat up in the bed, momentarily forgetting about his wounds, but a piercing pain in his chest and shoulder quickly forced him to lie back down. He recapitulated the events. Eva must be a State Security agent, he concluded. He shuddered at the possibility. But what if she was not? What if someone else, although he could not think who that would be, reported to the secret police about the planned exchange, and Eva was caught, too.

An unsettling picture either way.

Roman wished he could get out of bed and just go, walk, wander aimlessly. When you're upright and your legs carry you, your thinking becomes clearer, byzantine schemes are reduced to childhood puzzles. He felt buoyed and disinhibited; his brain was still saturated with anesthetics and sedatives and analgesics. He wanted to find Goldfarb. He wanted to know.

The door opened and the nurse, with a stern and determined expression signaling that no protestation was allowed, checked his pulse and blood pressure and injected morphine through the plastic tubing. *I hope I'm wrong on all this*, went through Roman's head as he was drifting away.

CHAPTER 23

ROMAN BEGAN HIKING UP THE STEEP TRAIL. The star-speckled sky coalesced with the black mass of trees covering the mountains, and the orange glow of the city lights below was quickly diminishing. It had been two and a half years earlier that he had walked across moonlit fields and meadows and through pristine woods toward the West German border. Back then, the allure of the landscapes had been hiding from him behind the black curtain of his fear.

But this early morning, his mind was free. It was late summer, but, due to the high elevation, the temperature was cold, his fingers were freezing in the liner gloves. A dark figure with a head lamp suddenly appeared from behind a turn in the trail, dragging a large pine tree bough with multiple smaller twigs forking off its center, a veritable peacock fan. "Protection against bears," a female voice said, "I ran into one here the other day."

Gradually, the total darkness of the night gave way to a misty gray twilight, and the landscape opened, rugged and expansive. The solitude was vast and heavy. Large tan boulders infused with ochre and purple horizontal stripes were strewn about the mountain slopes, pale-green blades of tall grass, sprinkled with petals of bluebells and fireweed, undulated in the breeze. Sparse trees. An abandoned lumberjack camp. A wooden shelter. A headstone.

Soon Roman was above the timber line; the air has thinned, and the switchbacks began. He had to stop to catch his breath. A young man wrapped in the American flag walked past him. More switchbacks. The summit is straight above him. It appears to be very close. Hairpin turns again. Lightheaded and nauseous, he stumbled over a rock, but he pushed on. Another switchback, and another one. It is unceasing. Then finally the summit, and below him an ocean of rocks, an emerald lake, and, in the distance, the glinting surface of a river spanned by a suspension bridge, cutting through a deep narrow red canyon. Somewhere down there was also his new home, the city where he now lived, its view hidden by the mountains.

AFTER ROMAN'S CONTRACT WITH THE CIA ENDED, the family moved west. Sebastian was already a first grader and the round-cheeked Cassie was two. They loaded all their possessions into the trunk, and on top, of their silver Corolla and drove thousands of miles across two thirds of the country, staying overnight in obscure roadside motels with squeaky beds and desiccated breakfast muffins. They passed through monolithic gray cities, through weathered mountain ranges veiled in blue mist. They crossed the Mississippi River flanked by multiple swampy rivulets like a primordial matriarch surrounded by her unruly brood, with marshes around it covered in water lilies and with fishing boats nestled in tall reeds.

They rode across endless rolling turquoise grasslands cut through with infinite miles of railroad tracks and dotted with feed yards blackened with cattle already condemned, and with tall silos resembling peculiarly shaped enchanted castles in the morning haze. They crossed neat small towns that had palatial courthouses on the main square, places where hearty people were tending to their homes and land and public spaces with the determined diligence of their German and Norwegian ancestors back in the old country centuries ago. They made a stop at a museum that spanned the highway, containing the testimony to the irresistible and desperate drive to push west.

They kept riding until they were exhausted and their bodies ached and the children in the back seat grew annoyingly restless, until, suddenly, tall jagged snowy peaks emerged in front of them, rising above the horizon. They settled in a mountain town in a rented house, in a neighborhood of people with long hair and tattoos, backwoodsmen, tramps with leathery skin and fortune tellers, with bars and cafes and stores selling Turkish lamps and semi-precious rocks and Oriental wisdoms and art objects of variable standards, and where, in the background, the giant Atlas turned into stone was propping up the sky.

FOLLOWING ROMAN'S RETURN from his Czech mission and prior to the relocation to the west, he had again been assigned to translating at Langley. How does one explain that he is still here when he should be dead? How does one resolve having triggered a chain of events that have possibly led to someone losing their life? During that time, he had been running hot and cold—between the ecstasy of being alive, and the anguish of disbelief and guilt.

"It's not like you survived it by accident," Mike Corsi, his case officer, told him. "You fought for it, and you had help. You had some luck too, but a little luck is indispensable. As far as the guilt is concerned, you'll need to put it behind you. Sometimes our missions pan out. Sometimes they don't. You served the country the best you could."

"Any news on Stránský?"

"Death sentence. Same for the other agent, the one we thought Stránský reported on. But," Corsi raised his voice sanguinely and lifted his index finger, "as far as we know, they are still alive. Which is somewhat unusual because the Czechs are fond of quick justice, or injustice, I should say. Lately, a gentler breeze has been coming from the Russian steppes. Maybe that's why they haven't offed them yet. Let's hope that the good winds keep blowing."

"Were you able to find out anything about Eva Kubová?"

"No. I asked Jones several times. He has no information on her."

Roman was not sure if he should believe him.

"Roman, you've been through purgatory, but now it's over. Enjoy yourself, enjoy your family. Just be. Gee, maybe I should quit this business and become a psychologist!" Corsi laughed and slapped Roman on the back.

THEY WERE BOTH WORKING on a military base, Roman as a contracting special-ist, Andrea in the notary's office. Mike Corsi had helped them secure the jobs. The present was busy and new, but the past refused to yield. The nightmares crept in slowly, understatedly, once or twice a week at first. Animals hunting him down, tigers in the initial dreams, then dogs took over, big dogs, Dobermans, German Shepherds, Rottweilers. Driving down a steep hill in a car without breaks. Being lost in a dark, eerie neighborhood in his hometown, a neighborhood he's never been to, surrounded by ghoulish characters who carry razor-sharp knives.

Then the dreams became more frequent, they settled in, his nightly companions, and grew specific. Eva in a gray cell, sitting on a gray sheet on the floor, raising her gracile shackled hands in desperation, asking him why he set her up. Eva waking up in the middle of the night, going to the kitchenette to get something to drink, and vanishing from the apartment. Stránský under the gallows, in a white coat and with the proverbial blue stethoscope still around his neck.

To battle the nightmares, Roman kept the windows open at night. He raised his head with multiple pillows. He had read in a popular psychology journal that writing down the content of a dream can help prevent it from coming back; he wrote down the dreams. Nothing worked. He was afraid to go to sleep, and when he did, his violent thrashing would wake Andrea. He wanted to sleep in the living room, but she wouldn't let him. During the day, he couldn't shake his guilty conscience, or the paranoia when someone was standing too close to him in the store, or the startle reaction to every loud noise.

"I think you have that post-traumatic stress condition," Andrea told him one day. "You should go see someone."

"You mean post-traumatic stress disorder? I don't know. Maybe I do have it. But I don't feel like talking to therapists and shrinks. They are useless, in my opinion. Let's give it time."

But time did not help much.

"HITLER WAS STUPID to attack the Soviet Union. I have a theory on what made him do it. He was an admirer of Napoleon. One of the high points of his life was when he could rest his hand on Napoleon's tomb in conquered Paris. Napoleon was badly beaten by the Russians, and I believe Hitler wanted to best him. 'Napoleon did not succeed but I will. I am a greater military genius than he was.' They both even attacked in the same month, June. Germany had a formidable military force, but in the end, it was no match for the vastness of that country, and their winters, and the size of the army they could build."

Major Westcott reached for a cracker and a tiny cube of Gouda and took a sip of Pinot Grigio. He was an athletically slender man with a shock of silvery hair, a pencil mustache, and a pair of rimless glasses sitting lightly on the bridge of his narrow nose. He and Roman and another two guests, a stout dark man and his blond companion, were sitting in plastic chairs in a semicircle under a giant cottonwood tree, its succulent triangular leaves rustling above their heads.

"You must be a history buff like me," Roman said, nodding in acknowledgement of a commonality of interests.

It was the July 4th party held in the home of the manager of the Civilian Personnel Office at the base. Roman had come alone; Cassie had strep throat and Andrea had stayed home with the children.

String bulbs wired to tree branches were emitting a soft glow. The tops of white cloth-covered rectangular tables buckled under platters packed with raw vegetables and dips, with cheeses, potato salad, steaks, burgers, hot dogs, chicken, french fries, buns, cakes, pies, ice cream, cookies, fruit. Scattered among the dishes were two-quart bottles of Pepsi and Club Soda. There were stand-alone trays with wine, hard liquor, and beer.

"Napoleon was my childhood hero, and to a degree he still is to this day," Roman said. "The charge across the bridge at the battle of Lodi, in front of his soldiers with the sword drawn, that was an epitome of bravery in the mind of an eleven-year-old. My dream is to visit the Saint Helena Island one day. To experience the remoteness and the inhospitality there. To see Longwood House. They kept Napoleon in that building because it was so isolated, and the area around it was so barren that it was easy to secure and surveil. It was also rat-infested. They were still afraid of him escaping, notwithstanding that the island was more than four thousand miles away from France. Apparently, the garden of the estate still bears Napoleon's original design."

The major was gazing at Roman intently.

"I've often wondered about the fascination with Napoleon. Mine and others," Roman continued, having cleared the remaining potato salad from the paper plate. "Millions of people died during his wars. The male French population was decimated. But he also spread the ideals of The French Revolution across Europe. He was a military genius, and a reformer, and an innovator. He was not a typical despot. Maybe that's where the appeal comes from."

The major was still staring at Roman, or, rather, at his mouth. His lips curved into a conspiratorial smile. "Let me guess. Slavic?"

"What? What do you mean? I thought we were talking about Napoleon."

Westcott curved the five fingers of his hand as if he wanted to grab a tennis ball, and, with the fingers still bent, moved his hand in the direction of his mouth in a forceful gesture, creating the impression of a dog muzzle. "Your accent. It's Slavic, right?"

"Yes. Czech, to be exact."

"I thought so," Westcott said. "Our cleaning lady is Czech, a nice person, and pretty, very pretty," his smile morphed from conspiratorial into desirous. "Do you miss the old country?"

"I'm glad I'm here."

"I bet you are."

"How did you get out?" the stout man asked.

"Yes, how did you?" his blond companion echoed.

"In retrospect, getting out was the most straightforward part of the journey," Roman said, then quickly turned to the major. "Where were you stationed during your service?"

"I taught history at the Naval Academy for ten years before I retired," the major said. "Prior to that, I was with the Navy special operations."

"What history subjects did you teach at the Academy?"

"Mainly wars. The Norman Conquest, The Crusades, The Mongol Wars, The Hundred Years' War..." he paused and smiled at Roman again. "I'll have to get you together with my physical therapist. You would like him."

"Why would I like your physical therapist?"

"He's from Poland so you'll have something in common for sure, both of you refugees from communist Eastern Europe. You could converse in a Slavic language. Should be easier than English for the two of you. Even though I have to admit, your English is fairly decent. His, not so much."

"Czechs and Poles can't understand each other, Major. We'd have to speak in English."

"Oh, I didn't realize that. Forget it then."

The stout man gestured to Roman. "Have you been back home since you left?"

"This is my home now." They will not let you be part of the tribe, he remembered Chief Svoboda's admonishment while looking at the fellow's bewildered, uncomprehending face.

The blond lady must have sensed that there was some tension present. "I don't know about you, but I'm having another drink," she declared chirpily. "Come on guys, it's 4th of July!"

Roman stood up and sauntered toward the lines winding around the alcohol trays. The beer line was the longest, the wine line the shortest. The food trays were relieved of their load by now. With a can of Coors in his hand, he rambled around the evening garden, zigzagging between tables and chairs and groups of chatting, smiling people. A man came up to him from behind a bench. "Are you Roman?" He held out a hand in greeting. "I'm Joe Stewart, Captain Stewart. Your wife is friends with my wife Claudia."

Roman shook his hand. He knew Claudia, a cheerful young woman who would come by their house a few times a week after work to pick up Andrea for an evening jog, sometimes bringing along a plate of cinnamon rolls or a pie, and who always had a few kind words for the children.

"I thought it was you but I wasn't positive," Stewart said. "We should get together sometime. You must tell us about your home country. I'm sure you have fascinating stories to share."

"Everyone has a fascinating story to share, Captain, it doesn't even have to be about the home country," Roman smiled and ambled on. *There is more to a person than just where they are from or how they sound, isn't there?* He felt somehow reduced by these people, pigeon-holed into a category of a curiosity, of foreignness. He strolled past the house, walked out to the road and unlocked the car door. He positioned himself behind the wheel. It felt calming to be sitting at the wheel, only him inside, all tranquil. He fastened the seat belt and turned on the engine.

THE GENTLE BREEZE from the East kept on blowing. Stránský's death sentence was commuted to life in prison. The Czechs, having decided that it was safe not to be timid any more, flooded the streets, jingling their keys, and bloodlessly kicked out the puppets. That was the Velvet Revolution. Roman was following all this on the television at home, and, today, in a recently rented space where they would soon open a coffeehouse, after they make some repairs and paint the walls. Seeing the exalted crowds on Wenceslas Square made him tearful. He wished he were there, sharing in the ecstasy of newly gained freedom. It wasn't so long ago that he had been hiding somewhere near that square behind a giant refrigerator. The men who chased him that day are, no doubt, celebrating with the rest of the nation, waving the flag; they know well how to conform.

Now he can contact the medical school and ask for a duplicate of his diploma. He wasn't sure that he was ready to reenter the battlefield of medicine after a five-year gap, but possessing again that vital sheet of paper would at least give him that option.

He covered the floor of the room with a huge tarp that looked akin to a Pollock creation, with its random overlapping varicolored blots of dried paint, and started coating the walls in the shades of black and gray Andrea had selected.

"WHAT ARE YOUR THOUGHTS about opening a coffee bar?" Andrea had asked Roman a few months earlier during a stroll in a grassy canyon flanked on both sides by huge red and white sandstone rocks set ablaze by the afternoon sun. The air was saturated with the heavy, heady aroma of ponderosa pines, azure bluebirds busily darted in and out of dense bushes, and small herds of mule deer impassively fed on pine cones and twigs.

Before Roman could answer she added; "Brewing coffee, baking pies, talking to people, being our own boss, I would love it. I know it would be hard work, but if we approached it as people business, not just coffee business, I think we would come off well."

"There was a Czech man in Germany who tried it and got behind on rent and ended up in court," Roman said, as he picked up the tired Cassie.

Andrea persisted, and, in the end, they decided to take the risk. They found the rental space on the eastern side of town, in a community of family homes where coffee bars were scarce. Andrea quit her job, Roman kept his. They named their enterprise Coffee under the Wire.

CHAPTER 24

ADAM **N**EDOMA **MADE HIS ENTRANCE** to the coffeehouse with a slightly stiff swagger, without crutches, not even a cane, his hair spiked and dyed blond, wearing a white shirt, black pants, a tie with black and orange stripes, and a lemon-colored sports jacket. Looking at his friend's rugged, tanned square-jawed face, Roman couldn't help but hark back to the time he had last seen him seven years before, wan and semi-suicidal, his body buried under the covers of a decrepit hospital bed. A young woman with red hair and fair skin was walking next to Adam, the simple elegance of a low-cut purple satin shirt and tight-fitting black jeans accentuating her sensuality. This was not Lenka, the startled Roman realized.

"We will be going on a road trip across America," Adam had told him over the phone a month earlier. "We'd love to stop by and see you."

And the boys are already embracing, the gal's name is Anneliese, she is from Hamburg, the trip has been a blast so far.

Since they had recently hired a barista, Andrea was able to join the group, and the four of them took a seat at a table by the window.

"I see that I am outnumbered by three German-speakers. My German has all but disappeared. Only in English, please," Roman requested. Adam ordered a cup of Viennese coffee. Anneliese had a cappuccino and an apple strudel.

"The coffee is sublime." Adam looked around the interior. It was roomy, lit with electric lanterns that mimicked old gas lamps. Large black-and-white posters depicted walled-in cities, rolling landscapes, and thatch-roofed village huts, the Europe of old. Sentimentality was undeniable.

A wizened woman, a veritable mummy, was sitting motionlessly across the floor from Adam, a colossal, fluffy white dog resting at her feet, it had a gentle nose and lips and understanding eyes, it was a human face, ready to break into a smile or a cry. Even a suburban cafe can be a source of inspiration, thought Adam. He himself was gaining renown in Düsseldorf with his art. He had his own gallery, and paintings were selling well.

Their New World trip has been an experience. America is enormous and messy and gorgeous and a contradiction, said Adam, laughing. They first landed in New York, they've never seen anything like it, not beautiful but so sui generis. They got robbed in Central Park, they only had twenty dollars on them but the muggers took their watches, too. In Philadelphia, they visited the Barnes Collection and took a picture of the bronze Rocky next to the legendary staircase. Then on to Cleveland and Chicago for more art and jazz. In Iowa, they made a stop in Cedar Rapids to learn about Bohemian immigration, and drove through Stuart where Kerouac was once stuck overnight at the train station. Then they crossed the prairies to the West.

"What happened to Lenka?" Roman asked when Anneliese left to go to the bathroom.

"Sorry, man," Adam chuckled. "I should've told you over the phone. She absconded with the plumber. A big fat dude. He came to the house to fix some leaky pipes, and they must have hit it off down in the basement. One month later, she was gone. She told me to more or less go fuck myself, and she shared, mercifully," Roman rolled his eyes, "that she never loved me anyway. That was about eight months ago. Initially, it was tough going for a while. Then I met Anneliese at an art show. She's a former geometry instructor turned fledgling sculptor. She decided that she had to make herself embrace all the rhombohedrons and dodecahedrons and scalenohedrons that she had learned to loathe because she thought that her students' inability to comprehend them was the testament to her self-perceived pedagogical ineptitude. She not only made peace with those angles, she discovered art in them, and now she's creating geometrical shapes from clay and stone. That's all she makes, pointy, multi-angled structures. I believe it is a form of auto-therapy. I hope that, with time, she'll branch out to other configurations. Things have been good between us so far. We'll see what the future brings."

Anneliese was approaching from the lavatory. "Were you talking about me? I know you were. I have a sixth sense." She gently stroked Adam's hair.

"I was describing admiringly your artistic style. While we are on the subject of art, would you like to see a few pictures?" Adam turned to Roman and Andrea. "We brought them on the trip, in case a gallery or some other establishment was interested in showing them."

"Yes. We'd like to see them," Andrea said.

Adam and Anneliese went to their camouflage-colored rental van, took out a large wooden box, put it on a dolly and wheeled it into the coffee bar. Adam unlocked the chest and pulled out a framed canvas. It was an oil painting with different shades of red as the prevailing color; a delicate scarlet vase was faintly contrasted against a crimson base, and above the vase randomly arranged large petals were smeared on the canvas in thick maroon lumps with yellow rims. In the next picture, grayish-blue irises in a luxuriant green meadow were painted with similar heavy, rich, expansive strokes.

"This is beautiful, Adam. Would you like to leave them with us for a while?" Andrea asked. "We'd keep them on the walls until they sell, and I'm confident they will."

"Of course. I will price them at six hundred dollars apiece but that's negotiable. What percentage of the proceeds would you keep?"

"None." Roman shook his head. "All money would be yours."

An old man walked in, slight and hunched over, with a windswept deeply lined face, wearing a rumpled dark-blue suit and a wide-brimmed hat, a violin case on his back. He pulled a cracked leather valise secured with bungie cords behind him. He sat down at the table next to Roman's. "How are you, Eugene?" Andrea waved at him.

"Happy as a lark. A huge cockroach flew straight in my face at the shelter this morning, then it fell and splattered on the floor like a blob of grease. I heard that meant good luck. Sure enough, a few hours later they notified me that I could move into a basement studio apartment. After a year of no privacy, I have a place just for myself. I'm thrilled, guys. I am moving in tonight."

"That's fantastic, congratulations. About the cockroach, what means luck? That it flew in your face or that it splattered?" Andrea inquired.

"The former."

The barista came to the table and put a grilled cheese sandwich and a cup of milk in front of the man, who turned to Roman. "Do you have any Russian classics to spare?"

"I own *Resurrection* by Tolstoy. A tedious read," Roman said.

"I like tedious reads, they are calming, like meditation." Eugene opened the scratched instrument case and took out a flawlessly pre-served chestnut-colored violin.

"I used to play the cello," Anneliese said wistfully. "I quit when my teacher killed herself with the endpin rod."

"Did she kill herself over your playing, or someone else's?" Adam laughed.

"Makes you wonder, doesn't it? Are music teachers known to have high suicide rates?"

They were all having a swell time, drinking coffee, eating desserts, Eugene unobtrusively fiddling Beatles songs on his fine instrument, Eleanor Rigby and Michelle weeping under his bow. The sun was already hiding behind the mountains but the sky was still light.

"I was in Prague a few weeks ago, making arrangements for an exhibit," Adam said.

"How was Prague?" Roman asked with curiosity that concealed his unease.

"It's a changed city," Adam said. "Not so morose any more. It's alive. Freedom is a great magician. I went to the Old Town Square. There is a restaurant on the second floor of the building that's right across the sidewalk from the clock. The place has the ambience of old, reserved elegance, waiters in black gliding about the room, furnishings go back to the times of the monarchy. I'm sitting by a large window enjoying an exquisite sight of the square, that quintessential view you see in photos, and memories start coming out, some good, many not so much. I feel a tap on my shoulder. A sinewy guy with salt and pepper hair and a thin moustache is standing above me, with a little smirk on his face. He said he knew that I was your friend. I asked him how the hell he knew who I was in the first place, and his response was that he knew a lot of people and a lot of things about them. He said to pass on to you that he would like to have the opportunity to meet you someday. He told me that his name was Kohout and that he was a friend of Eva's. He said he had something for you."

Flashbacks came on quickly. Boisterous tourists. Eva in a red beret. The pursuit. The cold apartment. Border guards closing in.

"Are you alright? You turned very pale." Andrea squeezed Roman's hand. "I'll get you some water."

"I was debating if I should even tell you about this weird encounter," Adam continued, noticing Roman's reaction. "But I concluded I probably had to. I asked the dude for a phone number or an address, but he declined. He said he was confident that the two of you would cross paths eventually."

ROMAN LOCKED THE FRONT GLASS DOOR of the coffeehouse. Andrea was already at home with the kids. The evening was warm, pleasant. He was in a good mood. He was heading to his car when suddenly he felt a hard, circular object pushing into his lower back and simultaneously, he heard a voice whispering in Czech; "You have the barrel of a loaded

Magnum against your spine, so don't do anything stupid. Just keep walking."

"It's over for you, creep," another voice, vaguely familiar, growled quietly. They passed by his car. Roman's mind was racing. He had to wrest the gun away from the man directly behind him. They'd taught him how to do that at Camp Peary, the barrel had been in the same spot on his body during the training as it was now. He just had to move his right arm quickly behind his back, grab the gun, twist it, and then turn around and punch them and kick them and elbow them. But he was unable to spring into action, he was mentally paralyzed, so he just kept tramping on until they came to a black sedan parked by the curb. One of the men opened the back door, and the other guy pushed him inside, and they took off, driving toward the dark silhouettes of the mountains. Roman looked at the man sitting next to him in the back seat, aiming a gun at his temple. It was Milan Stránský. "You thought you would get away with this, didn't you, asshole," he hissed. "Not so, you snake. You're dead." The driver was silent.

"It was a mistake, Milan," Roman said quietly. "A horrible misunderstanding. We had to check you out. We had to make sure. We had no choice, and it went wrong. It was not intentional."

"What you did landed me on death row and then in prison for life. How about that for an achievement. Now it's your turn to pay."

"How did you get out? Did they pardon you or did they commute the sentence? Did you escape?" Roman tried to engage him in a conversation, but Stránský didn't answer. They were speeding up a narrow winding two lane road, pushing deeper and deeper into the mountains. The city lights disappeared. They turned onto a dirt road, the car was flying over bumps and potholes with high speed, the two men in the back seat were being tossed about in every possible direction. *I could take his gun and shoot them both,* Roman thought frantically, but he couldn't make himself do it.

The driver stopped the car and Stránský ordered Roman to get out. Both men turned on their flashlights. Roman glanced at the driver. He was lean and muscular, with salt and pepper hair and a thin moustache. This must be Kohout.

"Run!" Stránský yelled and shoved Roman forward. Roman took off and the two men followed closely behind, shouting directions at him and hitting him in the back with the handles of their guns. The initially flat terrain soon changed into a boulder-covered hill. Roman was proficient at bouldering, and he tried to get away, but his legs felt like jelly, and he was not able to gain speed. When they reached the middle of the boulder field, they had him turn toward the woods. He was stumbling over tree roots and fallen branches, barely catching his breath. Finally, they arrived at a small open area with a big rock in the middle, and they commanded him to stop. Kohout went behind a group of trees and returned with a long crowbar and a shovel while Stránský kept Roman in check with his revolver. Kohout lodged the tip of the crowbar underneath the rock and slowly pushed it aside using all his strength, then he shoveled away a several inch-thick layer of sand from the area flattened by the rock. A two-part square metal lid emerged. Kohout opened the sturdy lock that connected the handles and lifted both sides of the heavy cover, revealing a concrete cube-shaped underground bunker. He climbed in using a rope ladder and Stránský, with a kick in the ass and a scream, steered Roman to follow Kohout. The bunker was completely empty except for a heavy chain coiled on the floor in a corner, one of its ends embedded in the concrete. The other end had a metal leg cuff attached to it.

"We could kill you right away," Stránský sneered. "But that would be too easy. You will die here from dehydration and starvation like a lowly dog you are. Five days, give and take, doctor."

"And don't bother screaming for help. The structure is soundproof," Kohout said with a snigger.

"You built this just for me, you nutjobs?"

"Don't be so cocky." Kohout shoved him in the chest. "You're not the only one on my list. You're neither the first nor the last to croak here. In your case, I'm very happy I could team up with my friend Milan here, who also has had beef with you. Two heads are better than one."

"I don't know you. What do you have to do with all this?"

"I'm Eva's friend."

"What happened with her? Is she alive? Are you her avenger?"

Kohout did not react. He turned to the wall, rummaging through his backpack, grumbling about not finding the key to the leg cuff. That distracted Stránský, who took his eyes off of Roman and lowered the gun, and Roman leapt forward and charged him, realizing with agony that his moves were awkward, his hands too weak to take the weapon away, his feeble fists and feet and knees were barely touching Stránský who let out a condescending laugh and whacked him in the chin, and Roman fell on the concrete floor and his eyes closed.

SOMEONE WAS VIOLENTLY SHAKING HIM, and he heard a female voice calling his name. He tried to see but his eyelids were heavy, like they were weighted down with lead, and when he finally forced them open, there was Andrea next to him, her head and upper torso propped up by two pillows, her beautiful face, now worried, lit by the soft glow of a tiffany lamp. He was in his bed, in his bedroom, it had been a nightmare, the worst and longest of his nightly bad dreams, a horror film. He was drenched in sweat, his heart was racing. "You were yelling in Czech," Andrea was telling him, "your arms were flailing, you were kicking. What were you dreaming about? One of your usual nightmares, or did it have something to do with what Adam talked about the other day?" and Roman nodded, another variation on the recurrent theme but much more frightening, he softly stroked Andrea's face, he felt his heartbeat quieting down, he was glad that he was in his home next to his wife. He was glad that it was only a dream.

CHAPTER 25

NEXT MORNING Roman phoned Mike Corsi.

"Your call came sooner than I expected," Corsi said. "But that works out quite well because I was just about to give you a ring. Stránský's life sentence was reduced to fifteen years. We are pushing the Czechs very hard to pardon him. I believe it will happen."

Roman was not surprised to hear the news. He had called Corsi precisely because, after last night's dream, he had a feeling, his uncanny suspicion, that there would be fresh developments regarding Stránský.

"I'm very glad to hear that," Roman said. He was telling the truth; in his conscious mind there was an intense feeling of guilt about Stránský. Yet, in the subconscious, there must have also been fear.

"Something else," Corsi continued. "Several weeks ago, I spoke with a CIA officer who'd spent some time in Angola in the late eighties. You probably know there's been a civil war there for decades between the communist government and the anti-communist rebels. The US has been supporting the anti-communists, naturally. This officer I met had spent some time on the site with the rebel forces, and he fell ill there with an abscess in the ass from shrapnel. He had to go to the field hospital to get antibiotics, and to have his hindquarters drained. He was raving to me about a young Czech female doctor who took care of him. When he said 'Czech' my interest was piqued, and I started asking more question. She had told him her name was Zuzana Němcová. But I wonder. He said she was tall, with long, curly auburn hair, gray eyes, fair complexion. That matches Eva Kubová's description, doesn't it?"

"It does. When was this?"

"In the fall of nineteen eighty-six."

Roman's second escape from Czechoslovakia was in the early spring of that year. Intuitively, he had no doubt that this Czech doctor was Eva, and that her existence in Angola had some connection to what had transpired in Prague that spring.

"Did your guy say anything else? Did he mention any conversations they had?"

"He asked her how she wound up in that hellhole. She told him that a hellhole was exactly the place where she wanted to be."

"Corsi. Would that man know if she's still there?"

"He doesn't know. Another officer went to Angola a few months after this man returned to the States. That officer tried to locate the doctor at the request of the fellow I spoke with, but he couldn't find her. When this second officer asked about her whereabouts, he was given conflicting answers—shot dead during a raid, captured by the communists, joined the South African army, and such. It's a bloody chaotic war zone so there'll be a lot of misinformation and rumors."

"There's only one way to find out," Roman said.

"Which is?"

"Go to the source."

"You traveling to Angola? That may be a little dicey even for a badass like you."

"No, to Prague. One more thing, Mike. Would you check on an individual for me? He goes by the name of Kohout. He lives in the Czech Republic, most likely in Prague. I suspect he used to work for the State Security, but I'm not certain. Could you make some inquiries?"

"Are you trying to get yourself into trouble?"

"He may be the link to Eva."

"I'll see what I can do."

"I DON'T WANT YOU TO GO, Roman. What do you expect from venturing back there? Forgiveness? Maybe wait a few years and reassess. What do you think? The people who wanted you dead six years ago may not be in control any longer, but I'm sure they are still there, alive and well. That fellow Adam told you about is probably one of them. And the fact that Stránský has not been released from prison tells you that even the government is not ready to forgive former spies yet." They were standing at the kitchen counter, tensely chomping on chips and smoking.

"Stránský will likely be released any day now," Roman told her.

"Well, then he may go after you. If something happens to you, the kids won't have a dad, and I won't have a husband. Are you taking that into consideration?" Andrea's forehead was furrowed and her voice raised.

"Andrea, communism is gone, so I am not that much concerned about the government. As far as the chance of an individual person wanting to harm me, I'll take precautions to prevent that. I'll be alright." That was an attempt to reassure Andrea, but he needed to reassure himself, too. Adam's ominous Prague encounter never completely left Roman's mind.

"I think you're seeing it through rose-colored glasses, Roman. It's risky. Is this about Eva?" Andrea could be direct.

"It's about Stránský. It's about her. It's about me and my guilty conscience. And my fucking nightmares and flashbacks and crazy thoughts. It's about all of it, don't you understand? Are you jealous of Eva? Is that the issue?"

"If I was, it would be my problem to deal with, but I'm not. I'm worried that you will be putting yourself in danger by going back, and that you may not get out of it what you are hoping for."

Roman reached out for Andrea's hand. "It's a continuing saga. First, I voluntarily left that country because I couldn't bear what was going on there. Then I was ordered to return on a covert mission, and now I feel I have to go back to try to settle the consequences of that mission. To try to untangle all the mess it has created. I think I need to do it. I need to do it for us."

"But I have a very uneasy feeling about your plan, Roman. There are better and safer ways to deal with this. Make an appointment with your doctor and ask him to refer you to a therapist."

"I would not go see a therapist. I already told you that. Therapists have a tendency to bring you down much lower than you already are. It makes them feel in control."

"How many therapists have you been to in your life?"

"Two. I saw one, a female, after a breakup that left me completely paralyzed. She kept reproaching me for having gotten involved with my former lover in the first place, considering that I saw how attractive she was, considering that I knew how smart and intelligent she was. The therapist was making it clear to me that, in her view, that girl who threw me over for another man after four months—one day searing passion, next day out in the cold—was superior to me in everything. That I should have realized early on that the relationship was doomed from the start because of all these glaring inequalities between us."

Andrea gave him a look of surprise. "Yeah. It's true," Roman said. "The other one was a male therapist whom my parents sought out when I was in elementary school. I had difficulties handling some rather extreme bullying by a couple of classmates. His message to me was that I was a little coward."

"Who was this chick? The flame that burnt out so soon?"

"Another medical student. She ended up a surgeon. I still don't know why her giving me the boot had such a devastating effect on me."

"Wounded pride. She left you for another guy."

"That was probably part of it."

"That was probably all of it. Was he good-looking?"

"Yes."

"Better-looking than you?"

"I would say so."

"See? That made it even worse, didn't it? I'm sorry for the bad experience you've had with the psychologists. They belittled you and underestimated you and pushed you down, but they are not all like that. I have fond memories of the one I was seeing because of my disastrous home life. She helped me get out of the quagmire, to find myself, to realize my self-worth. You have to give it a try."

"She helped you realize your self-worth? That sounds trite. I don't need to see a therapist for that."

CHAPTER 26

COOLERS AND BAGS WERE STOWED in the trunk, children placed in booster seats and the gas tank filled. Andrea had insisted on a road trip. She thought that spending a week together, away from work, surrounded by the countryside, could dampen his internal anguish, make the past recede, at least somewhat, and magnify the importance of the present.

It took only a few miles of driving to leave the city behind. They rode on a twisty highway mirroring the path of the foaming river flowing adjacent to it, with its rapids and cascades and fords, and groves of cottonwood trees along its shores. Towering rubicund rock formations demarcated both sides of the canyon.

Roman was negotiating the sharp curves by rapidly and repeatedly jerking the wheel ever so slightly rather than turning it in a single, fluid motion. Andrea disliked his driving style, but it worked fabulously. He had learned it from a trucker he was riding with on a summer job in Bohemia, delivering building supplies to agricultural cooperatives and villagers and to Prague weekend warriors toiling on their modest country homes. It had been late in the season. Capacious, undulating golden wheat fields stretched for miles, and, further away, green hills were visible, remote hamlets with red-roofed houses scattered among them. The bestubbled driver with missing front teeth barreled down asphalt roads full of potholes, laughing with crazy delight, gently tapping the brake pedal before a turn, then the artful iterative tugging at the wheel, balance was restored, loss of speed was minimal. When there was a longer segment of straight road, the driver would pull a violin from under his seat and fiddle, steering with his knees. "A sullen old lady is waiting for me at home, I have to have some fun while I can," he used to say, and there was a smattering of bitterness in his voice, of apprehension.

"Bighorn sheep!" Andrea shouted. There was a conveniently situated pull-off and Roman stopped. A herd was ascending a steep smooth rock, nimbly, gracefully. How effortless, how natural it is for animals to be scaling the heights, the depths, how lumbering, inept the humans are in comparison when they attempt it. Sebastian was running along the road trying to keep up with the sheep, Cassie toddled behind him, squealing.

They arrived in a mountain town and had a picnic in the park by the river, and they sauntered along its banks and rested on large flat gray boulders made warm by the sun rays, watching the rafters and kayakers clear the churning white rapids. They ambled down the main street, pushing Cassie in the stroller because she had a tantrum and refused to walk.

A spacious antique shop that piqued their curiosity was filled with an amalgam of utilitarian objects of yesteryear, esoteric items, and folk-art creations. There were gracile Japanese porcelain tea cups and saucers with fine flower patterns, ornate copper and ceramic samovars, a hanging kerosene lamp with a delicately painted shade. Several shelves were filled with polished oval stones of varied colors that snugly fit in the palm of the hand, and gem-made rings and bracelets and necklaces were displayed in an antique vitrine; the Green Turquoise restores passion and protects from wickedness; the sage-hued chrysoprase brings good fortune and helps avoid speaking out in anger; the variegated sardonyx with ochre, white and auburn bands bestows courage on the wearer; the pale-blue angelite confers peace of mind. Roman wished he was able to unconditionally submit himself to the power of stone healing.

A large map of the seventeenth century Europe hung on the wall. Poland was surprisingly vast, Hungary was divided up, Germany and Italy non-existent, Turkey occupying the whole South-East, Scotland still independent. A hundred and fifty years later the political landscape would look unrecognizably different. How many more times will the map have to change for the continent to come to its senses?

Massive pipe wrenches, and scythes and sickles with thin, worn-out blades in the next hall. A set of old German stainless steel dental forceps, a sentimental dentist may purchase them, or an admirer of Doctor Szell. Pocket knives that had been carried by nineteenth century explorers, World War I daggers, hussar sabers. Mahogany tables with intricate wooden inlays, elaborate Waterford crystal bowls, siphon seltzer bottles covered with a metal mesh. Regal brass lion bookends, an old gramophone with its carmine-colored horn shaped like Triton's conch shell. A collection of bulky, brittle, shellac-made 78 rpm Soviet war-song records. An Austrian manual bread cutter with a round blade reminiscent of a circular saw, with adjustable positions allowing to vary the thickness of the slice. How liberating it would be, Roman thought, to escape into the realm of objects, of things, things are uncomplicated, things are honest, things are faithful.

Window panes of stores further down the street displayed flyers asking for any information on an Adrienne Smith, last seen leaving for a jog in her neighborhood park before her disappearance, a cheerful, loving person, always there to help others, the distraught husband wants her back desperately, offering a reward.

They left the town and drove through a mountain pass beneath the snow-capped peaks, across the Continental Divide. On the precipitous descent, the gorge widened into a canyon and the canyon into a broad valley. The mountains retreated, but they were still visible in the distance, blending into the blue horizons. Horses stood on pastures alongside the road, necks gently bent, dignified, motionless, statues of calm powerful magnificence. Twilight set in, and it was time to find a place to rest for the night.

Crowded breakfast buffet next morning, people competing for space at the food trays and at cooking appliances. Roman poured half a cup of Golden Malted onto the hot waffle iron and when it was ready, drowned the waffle in maple syrup. Andrea picked an omelet. The children ate Fruit Loops and drank juice. Roman and Andrea sipped on coffee and the little ones were asking for some. Roman put a few drops on a spoonful of sugar, the granules turned tan, and the children consumed it with delectation.

Soon they were heading south, through an old railroad town that had been marked for demise but refused to die and recovered. Mountain peaks were closing in again. In twenty miles came another municipality, colorful low buildings lining the central avenue, interspersed among tall gilded edifices, a charming architectural dissonance. At the edge of town the road began to narrow and rise suddenly and dizzyingly. Switchbacks were carved into a looming giant granite mass. Sheer drops on both sides of the highway, no guard rails, no shoulders.

Roman's palms started to sweat, and Andrea instinctively moved closer to him in her seat and shut her eyes. In the back, Cassie was screaming at the top of her lungs. Sebastian must have pulled her hair. A semi-tractor was coming down from the opposite direction, the trailer was loaded with miles of lumber, and it was swerving over the median. Roman glanced to the right; no more than four feet between the passenger side of the vehicle and the edge of the cliff. A nasty feeling, yes, fear, twisted his stomach, then the truck was gone, and they were still on the road. They lived.

The pavement widened slightly, and a red, block-shaped mountain jutted out in the near distance. Mining relics were scattered on its steep slopes, orange-colored brooks swirled through the gulches. The car was now on the descent, vegetation reclaimed its right to adorn the mountainsides again. Below them a single road weaved along a deep valley, cutting through a triangle of densely packed roofs.

It was a rugged little town, just one street and the buildings flanking it. Instead of horses, dust-covered all-terrain vehicles were parked by the curb. The hotel receptionist wore heavy makeup, oversized round glasses with maroon frames, a beige felt cowboy hat, and a lavender-colored ruffled dress, a throwback to the saloon dress code or a personal fashion taste. "There's a twenty-five dollar fine for a lost key," she said with a Southern inflection.

The key was made of brass, it was huge and ornamental. The room was on the third floor, no elevators, just a labyrinthine mesh of dark creaky staircases with white balustrades, on the hallway walls photographs of the pioneers, groups of men in work clothes, none of them smiling. Nowadays the wider the smile, the more of the teeth and gums show, the closer we feel to the person, the more we trust them only to be disappointed later, but these men weren't smiling, they stared, their lips formed a narrow line, they were tough, determined, uncompromising.

Roman unlocked the door and took Cassie off his shoulders. The beds in the room had large headboards with forest-green upholstery matching in color the wallpaper motif of leaves and branches. The nightstands were adorned with intricate carvings and floral ornaments. A Victorian room but very small, scarcely any space to move around. There was no telephone. They quickly settled their luggage and headed back out for dinner.

The Southwestern restaurant up a block was packed, the streets were empty but the eateries were full, where did all these people material-ize from? The crowd inside was mostly middle-aged or older, rugged tanned faces, men with ponytails and beards down to their chest, plenty of leather, but it was not a biker bar; probably a local hangout. "Let's keep it simple and order burritos for all of us," Andrea said. To drink, Roman had a shot of Makers Mark with cream soda, Andrea went with a Tequila Sunset. Kids were begging to try it, but this time the request was denied.

Sudden fatigue set in. Back in the hotel room, the children quickly fell asleep in their Victorian bed, and Andrea and Roman took a shower and from the window caught the last glimpse of the mountains before the sky turned black.

ROMAN HEARD THE DOOR being unlocked. The receptionist was standing in the entrance, illuminated by the ash-gray rays of the hallway light like a figure in an El Greco painting. She tiptoed to Roman's side of the bed, pushed the covers aside, climbed onto the mattress, pulled her dress up to her waist and straddled him. She took her glasses off but kept the hat. Roman turned his head. Andrea was not next to him; she must have gone to the bathroom. The receptionist smiled, leaned forward, put the palms of her hands on Roman's chest and started moving her hips, slowly, rhythmically. Her gaze was fixed on a still-life with a Bible and candles hanging on the wall above the bed.

"Is your shift over or are you taking a break?" Roman asked and watched her face, watched the smile change into an angry grimace, this is not the receptionist, he realized, this is Eva, reaching into the depth of the ruffles and frills of her gown, pulling out a gun, aiming it at his forehead and putting her finger on the trigger, "No," he screamed, "no, doooon't!" he heard his voice reverberate down the hallway.

"You are waking up the whole hotel," Andrea was shaking his arm. "Who was after you this time?"

Sebastian and Cassie were sitting up in their bed next to each other, like two mushrooms, one tiny, one a little bigger. Roman went to the bathroom to splash cold water on his face, Andrea tucked the children back in. "Dad's fine. Just a bad dream."

She slipped into the bed beside him. "Makers Mark probably didn't help," she said after turning off the light. She held his hand. "I am sorry that this keeps happening. We're here with you. You are safe."

She soon fell back to sleep but Roman, as was usual after a nightmare, was not able to. Then there was a rap on the door. The door handle moved. He pinched himself. Yes, he was awake.

"A guest came down complaining about bloodcurdling screams

coming out of your room. What is going on? Everything okay?" the receptionist demanded to know, he recognized her voice, the Southern twang.

"Everything is fine. I am sorry for the noise," Roman called out.

"Please let me in, I have to see for myself."

"We are all fine, really," Andrea said, surmising that the clerk would be reassured by hearing her voice in addition to Roman's.

"You need to let me in. If you don't, and I have to break in, it will be at your expense."

Roman rose, opened the latch and turned the key in the lock. The receptionist strode in. She had changed her attire, she was now in blue jeans and a tight-fitting emerald-colored mohair sweater, but she still wore the hat, she looked different than downstairs, the new clothes transformed her into an attractive woman, a little ample around the waist but that did not diminish her appeal. *The first part of the dream should have been real.* He immediately felt guilty about his thought, but he could not help having it. Her right hand was close to her belt, he noticed she had a gun, a big black pistol holstered on the hip. What the heck, had it been a dream, or had she indeed been on top of him, training her weapon on his head? No, it had been a full-fledged nightmare, everyone is probably packing in this neck of the woods, they must not be calling the cops for help, they settle disputes themselves.

The receptionist quickly inspected the room, the children were quietly glaring at her, holding hands, terrified, and her tense countenance softened.

"There needs to be complete quiet, guys. The people around you paid for a restful night. If I am forced to come up here one more time, you will have to leave."

"We'll be as silent as the grave," Roman said.

"DID YOU GET ANY SLEEP?" Andrea asked him the next morning.

"No. I was afraid of having another nightmare. I didn't want us to be kicked out of the hotel in the middle of the night. I think we should terminate the mission and go back home. I cannot control my crazy dreams. I know you had good intentions planning the trip, but it's not doing the trick."

"We've been gone only a couple of days. You can't let your flashbacks and nightmares run your life. Our life. We are continuing the vacation. I'll drive today."

SHE WANTED TO HELP HIM, but she felt he was not amenable to any assistance. He was convinced that the only remedy to his emotional quandary was to go back to Bohemia and settle the past. Like her mother who decided that the only way out of her suffering was suicide, a much more extreme circumstance but comparable. The first time she tried was by cutting her wrists. Andrea came home that evening earlier than expected and found her in the bathtub semi-conscious, dark blood trickling from her wrists, along her legs, down to the drain. This was a tough sight even for a hardened, disengaged thirteen-year-old, but she handled it calmly, perhaps because she was high on grass, she lifted Mom's legs up by putting her feet on the edge of the tub, bandaged her wrists and called an ambulance. They stitched her up and kept her on the psychiatric ward for a week.

One year later, it was a drug overdose with Valium, this time Andrea's aunt found her. It was serious, she had to be in intensive care on a ventilator. She truly wanted to be dead, but the time was not right yet. In another two years, it was a gunshot to the chest, neighbors heard it and called the police. She survived.

By this time, Andrea was maturing and coming out of the continuous drug haze. They started having conversations, conversations Mom should have had with the psychiatrist instead, but she was not keeping the appointments.

She told Andrea that when her father, Andrea's grandfather, first climbed on top of her during the night, this was right after her twelfth birthday, she sensed it was wrong, she felt betrayed, her daddy, who over the preceding few years had been more attentive to her and kinder and huggier than ever before, how could he? It was shame, it was fear. It continued for two endless years, until finally during one of these moments of perverted intimacy, she sank her long fingernails deep into his cheeks, and he never came back. She suspected that her mother knew about the abuse all along and decided to ignore it, to tolerate it.

The pain of abandonment and betrayal never went away. As Andrea, an only child, grew older, that pain intensified. "Mom, do you see the psychiatrist?" Andrea would ask her. But mom did not need a psychiatrist, she was able to secure sedatives and analgesics from multiple other doctors to blunt her torment. They prescribed them to her for headaches, for severe lower back pain, for insomnia, for anxiety. And then, when Andrea left for college, Mom succeeded at last.

A few days earlier, Andrea had spoken with her on the phone. She was in the habit of calling her mother several times a week. Mom was more engaged during that final conversation than what was typical for her. She inquired about Andrea's classes and friends, and said three times that she loved her, Andrea later remembered. Andrea told her that she would be coming home for the weekend. "I'm looking forward to seeing you," Mom replied. And when Andrea arrived the next Saturday, she found her lifeless on the living room floor with a dark hole in her temple, a small handgun lying next to her body.

Almost no day went by that she would not think about her mother. Sometimes fleetingly, just for a few seconds, asking Mom if she was watching her from above, sometimes for much longer. What could she have done, what should she have done to save her? In the end she always had to conclude that no matter what measures she would have taken, it would not have made any difference. Her mother's aspiration was to die, and she was determined to realize that goal, and she did not relent until it was reached.

CHAPTER 27

T HE PREVAILING COLOR WAS BROWN, brown soil dried out by the heat, brown rocks, there was only an occasional pinyon pine or a patch of grass with a few lonely cows grazing. Sprawling, bizarrely shaped one-or two-story brown buildings with huge windows and strange chimney-like spirals, enclosed in gated communes, were abutting the sun-drenched highway. "These are called Earthships," Roman said to Sebastian. "They're made with earth-filled tires, and cans, and other recyclable materials. They can produce their own electricity and heat and water. They are off the grid."

"So, they are good for the environment," deduced Sebastian. "Why aren't they around where we live?"

"I am sure there are some, but most of these homes are in this area because the whole Earthship idea started around here."

They made a stop at a narrow deep canyon, the river at its black bottom was so faraway that it seemed to be standing still, only a distant steady rumble gave the clue that it was a powerful, fast-moving flow. Ravens were gliding above the gulch in slow, wide circles, emitting their low, raspy, portentous calls. Dark-skinned girls with braided shiny black hair sat in wicker chairs by the side of the road, selling richly colored war shirts. A broad-shouldered man with a handlebar moustache, his massive gut spilling over the belt of his low-hanging pants, was grilling green chiles in a giant pepper roaster just past the bridge that spanned the canyon.

The town they drove into was brown, too, with lackluster adobe houses lining the streets, but in the dark vaulted passageways, inside the cooled buildings, a multitude of shops, bars, hookah lounges were hidden, along with galleries filled with art harking back to the Western lore, and with one-room museums celebrating the heroes of times past, the gambling lawmen, gritty explorers, saloon brawlers, gunslinger desperados.

They stayed overnight in a hotel where the bullet holes in the ceiling of the dining room bore testimony to the town's unruly past a century ago. They took off the next morning and rode across the arid country until they arrived at the base of huge sand dune formations. Roman parked the car, put several water bottles in his backpack, and the family started climbing up the nearest mound under the hot sun, feet sinking into the sand, yellow particles whirling in the wind, invading the mouth, the eyes. Roman lifted Cassie and carried her on his shoulders. They ascended a few more yards and they had to stop, and looking back on their way down, their forsaken tracks were still visible on the hillside.

They shook the sand out of their shoes before getting back in the car. They drove on, along a ridge of craggy, lavender peaks, the road ending in a small town lodged against the foot of the mountains as if blown there by the gales of the vast valley on whose edge it was sitting.

Thin, long-haired men and women were strolling down the narrow central street, milling around in front of the drugstore, drinking tea, rooibos tea has salutary effects on the liver and the lungs and diabetes, but it has to be steeped correctly, the leaves have to have enough space to expand, they learned from the saleswoman in the store just a few minutes earlier.

Someone was playing "My Back Pages" on a worn guitar. There were churches, Buddhist shrines, Hindu temples, and tarot-reading huts strewn about this peculiar pueblo. A red fox was creeping lazily through unmanicured yards, wearing its cunning smile. "Look," Roman turned to Andrea and pointed to a sign, *Mental Health Experts, walk-ins welcome*, written on a wooden board hanging above the door frame of a one-story log house. "Should I check it out? The folks here must have absorbed at least some of the wisdom of those peaks. They stare at them all day long. They might be able to give me some nontraditional advice."

"I thought you didn't trust therapists. This would be a total shot in the dark. The *Mental Health Expert* is probably a quack or a stoner. Or a New Age mystic."

"Or a sage, wizened mountain man. I'll try it. A one-time consultation."

A TINNY SOUND RANG OUT when he crossed the threshold. The anteroom was dark. A narrow ray of light was squeezing through a door in the back that was left ajar.

"Enter, whoever you may be," a raspy voice was inviting him in. Roman trod carefully across the dim lobby, knocked on the door and slowly pushed it open. A woman with lumpy, ruddy cheeks, full lips, slightly protruding dark eyes reinforced with black-rimmed glasses, straight, long chestnut-colored hair almost completely concealing her shoulders and chest, sat behind a black laminate desk. She was wearing a royal-blue tee shirt or tunic of sorts that revealed cachectic arms with faded tattoos. The air was saturated with a strong scent of cologne. "I am Doctor Lundquist," she reached out with a slightly tremulous hand. "Have a seat. What brings you in, young gent?"

Roman was taken back by her forbidding appearance. Andrea was right. Most likely a quack who likes to get stoned. "Are you a psychologist, Doc?"

"I am an endocrinologist by training, but I took psychotherapy courses. I gradually drifted from hormones to the mind and from a big city to a mountain village. It's all connected, you know. My granddad came to this country from Sweden. He was a lumberjack. He settled in Duluth, Minnesota. I grew up there, on the frontier, with water, ice, snow, and ships and steel. Where are you from, tormented soul?"

"Originally from Bohemia. Now I live not too far from here. Why do you assume I'm tormented? I may be just having a transiently bumpy ride."

"You wouldn't be sitting here gazing at my dour face if you weren't tormented. What nags you?"

"Guilty conscience. Nightmares."

"What have you done, sinner?"

"I hurt some people. They were my friends." He paused.

"You are very parsimonious with words."

"Some years ago, I was sent on an assignment to Europe, and I got them in trouble during my mission. I didn't have much choice in that. I prefer not to go into any more detail right now."

"You're wrong on the choice. There's always a choice. People are free to make a choice under any circumstance. Nothing and no one can take that away from us. That's the real freedom. Not what's written on a sacred piece of parchment."

Here we go. When you feel low, they'll bring you even lower, Roman thought. But he didn't dislike her.

"How does one deal with guilty conscience?"

"Head on."

"Can you be more specific?"

"Head on. Push the thoughts out of your mind. Nip them in the bud, don't open the door when they knock. Or let them linger and ignore them, let them evaporate into the ether. That works too. Going back to the places where it all happened, seeking out the people you have harmed, or you think you have harmed, because the perception of what you've done may differ from what you actually did, that might help, too. But it may not. You'll need to be the judge of that. I don't know enough about your situation."

"One of those people is in prison. He'll likely be released soon. The other one may be dead. I see myself as having played a part in their misery."

"Wow, so you were involved in a high stakes game. Are you ready to let your memory completely unwind? Are you prepared to share with me in detail how you feel? I'd like to help you ease the pain."

Why not open up to her? Without doing that, she could not offer much more, and Roman had a curious intuition that this strange person, this possible junkie without a professional degree in psychology, might have the capacity to help him. He hesitated. He glanced at the bare gray walls, at the empty desk, at her fidgety hands and toothpick arms, the smell of cologne still lingering in his nostrils, and he realized he did not know anything about her, and a more sober, stifling voice prevailed. He shook his head. "Maybe at the next visit."

She opened the desk drawer, pulled out a half-empty bottle of Jack Daniel's, and took a swig. "I could never understand the people who have an issue with physicians using limited amounts of alcohol on the job. Using, not abusing. Outdated, orthodox thinking. In this town no one gives a shit. That's one of the things I like about this place. That, and the blue air, and the purpleness of the mountains, and the multitude of herbal potions you can lay your hands on in the drugstore." She meticulously cleaned the rim of the bottle with a disinfecting wipe and dried it with a tissue. "Here. Take a gulp. You're so taciturn. It'll relax you. It'll make the session more worthwhile."

Roman was wondering what the whiskey was spiked with. He felt a certain affinity for her, suspecting that she, like him, was forced to abandon the practice of medicine, only that in her case the reason must have been addiction to firewater. Yet, he also had a sudden urge to get up and leave. She will not tell him anything other than the variations of what she had already shared; and her behavior was getting a little too odd for the role she assigned herself. "I'll pass. I think I'll get going. I know I wasted your time, and I'm sorry for that."

"No worries. I could offer you something else that may help loosen you up. Something far more enjoyable than good old-fashioned Jack."

"No, thanks. I really need to go."

"As you wish. I understand. We're all just trying to do our best during this brief terrestrial sojourn. I hope I was at least of some assistance. It'll be fifty bucks."

"I KIND OF LIKED HER. But you were right. She was a drinker and a stoner laced with New Ageism. A nice complement to the ethos of the town, but I didn't feel comfortable baring my soul to her."

Back in the car, they soon left the town behind. The landscape was still dry. Tall, bizarre sandstone formations lined the sides of the narrow, winding road.

"Stop at these rocks," Sebastian demanded from the back seat, "I want to try climbing!"

"Why not," Roman said and pulled into a small parking space. "The bluffs are too steep, but we can do a little scrambling at the base."

"Cassie and I will stay down here," Andrea said. "Don't go too far. He's wearing only sandals. Be careful."

The sun was beating down on the granular sandstone surface. "How old are these cliffs, Dad?"

"Probably millions of years."

"How were they made?"

"Winds and water brought in sand and other materials, and over many, many years the sediment turned into rocks. The water and the wind kept working on the rocks, and chipped away and carried off their weaker parts. The cliffs that are here now were the hardest part of the rocks. That's why they stayed."

They scrambled over a ridge, and the parking area disappeared from the view. The elevation grade was still fairly mild, and they continued hiking upward. "Pinyon jay," Roman was pointing to a bird with a gray belly and blue wings perching on a bare branch of a pine tree, when a dark, hissing and buzzing sound pierced their ears. It was coming from a nearby boulder, and when they looked, they could still catch a glimpse of a slithering stocky tubular body disappearing behind the stone. Sebastian grabbed Roman's hand and almost whispered, his eyes widened. "Was it a rattlesnake?"

"Yes. That was a rattler."

"I didn't know they were green."

"Some of them can be."

"I'm scared. Let's turn back."

"You don't need to be scared. It was just warning us to stay away from its home. We have to remember not to get close to that boulder on the way back."

"OK, I'll remind us," Sebastian said, still shaking.

Roman pulled him closer. They continued with easy scrambling for about a hundred more yards until they arrived at the escarpment. "Alright, here's where the real climbing begins. Let's stop and have a drink of water. Then we'll go down."

They started descending. "Lots of scree. That comes from the rocks," Roman told Sebastian. "Position your feet sideways instead of straight down so that you don't fall."

"Dad?"

"Yes?"

"Are you going back to Prague? I heard you and Mom arguing about it."

"You should not worry about that, Seb. That's between your parents."

"Mom doesn't want you to go. I don't want you to go either."

"Seb –" Sebastian's shriek drowned out the rattler's hiss, and the boy dropped to the ground holding his ankle. The snake sinuated quickly and smoothly between the rocks and vanished. They'd forgotten to keep away from its den under the boulder, and Sebastian must have stepped on the rattlesnake, or he just came too close. Roman inspected the boy's leg. There were twin puncture marks right above the ankle. Sebastian was crying. "Am I going to die?"

"You won't die if you calm down." Roman picked him up. "I'll carry you. Don't move that leg."

You should have listened to the boy and turned back when he asked.

He had a sense of foreboding, went through Roman's mind when he clambered over the ridge with the child in his arms. Andrea was sunning on the rocks above the parking lot. She noticed them approaching and ran in their direction.

"What happened?"

"Snake bite."

AFTER ANDREA GOT CASSIE SETTLED in her car seat, she took Sebastian and held him in her lap. "Make sure his bitten leg is below the level of his heart," Roman told her and unfolded the state map. The closest larger town was about thirty miles away. Roman sped through the serpentine roads. Sebastian was crying and whimpering and then he turned quiet.

"He's very pale and sweaty. It looks like he's fainting." Andrea's raised voice trembled.

"Put his head down, and lift both his legs up."

"A minute ago, you said to keep his bitten leg down. Make up your mind."

"His blood pressure may be dropping. He needs to have his head flat and both legs up"

"Is he going into shock? Oh Jesus!"

They reached the town at last, and ten minutes later they were crossing the hospital emergency room entrance, Sebastian limp in Andrea's arms.

"What did the snake look like? What skin pattern? What color?"

"Olive green."

"Most likely a Mojave rattlesnake. The most poisonous kind in the area," the doctor said.

Blood was drawn, EKG leads attached, intravenous fluids started. Then the nurse turned to Roman and Andrea. "We don't have any rattlesnake antivenom left. We used the last dose a couple of days ago, and it hasn't been replenished yet. We just called the university hospital to have some delivered. But it may take several hours for it to get here."

Sebastian was unresponsive, his blood pressure was unstable, his oxygen level was dropping, and he was transferred to intensive care.

It was a small unit, Sebastian its only patient. "This is very serious," the intensivist told them, a young doctor with dark curly hair down to his shoulders and a foreign accent.

"Save him," Andrea said. It was not a panicked plea, it was a measured and quiet request, but the doctor recognized the anguished tension that was underlying it. He held her hand. "I'll do my best."

A ventilator was brought in, they were asked to leave, and when they returned, the grating sound of mechanical respirations was filling the room. Sebastian was motionless, yet, as if in conflict with the cube-shaped metal machine that was helping him breathe, his body quivered with each puff the ventilator delivered. In front of them, visible through the glass wall, was the peaceful nurses' station, the doctor sitting behind the desk, watching the monitor screen. "We've been here for several hours, and he hasn't left. It makes me feel safe that he is here," Andrea said, and Roman thought of all the sleepless nights at the hospital, and the victories and the defeats, and suddenly he missed it, he missed the struggle, the intensity, the purpose, the fulfillment, *That's how I used to be, like this young doctor, that's how I still could be had I stayed, but destiny had other plans.* He was exhausted. His head slumped to his chest, and he fell asleep.

HE WAS WOKEN BY THE SOUND of the door sliding open. The doctor and the nurse both walked quickly to the middle of the room. The nurse was holding a syringe in her hand. "The antivenom has arrived," she said.

Andrea and Roman jumped to their feet and watched as the nurse slowly injected the contents of the syringe into the drip chamber of the IV tube.

"How soon will it kick in?"

"The next few hours will be crucial, but I feel much better now that it's on board," the doctor smiled. Andrea was crying and laughing, Roman was thanking the doctor and the nurse, Sebastian's chest was heaving rhythmically, but soon he would be awake and taking his own breaths, and they'll have their walks again, and their games and their laughs. He loved that boy as if he were his own.

There was a cease-fire between Andrea and Roman after Sebastian's encounter with the rattler. Cease-fires, however, are destined to be broken, and a week after returning home from the hospital, Roman announced to Andrea that he would be going to Prague after all. That he had to.

"No, you don't *have to*. You have a one-track mind. Even after what we just went through, that's all you can think about. There's more to life than what happened with Eva and whether Milan will forgive you. Don't live in the past. I don't need to be a psychologist to tell you that."

"I wish it were that simple."

"If you lived in the present, the nightmares and the pangs of conscience would go away eventually. You don't even bother trying. You are selfish," Andrea persisted. She was standing in the living room with her arms akimbo, her cheeks beef-red, a sign of burning anger, and Roman felt he had no strength to face it, so he left, he drove to his favorite place, a hill overlooking the long spiny string of red rocks running diagonally across the city, and the snowy peaks behind them. He sat in the car, engine running, and stared through the windshield, trying not to think, trying to escape into a transparent emptiness.

When he came back and opened the door, Cassie put down her beloved teddy bear with one missing eye due to rough handling, and ran to give him a hug. Sebastian walked slowly behind her, not entirely back to himself yet.

Andrea was now calm. They sat down at the kitchen table. "You know well what I think about this," she said to him. "But if you're so adamant about going back there, do it. I'll be by your side."

CHAPTER 28

GREEN ROLLING HILLS AND RED ROOFS below were coming into view. Roman was recapitulating the focal points of his upcoming mission. Corsi had called just before he left. There was indeed a captain Kohout who used to be a State Security officer until the organization was disbanded after the Velvet Revolution. The agency had no information on his current whereabouts. Regarding Stránský, he had been released from prison about two weeks earlier.

He will seek out Stránský. He will search for Eva, in spite of having resigned himself to the reality that Kohout was probably the only one who would be able to apprise him of her fate. He was not sure yet how he would go by locating Kohout, but he had an eerie feeling that that particular encounter would occur on the captain's terms rather than his.

FOGGY DRIZZLE and then the landing. The small dreary blue-tile terminal was gone, replaced with a new sprawling glass structure. A cab ride to the city center. Cracked and peeling facades of buildings have been repaired. No more hammers and sickles rippling in the wind. The Castle and the river emerged in front of him, and a soft arrow of sentimentality fleetingly pierced his chest.

Roman booked into a small hotel on a hidden square in the Lesser

Town, took a quick shower, then looked for Eva in the phone book. Her name was not listed. He grabbed a cup of coffee in the lobby and went to the streets. Was it the whiff of freedom he smelled?

He had to see his former hideaway apartment; it was just around the corner. The gate to the building was ajar, and he fully opened it. A long creak echoed through the stillness inside. The same old damp and musty smell hit his nostrils. Upstairs, he rang the bell, and a bearded young man appeared at the door. "I stayed in this pad in the eighties for a few weeks. Can I come in for a minute?" Roman asked. The man hesitated but then stepped aside and let him enter.

"There used to be a stove here," Roman remarked.

"It's central heat now. I heard this was a CIA safehouse in the communist days. Are you with the CIA?"

"Not to my knowledge."

The room was homey. A saxophone rested on the couch. Roman pointed to the window. "When I lived here, a huge raven flew in through the pane once during a late-winter storm. It must have been blinded by the snow. It landed on the floor. Its head was almost cut off by the glass, save for a sliver of the neck that was still connecting it to the body. It was thrashing and flapping its wings for a few seconds, then it died. I'll never forget that sight."

Why did he bring up this memory? Roman wondered, noticing the dumbfounded look on the young man's face. Was it because this short, violent episode that had happened right here was symbolic of his Prague undercover ordeal?

"You have it nicely furnished here," he said with a smile. "Are you a musician?"

"I am an underwater welder," the man replied, his eyes still wide, and opened the apartment door. The time for reminiscences was over.

ACROSS THE BRIDGE and up the hill, walking by baroque churches, beer halls, antique shops, bakeries, ice cream parlors, through green parks with flower beds of purple asters; he was heading to his parents' apartment.

He had called them before leaving the States to let them know he would be coming. He was intensely looking forward to seeing them, but, at the same time, there was a trace of awkwardness and unease inside him. He understood that this was natural after not having seen them face to face in more than seven years, but he was annoyed by this sentiment nonetheless.

He crossed the last intersection before turning onto their street. Here is the building, this is where he grew up, the gate is unlocked, the familiar message board is still on the wall in the lobby, the elevator button still lights up in carmine color when pushed, a fascinating phenomenon for a small child. He remembered holding his thumb against the light and the thumb becoming sort of gently transparent, with a red glow. He tried it now, but the thumb barely glowed, it was much thicker than it used to be those decades ago.

He was on the fifth floor in no time and ringing the bell. Mom opened the door, her whole face transfigured into an enormous smile, and his apprehension instantly vanished. "Roman, my dearest!" she cried out. Dad was standing right behind her. "Roman, son, finally!" he roared, and Roman's eyes were moist and he felt tears trickling down his cheeks; it has been a long time since he last cried. He was hugging and kissing them. Their faces were more furrowed, and there was plenty of gray in their hair, but they were still trim and fit like they used to be.

"You look fabulous," Mom beamed. "You're much more muscular than how I remembered you. Come inside, my dear, don't stand in the doorway," she said, not realizing that their embraces were not letting him in. They moved aside, and he entered the apartment. He opened the kitchen door and was engulfed by the heat flowing from the range, pots and skillets making bubbling and popping noises on the stove. The oven lights were on, he could smell beef tenderloin and French bread. Mom, as usual for her, was preparing a royal feast.

He walked across the hallway and into all the rooms, nothing changed here, as if time stopped at the threshold and was barred from entering. Same carpets on the floors, the same narrow bed in his tiny one-time bedroom, the chandelier lights in the study still dimmed, the encyclopedias in the same location on the heavy book shelf.

"Let's sit in the kitchen," Mom said, "that way I can keep cooking, and chat at the same time. The meal is almost ready."

Dad took a bottle of Slivovitz out of the cupboard and poured the strong distillate into shot glasses. "To the reunion with our dear son!" he proclaimed with a trembling voice. They clicked their glasses, sat down at the old kitchen table and started talking.

Dᴀᴅ ᴡᴀs sᴛɪʟʟ ᴛʀᴀɴsʟᴀᴛɪɴɢ but competition was getting tougher, fighting with young pushy folks for gigs was not enjoyable. He has recently taken up bird-watching, a gentle passion. All he needed for this hobby was binoculars with a decent magnifying power and a pair of comfortable, reliable shoes and a field guide. It can be challenging, especially for a novice, to identify the rarer birds, Dad said, there are many similarities within a bird genus, one has to look for distinguishing features, for detail, a patch on the chest, the shape and length of the tail, stripes on the belly, the size of the bill, the color of the wing bars. He brought a leather-bound notebook from the study to show that he had already identified eighty species, with dates, locations, common names, and occasionally scientific names, all neatly recorded.

Mom volunteered in the City Library, and she was writing her life story on the green Singer typewriter that had been part of the family since the early sixties. It took her this long to finally decide to put it down on paper; growing up in an extended family in a small tucked-away town in the East, six siblings, she the youngest. Her father was a shopkeeper selling fabric, mother a schoolteacher. Idyllic early years through a small child's trusting eyes. Magical Shabbat nights, Dad singing the blessings and hymns in a beautiful tenor. On warm evenings, multiple generations gathering in the wooded back yard, humming soft melodies, bantering playfully, snacking on delicious pastries, the youngest ones always at the heart of attention.

She remembered the enthralling din and sights and smells and tastes of the outdoor market, the plenitude of colorful produce and other foods on the trays, blueberries, huge and sweet, picked in the mountains by Ruthenian peasants, ripe watermelons with large black seeds embedded in the moist crimson flesh, the mild cream-colored sheep-milk cheese, its blocks consisting of a multitude of long interwoven strips. As a child, she relished unraveling the strips and slowly lowering them into her mouth, one by one, and letting them melt. They knew personally some of the vendors from frequent encounters. She could still picture the dairy farmer, a stocky red-faced Bulgarian woman wearing elbow-length black gloves, cutting up large ivory-colored cuboids of butter into smaller chunks with a hefty knife, weighing out the pieces and wrapping them in waxed paper. Once her mother bought the butter, she could not wait to get home to spread it, in a heavy layer, on a slice of crispy-crusted dark bread.

In the summer, they took swims in the eternally ice-cold river and went for walks in the pristine woods and verdant meadows, in God's country, as the folks there used to say. When she grew a little older, she started helping in the shop after school, and later, a teenager, she would don her turquoise dress for special occasions on Sunday afternoons and take off for The Corso, the promenade in the city center, lined with upscale shops and coffeehouses. She carried a book under her arm to give the boys a pretext to start a conversation, a time-honored tradition among the town youngsters.

It was not an easy life, life never is, but for her it was harmonious, happy, hidden from the tumult of the big world, and the war swept it away, tore it apart, uprooted those very few who survived, but at least she was blessed with having been able to escape and fight back. Then came dealing with the aftermath and slowly putting her life back together piece by piece. Five years in Hungary, already married to Dad, working on developing a cultural exchange between countries. That was in the fifties, dangerous times, commission of high treason against The People's Democracy was not a rare accusation to be leveled in those days; they were glad to be tucked away in a different land.

The thaw of the sixties followed, and The Prague Spring, and the invasion and the ensuing repression, called The Normalization by the apparatchiks. She completed her education in middle age. Roman remembered her coming home from work in the evenings, never failing to make dinner, and then burying her head in books for hours, exhausted but determined.

"Three hundred pages already written," said Mom, "and more to come. It helps me to look back and take stock, and I'm not unhappy with what I see."

They wanted to know if he had grown accustomed to America. He laughed. "I adapted to the business of daily living. What's much harder is to adjust to the social habits. I think it will take at least twenty years to feel like I belong, but it may never feel that way completely. After a few years we've accomplished the basic acclimation, and now I'm realizing, wait, something is still missing."

"Like what? Give us some examples." Mom took her glasses off, laid them on the table, then picked them up and put them back on.

"Subtle aspects. Your coworkers don't talk to you socially as much as to their native colleagues. You don't get invited to parties much. Friends are scarce. That's the stage we are in now. We've lived there for only seven years, though. Things may change."

"I'm sure it takes time," Dad said. "Just be who you are. Put some effort into building relationships." For a former resistance fighter, he could be sententious. "Does Andrea feel the same way?"

"She spends most of the day at the coffeehouse so she's bombarded with a variety of social interactions, most of them superficial, of course. She sees it like I do. But you may be right, Dad. We'll need to put more work into it. I've been preoccupied with the past. That's not helping."

"What's bothering you? The stolen diploma?"

"Not so much that any more. Just minor stuff for the most part. I could have done some things differently." They had no knowledge about his stint in the country six years earlier and about his current state of mind, and it was not his intention to tell them.

"We all could have done things differently. What's past is past. You can learn from it, but you can't change it. Are you planning to get a duplicate of the diploma?"

"At some point. It's on my list."

"Would you ever consider coming back, son?" Mom sounded concerned. "I'm sure you could easily return to practicing medicine here."

"No, Mom. I love it there. We both do. There is something irresistible about it. I love how big America is, both in ethos and in size, and how free it is. I'm staying."

"Good," his father said, lighting up a filterless Sparta cigarette like in the old days. "Roman, do you remember the original nineteen-forty-five Soviet liberator tank that's on the pedestal in the Tank Commanders' Square?"

"How could I not."

"Well, it's still there. Make sure you go see it. Someone painted it pink."

IT WAS NOT DIFFICULT to locate Franta Penízek, his old friend from Ostbaum. Roman had an intuition that he would be back in Prague. There were four people by that name in the phone book, and the voice of the second person whom he dialed up was unmistakably Franta's. They met at a garden restaurant on top of a hill overlooking the city, allowing for a sweeping view. On the left, The Castle compound, with the dark steeples of the Saint Vitus church dominating the skyline. Below them, an ocean of red roofs and the dense crooked streets of the Lesser Town, and further east, the New Town neighborhoods on the other side of the river. The National Theater was easily identifiable by the golden brim of its rooftop; during the time of patriotic awakening the citizens of Prague donated money to have the theater built. Up higher stood the National Museum with its prominent green dome, and far back, aloft, the enormous television tower lorded over the capital like an embarrassing jest, a cursed communist gift to the city.

"They should blow up that tower," Franta sneered.

"They won't. Not now that they have those precious bronze naked babies climbing it."

"Yeah. The fellow who sculpted them also created the two men urinating into the pond in front of The City Museum. Did you have a chance to see those statues?"

"Not yet."

"Worth checking out, especially at night when their metal penises glow blue under the reflector lights." Franta chuckled. Then he turned pensive. "I came back to Czechoslovakia after what had happened in Ostbaum."

Roman nodded. "I followed the police into your apartment after you had gone missing. When I saw the empty closet, I was quite sure about where you had disappeared to."

"I went off the deep end, I know. Second thoughts started creeping in once I got closer to the border, but I've always had a hard time changing my mind on a short notice, so I just kept driving. The guards almost showed compassion and understanding. You've made your decision, they said, now you'll get arrested. I was in jail for a couple of months. I went to court. I was expecting three years of hard labor, but the judge gave me two years' probation. I don't know why she didn't send me to prison. It could have been my parents' working-class pedigree. Once I got out, I found a job as a paver, and then I switched to trucking."

"What do you do now?"

"Still trucking. I don't venture out too far. Poland, Slovakia, Hungary. Hungarian women don't wear bras!"

"I remember. Tell me, what happened with Jiřina and the dude who robbed you? Did the cops ever track them down?"

"They did. They found them in Monaco, they were living it up in the casinos down there. They led the police on a chase through the hairpin turns in the hills above the city. The man was driving and lost control, and the car flew over the guardrail and down a sheer cliff. Both dead, of course."

"Shit. Bad karma."

"Yes. You know, for months and months after all this I was mad and resentful, and at the same time I was mourning her death. I still loved her, and I hated her at the same time. It was consuming me. Then I had the epiphany that in order to put an end to the emotional craziness, I had to forgive her. It wasn't easy, but eventually I was able to do that. I forgave her. I still think a lot about what had happened, and about her, but I can do it without anger, without hate. I feel better."

"I am glad for you. So I guess forgiveness can be healing. Tell me, how is your life now? Are you married?"

"No, I'm not married. I have a live-in girlfriend, and another woman on the side. Worries, just worries all the time. The primary girlfriend has a teenage son who's gotten himself in some legal trouble, so we're dealing with that. The backup girlfriend just broke her leg in multiple places falling through the rotten wood floor of her attic, and she is needing my help, so I have to carefully juggle that part. Always something."

"You'd have less on your plate if you only had the primary girlfriend. Or only the backup one."

"Monogamy lost its attraction for me, Roman. I may go back to it at some point, but for now it feels safer to have a reserve."

They ordered another bottle of Chardonnay. "Have you tried pot since that evening years ago in Ostbaum?" Franta asked.

"Of course. But I did take the priest's advice. I've been only smoking indicas and only in moderation. Four, five tokes and that's it. Works great."

"I love the day after smoking," Franta smiled, "when the big high and the stoned state are gone, but I still feel this residual lightness and I'm relaxed and still horny and I have a wonderfully easy-going attitude. I'm told that I'm fun to be around then."

Four Buddhist monks sat down at the table next to them and started chanting, "*omm...omm...*"

"It's very unfortunate we don't have any weed," Roman said. "A wonderful night spent with a friend, alcohol, *omm*, and weed, I'd call that transcendence."

After finishing their drinks, they walked down the steep descent of narrow tree-lined streets. People sat at tables on restaurant patios under outdoor lights. Sounds of the organ seeping from churches, laughter, singing, and echoes of a miscellany of languages filled the warm air. The city was alive.

On Charles Bridge, a band of old buskers took up a narrow space by the parapet, playing the trumpet, the fiddle, and the washboard, how Bohemian, tourists in their own carefree world moved across in a slow, roaring relentless wave, pony-tailed vendors quietly stood at displays of wooden marionettes, amber earrings, and fake garnets, their gloomy faces betraying paltry profits, and dark sandstone saints on pedestals along the parapets of the bridge bore impassive witness to the human folly and futility.

They were now on the other side of the river, strolling down a cobblestoned street lit with ersatz gas lamps. This is where the exchange with Eva had taken place.

"There used to be a good eatery here," Franta said, "before it was replaced by this pizza parlor. You could get a slice of lard-layered wheat bread sprinkled with salt and chives. Yum! And potato pancakes loaded with garlic, and kielbasa, and other authentic fare. It didn't survive. Globalization, my friend, fucking globalization."

They said goodbye in front of the gray prefab high-rise in the southeastern suburbs where Franta lived. "I am going on a run in a couple of days. I'll be taking a truckload of gas masks to Krakow."

"Good luck with the delivery. Is chemical warfare in the offing?"

"Could be. Listen Roman, next time you are here, we'll have to go on a little expedition. I've always wanted to go down South in the footsteps of Švejk's[8] arduous journey. We could end the trip conveniently in The Meat Shops in Budějovice,[9] with some pork and cabbage and dumplings and a few pints of Budweiser. Sound like a plan?"

They hugged and Roman walked to the subway and caught the last train to town just before midnight. Tomorrow, he planned to take a bus ride to his old hospital to try to glean some information on Eva and Milan. Does the hospital still exist? Or was it converted into a warehouse or a sordid motel or a monastery or simply abandoned and now lies in ruins? And if it stayed in business, does it reek like it used to? He had no doubt that if the hospital was still standing, chief Svoboda would be there. He had made himself rich in that forlorn place, working hard to build his kickback empire. Would he welcome Roman with open arms, or would he give him a cold shoulder?

Roman got off the train onto an empty platform that immediately filled with disembarking commuters. He was always fascinated by the phenomenon of rapid appearances and disappearances of crowds, they were like flash floods, like shifting sands. A store can be vacant one minute, packed with people the next, and then deserted again. A long line can form at a cash register within seconds. A hitherto empty road suddenly fills with cars. He found something unsettling, something ominous, about these human ebbs and flows. He stepped off the escalator, ascended the staircase leading to the street above and walked toward the soft blue neon glow of the hotel about a hundred yards away.

CHAPTER 29

ROMAN OPENED THE HOTEL ROOM DOOR, turned on the bedside lamp, glanced around, and froze. A man was sitting at the desk by the wall, legs crossed, with a wide grin on his face. He was lean, with silvery hair and a thin moustache, dressed all in black. His large hands rested comfortably on his lap.

"What the fuck is this? What are you doing here? Who are you?" Roman yelled. His fingers wrapped themselves around a kubotan stick in his pocket. He knew who the man was.

"I am Petr Kohout. I mean no harm. I just came to talk." As Roman had suspected, Kohout would choose to meet on his own terms.

"Your name doesn't mean shit to me. You broke into my hotel room just to chat? Get out!" Roman moved toward the phone while not taking his eyes off of the man.

"Leave the phone alone and have a seat, Roman. I came in here so we can have a private conversation, that's all. I don't have bad intentions. Would you like to know what happened with Eva?"

Roman was staring at the intruder. He seemed calm and non-threatening and his words sounded reassuring, but that was most likely a ruse. The chances were not too high that a person would take the effort and the risk of invading someone's hotel room just to have a friendly one-to-one. On the other hand, Kohout probably was not a conventional individual. Roman weighed his options. He could attack the man, with a very uncertain outcome, or he could run, but somehow he was not convinced that his life was in danger. He wanted to know about Eva. He moved slightly closer to the door and continued to watch Kohout.

"What is your connection to Eva?"

"I used to be a captain with The State Security. I was her supervisor. She was an agent."

Roman's eyes opened wide. Notwithstanding that this was what he was surmising all along, the confirmation of his suspicion hit him hard. She was an agent. It was true. Why would Kohout lie? The woman who used to love him. The woman he used to love, and still cared about.

"What happened with her? Where is she now?"

"I will tell you." Kohout looked down at the tips of his shoes. "She notified me after you made your first contact with her. Our men came to the exchange, as you well found out. Then once she read your documents, she called me about Stránský."

Kohout paused, as if he wanted Roman to have a few moments to process what he'd just heard.

So she did all that. Now you know for sure. She still may have had feelings for you, but she did it all the same. She was programmed.

"Next morning," Kohout continued, "she came to see me. She wanted to know where we were holding you. She told me that the night before she was just millimeters away from committing suicide. She had the barrel of a loaded gun against her temple but couldn't make herself pull the trigger. She said her world had crumbled. We were friends, you see, beyond our professional relationship. She confided in me. I confided in her."

Kohout fell silent, gazing intently into Roman's eyes. "She said that she suddenly realized that what she had been participating in for years was a deadly charade," he resumed a few seconds later. "She told me about the history the two of you had had. She thought that the very personal, visceral recognition that you, and possibly Stránský too, would likely hang, triggered this sudden change in how she saw things. I tried to reason with her, but she was not up for an ideological or psychological discussion. She told me she wanted to disappear for a while, to purge her mind. She wanted to go on a risky assignment. I wondered if she meant a suicidal mission. I offered to arrange for an emergency psychiatric hospitalization. During my career, I've seen other folks break down like this. But she didn't take my suggestion well. In the end, I made plans for her to vanish to Angola to join the communists in the fight against the renegades. I reckoned it would be a challenging enough mission but not quite suicidal. We had a few Czech advisors on the ground there, who, I thought, could watch over her, keep her under their wings. And I hoped that after a few weeks, or months, she would cool off and come back."

Roman was listening and observing Kohout. The captain remained unperturbed, but as he was speaking, his face and his voice acquired a solemn dimension.

"She began working in a military hospital in Luanda, the capital, but a few weeks later I got word that she had deserted to the rebels. The rebels were on the losing end, so I guess that's where the real danger was, and that's where she wanted to be. She took care of the wounded and the sick in a field hospital. In the winter, before the end of that year, there was a communist offensive, and a bunch of rebels were killed. She, along with some others, were taken captive. There was an argument about what to do with her. One faction wanted to keep her as a valuable hostage. Another faction wanted her dead. The party that preferred her alive prevailed, but before they could move her to a prison in Luanda, some soldiers from the other group broke into the hut where she was kept and shot her dead. It apparently happened within two days of her capture."

There was quiet in the room. So, Eva was gone. She has been gone for almost six years. Roman's chest heaved and tears started rolling down his cheeks. Tears of guilt, frustration, sorrow. Tears of the memory of love.

Why wasn't he angry with her for her betrayal? She stabbed him in the back, true, but then she had guilty conscience. She tried to atone for what she had done. She was programmed, but the indoctrination wasn't foolproof. It was a tragic tale.

Kohout smiled. "That's Eva's story."

Roman wiped his face with the palm of his hand.

"You are a hard man," Kohout said after a while. "It almost never happened that someone we wanted to capture would get away. But you did."

"I had no other choice, did I. Either escape or death. So, I gave it the best shot."

"We were very close to catching you at one point. Remember the dogs?"

"The dogs barking? Yes. I was hiding under a pile of leaves. I thought that was the end."

"It almost was. But somehow the dogs got confused. We couldn't explain it at the time. Until later. After the revolution, I found out that one of the men on the canine team that was searching for you was a CIA agent. He managed to disorient the dogs."

So, it had not been the rain that covered his scent. Jones, the reticent, unassuming man, never told him about this.

"Milan Stránský was released from prison not so long ago. Would you know where I could find him?" Roman realized with a surprise that he was speaking to Kohout as if he was someone he could trust.

"I do know. I still have some contacts in the right places. He got his previous job back. He is at Pinnacle Health. Are you sure you want to seek him out? I don't think he has fond memories of you."

Kohout turned his head toward the dark window. He sat quietly for a good thirty seconds, then he rose. "Time to leave. Sorry for the intrusion. I wanted to meet you face to face, and I am glad I did." He walked past Roman to the door. Roman did not move, realizing belatedly that he had let his guard completely down.

The captain put his hand on the door knob. "You seemed very unsettled when you first spotted me here. You had a good reason to be.

I did break into your room with the intent to kill you. You and your CIA buddies, those bumbling idiots, you humiliated our agency. You humiliated me. My name was dragged through the mud for months after you got away. They demoted me. They wanted to fire me. And if you hadn't shown up here on your stupid mission and if you hadn't contacted Eva, she would still be alive today. I am blaming you for her death."

He paused and stared at Roman. "I loved that woman," he said in a suddenly changed, quiet voice. "I loved her." He shook his head as if embarrassed by the revelation. "I began to change my mind about killing you when you showed tears after I told you she was dead. I understood then that you had true feelings for her. And when you asked me about Stránský, I saw that you carried a lot of baggage, just like me. I saw that you had your own demons to fight. I also came to realize that if I killed you, I would close one chapter but another chapter would open. I'm tired of starting new chapters. Consider yourself a lucky man tonight."

Kohout walked out and the door closed behind him, slowly and noiselessly.

ROMAN SAT ON THE EDGE OF HIS BED, stupefied. This was not a nightmare. This just came to pass. At least he was in one piece, he was alive. He had no doubt that what Kohout had said about his intentions was true. He pushed himself off the bed, dragged his feet to the door and locked the deadbolt and the latch. He opened the fridge, reached for a bottle of beer, poured himself a glass and took a swig. He walked back to the bed and lay down.

Kohout could change his mind and come back. He thought about switching hotels, but if Kohout had found him here he would find him anywhere if he wanted to. Roman could get a ride to the airport and board the first available flight back to the States. He pondered the idea. He was on the run the last time he left the country. He will not run this time. This surprisingly easy decision gave him a sense of peace and confidence. He finished the beer and turned on his side, hoping to get some sleep.

He woke after a few hours with a dull headache. Pale daylight was penetrating through the blinds. It was six in the morning. He rose quickly and left the hotel. The air outside was brisk. He trudged along the cobblestoned streets and squares and across dewy parks. The city was waking up. A sportsman's store was already open, and he bought a Swiss Army knife and a can of pepper spray. He crossed the bridge to the Old Town and had a couple of slices of poppy seed roll and a cup of coffee for breakfast in a side street bistro. He wandered back across the river, climbed up the steep steps leading to the Castle, and eventually found himself on top of the hill where his and Eva's favorite hangout used to be. An art gallery was now in its place. The glass door was wide open, and he walked in.

Paintings were affixed to the white walls in a slapdash pattern. All the canvases were uniformly black. There was a white tag with a number under each painting. Following the twisting walls, Roman descended down the squeaking stairs to the basement looking for an unalike piece, but he did not find one. "Do you have any questions about the art?" he heard a sonorous voice behind him. A tanned, thin man with a ponytail, a gray goatee and a long narrow scar on his cheek stood in the hallway, holding a notebook.

"Why are the pictures all identical? All black?"

The man let out a quiet laugh. "They are not all the same. There is a different story behind each of them. Let's see." He opened the notebook. "Number eighty-five. Yes. I painted that one after Charon nearly took me for a fun ride on the Styx. That was black. Really black. The one next to it, I painted after hearing Vláďa Mišík[10] sing. That wasn't black at all. Can you see the difference? This one I made when I was watching aspen leaves rustling in the wind and ravens gliding and circling aloft."

Roman nodded, and walked past the artist and through the door, and he wandered, up and down the hills, past the monastery, past the spot where a resistance fighter, one of the Three Kings[11], was ambushed and killed by the Gestapo, a simple monument, a brick base with a single slender steel rod bursting upward, stood there in his memory. Apartment buildings and houses were getting sparser. He was on a path among trees and rocks, here is the lake he used to go to with his parents to escape the hot empty city, beavers are building their lodges in it, big jagged rocks are reflected in the limpid surface. He kept rambling, across miles of woods and quietude, then an asphalt road appeared, and a bus stop.

He bought a ticket to the bus terminal. The ride will take three hours. Eva would still be alive if he hadn't shown up for his stupid mission. But Eva was no saint. "I caught a twelve-kilogram carp yesterday," the man sitting next to him on the bus suddenly spoke. "That's a monstrous carp," said Roman, remembering the tall tales spiked with ribald innuendos, told by grizzled men sunken in their fishing chairs strewn around the pond near his parents' weekend cottage. "Once I caught a twenty-kilogram giant redfish from a ramshackle ocean pier, with a tiny pole," he said to the man. "The village mayor came to meet me and gave me a plaque with the inscription 'You can have a small rod and still catch a beauty'," and the man didn't stop laughing until the bus arrived at the terminal in a small town down South.

A tall plague column[12] dominated the town square. In a side street stood a Roman Catholic chapel, the word "Ossuary" written in large Gothic-style black letters above its front door. "The monks did not know how to handle the multitudes of exhumed skeletons of the plague dead," the bronze tablet affixed to the entrance wall read, "so they put the bones to utilitarian and decorative use." A huge bone chandelier hung from the ceiling, a bone altar stood in the sanctuary, bone lamps and bone monstrances occupied bone table tops. *Memento mori*, the line between here and there is thin. Roman knew. *Is there a bar in this town?* He found one back in the main square. He walked in, sat down and ordered a pint of icy-cold Gambrinus, then another, and sausage with sour cabbage and boatloads of mustard and horseradish. A Gypsy man was sitting across the table from Roman, strumming a guitar, singing plaintively about when he did time in a Prague prison, "*I missed my sweet momma in the slammer, why did I ever grab that hammer?*"

"Hey Zoli. Honza is over there with his Gibson, why don't you play a duet together," a gaunt man with a tear drop tattooed under his eye prodded the Gypsy, motioning toward a fellow on the other side of the room.

"No, not today," said Zoli, "it would be a fight, and I don't wanna fight today. Today is peace. *Oh crowbar motel, that cold lonely night, no woman in sight.*"

"You dirty bitch, I'm gonna bash your head in!" the gaunt man suddenly screamed at a gaunt woman in the chair next to him.

"Oh, yeah? Yesterday you were pawing at me, groping me all over, your dick was stiff and bent in every which direction like a big nasty curved dagger, I was good for you then, wasn't I, you stinking asshole," the woman shouted.

"Your patience is saintly," the Gypsy said to the gaunt man. "*I miss those days, I miss that time, I miss my buddies, I miss the life of crime, should I go back or should I relent, God tells me stay! God says repent.*"

"I used to live a few blocks from that prison," Roman said to Zoli.

"Really? We jailbirds built an apartment building nearby." Zoli's face brightened with memory. "I was the crane operator on the construction site."

It was deep twilight when Roman left the bar. He was tired, he was drunk. He walked slowly to the edge of town and noticed a derelict barn with its door ajar. He pulled it open. No one was inside. He lay down on a pile of hay and quickly fell asleep. He had only one short dream; the gaunt woman from the bar French-kissing him and gently rubbing his hands.

CHAPTER 30

R OMAN WAS IN AN UNEASY STATE OF MIND. It reminded him of the stage fright he used to have as a young boy when he played the piano in front of a large audience. He had to learn the music by heart, and he was able to achieve that flawlessly, but when he sat down behind the keyboard and began his public performance, he could not help but start thinking about which key to push next, instead of just letting his reflexive memory guide him, and his fingers invariably betrayed him, they froze, he was unable to continue and a dark, hissing rush would flood his head, he would break out in a cold sweat and sit there in shame, with the audience deadly quiet, all eyes trained on him, until he heard the hurried steps of his teacher who would put the sheet music on the piano rack and Roman would finish playing in sheer humiliation.

This is the tram stop where he has to get off. He started slogging toward the edifice of Pinnacle Health, its high dark-brown brick walls as if converging at the top, its grotesque shape looming over the cityscape like an odd Gotham City structure. He found the location of Stránský's office on a large board in the entrance hall and slowly headed in its direction. *Attempts for contrition will fall on deaf ears, efforts to explain will be embarrassing, the wrath will be severe.* Whatever happened, happened. Why is he engaging in this masochistic exercise? He knocked on the white door. There was no answer. It was four in the afternoon, and Stránský should be coming back any time soon. Roman leaned against the wall and waited.

MILAN STRÁNSKÝ WAS FINISHING HIS AFTERNOON ROUNDS. It was going to take some time for him to get back into the groove. In prison, his fellow convicts occasionally sought him out for medical advice, but that was the extent of the exposure to his craft for the past six years. That is a damn long hiatus in medicine. But his old colleagues had confidence in him, and he had confidence in himself. His wife had left him, two stints in prison in short succession was just too much to take, that's when love is put to the test. He had had to make the death row journey alone, and he thought a lot about life in those days, all that he would miss, the sunrises and the warm summer rains, helping people, his daughters' laughter, them becoming adults. That is what matters in life, the rest is just things and glitter and vanity and greed. Too late to come to this realization while sitting waiting for the gallows.

He did not believe in afterlife, he feared the permanent cessation, he feared the nothingness. He soon learned from his former handlers that it was the CIA's bungled spying effort that got him arrested, and that Hollander was the assigned point man. Why would the CIA have wanted to put him under surveillance? Stránský couldn't think of a reason. The State Security officers didn't have an answer either, or at least they told him they didn't. The Americans' betrayal hurt.

Milan used to like Hollander. He thought Roman was a smart, compassionate young man and a quick learner and that he would go far, and he was helping him and considered him a friend, and this is what he received in return. But this was what he had chosen, the ruthless world of spies at black tie banquets and in desolate alleys, he had been playing the game, playing with fire, and he reaped what he sowed, yet with Roman it felt personal. Stránský would have liked to meet him someday, with the aim of laying his hands on him, but he would not have that chance any more.

When he was told that the death sentence was commuted to life behind bars, he, the non-believer, dropped to his knees and gave thanks, not certain whom he was thanking, Good Fortune, Providence, or was there a Supreme Entity after all? He cried; life eclipses death, always.

Then communism crumbled. The Yanks started getting involved in his case, pushing the Czechs for his release, maybe a level of gratitude was their motivation, guilty conscience more likely, and three years later a reduction in the sentence came, and then freedom shortly afterward. What was he to do after a stretch like that other than learn his lesson darn well and unceremoniously pick up the pieces where he left off?

His old friends from Pinnacle decided to give him another chance, he was a victim of communism after all, the drug racket was forgotten. For the previous six years Stránský had been slogging in a dark valley, now he was in green fields. He will not take anything in life for granted any more.

Roman watched Stránský round the corner and walk in his direction down the long hallway. He hasn't changed much. Still the horn-rimmed glasses, a gangly physique, the hair perhaps sparser than the way Roman remembered him. He was looking down, heading straight to his office not noticing Roman, a blue stethoscope, always blue, dangling around the neck, and a stack of papers under the arm. Roman took a few steps forward. "Milan."

Stránský lifted his head and their eyes met. He recognized Roman instantly. How he wished, when he was on death row, to inflict physical damage on him, but now he just felt a surprised annoyance, a low intensity exasperation. "You of all people. What the hell do you want?" he snarled while unlocking the office door.

"I came to talk to you. I had to. I am very sorry for what happened to you."

"You can take your apology and shove it up your ass." Stránský felt a strong urge to end the conversation by slamming the door shut but he stopped himself. He had just been given a fresh start on life. There were no winners in this story. He looked at Roman again. He was a student of facial expressions, and what he saw in Roman's countenance was contrition and sincerity. "Alright," Stránský relented. "Come in." He closed the door, and they sat down at the small round table in the middle of the room.

"Why did you spy on me? How did it feel to spy on me?"

"It was nauseating. I felt horrible. I tried to rationalize it. Not too successfully."

Roman paused, gazed at Stránský, then continued. "The CIA became suspicious when one of their agents was apprehended shortly after you had run into him during a bungled car pass. Apparently, the CIA crew arranged, by mistake, for two different agents to come to the same exchange. The CIA thought you may have denounced the other agent to the State Security. You were valuable to the Americans, and they saw no other choice but to put tabs on you to find out where you stood. They wanted to know whether you switched your allegiance back to the Czechs."

Two vertical furrows appeared above the bridge of Stránský's nose as he listened to Roman's account. "I was already in the States when that agent was arrested," Roman said. "I was a contracted employee with the CIA. The agency sent me to Prague to help the local team set up a surveillance mechanism so that they could get information on you. I was picked because the agency was aware that you and I had worked together at the same hospital. I'm very sorry, Milan."

"So that's what it was," Stránský said slowly. His eyebrows were raised, his jaw dropped slightly. "That car pass was a major screw up on the part of the Americans. I remember the other agent. A tall, good-looking fellow. I ran into him again later. In prison. I hope they let him out by now." He stared into Roman's eyes. "I didn't provide the State Security with any meaningful information while I worked for the Americans. I did not inform on that man."

"I know you didn't betray us, Milan. The CIA was wrong suspecting you."

"Someone obviously uncovered your scheme, Hollander. You used to be good friends with Eva Kubová, am I right?"

Roman nodded. He wondered what Stránský would say next.

"I think she was a State Security agent. I ran into her a few times in The Tiled Cage. Maybe she was the one who got to the bottom of your surveillance project. And then reported what she had found."

He is suspicious that Eva had a role in his arrest. But he is not certain. Should he tell him the whole story? What purpose would it serve, though? To disclose that there was another close acquaintance that had done him wrong? And Eva was dead. *Roman is not going to disrespect her memory.*

He just shrugged and shook his head in response to Stránský's comment. *Now he's going to ask me about her whereabouts.* But Milan didn't ask. He let out a short, bitter laugh and waved his hand. "With an informer on every street corner in those times, it could have been anybody." He gazed at Roman. "The cops searched my apartment and found a transmitter, photos, notes. I thought I was good at hiding incriminating items. I was wrong. The secret police had the whole picture within a few hours. They arrested me, then they sent me to The Little House for good measure, just to make sure there wasn't anything else they needed to know." This was the first time after he had been released from prison that he talked to someone about this part of his ordeal and, to his amazement, it felt cathartic. He wanted to continue, he wanted to tell Hollander about the beatings, the waterboarding, but Roman didn't ask any questions, he just sat there quietly, his face turned pale, and Stránský held back. Remorse was weighing this young man down and Stránský suddenly, inexplicably, felt sorry for him.

"Do you remember the guy with bad heart disease we revived together?"

Roman nodded.

"He is still alive after ten years. He's married, has kids."

"So that was a good thing we did."

"It was."

"Is Svoboda still running that place?"

"Yes, to my knowledge. Did you know that he stood up for you?"

"He stood up for me?"

"Yeah. After your conviction for sedition, the director of the Health Care District was ready to fire you. Svoboda told him he couldn't afford to lose a physician. He fought for you. He insisted. He vouched for your integrity. The director backed down. And then you defected."

"He never shared that with me. I wonder why."

"He didn't want you to know that you were close to losing your job. He understood that you already had enough to deal with."

"We had a conversation before I took off. He implored me not to stay abroad. He tried his best to make a reasoned case, and now I think I know why. He could have brought up his intervention on my behalf then and used it as a moral argument to convince me not to defect. He still didn't mention it. That was selfless. Did he have any difficulties after I left?"

"He was reprimanded by the director, and the State Security paid him a visit. For a few weeks he was quite distraught. He was worried about losing his lofty perch. Eventually, the whole issue faded away."

So, Svoboda's self-centeredness was not all-encompassing after all. Notwithstanding the vanity, the corruptness, the penny-pinching, the sycophancy, there was somewhere, resting in a neglected, forgotten crevice of his soul, a dormant nucleus of courage, empathy, thoughtfulness, that retained the capacity to be aroused from its stupor with the right spur. Roman misjudged him. In most people, Roman was convinced, that nucleus had already atrophied early in life.

"Roman, the spy business is ruthless," Stránský said, his voice muffled, as if coming from a distance. "If our positions were reversed, I would have done exactly what you did. I would have had to. Orders come from above."

STRÁNSKÝ'S WORDS REVERBERATED in Roman's head on the way back to the hotel. Was it true absolution or was it a momentary gesture of compassion toward a man with guilty conscience? The sufferer pitying the one who caused the suffering? That night he dreamed about Stránský somewhere in the jungle, naked, his shoulders, waist and ankles tied to horizontal planks supported by vertical beams about three feet high, with densely planted bamboo shoots, their ends sharpened, thrusting through the spaces between the planks and into his body.

Roman ascended the winding bluestone staircase to the fourth floor, opened the tall heavy door bearing a brass plate with the words *Document Study* and entered a large windowless space illumined by frosty white tube lights. Metal shelving units brimming with files of varying sizes lined the walls. Documents were stacked on chairs and on rolling carts. They were heaped in high columns on the floor behind a long wooden counter on the far side of the room where a young woman with long dark hair whose name tag read Marta Šťastná was kneeling down next to one of the piles, the azure color of her suit radiantly disrupting the monotony of the surrounding grayness.

Roman approached the counter, identified himself, and made his request. Ms. Šťastná stood up, opened a bulky notebook that was sitting on the desk and found his name. With a surprising effortlessness, she located a file among a pile of documents splayed on one of the carts and handed it to him. Roman scrutinized her countenance. He was hoping for a hint of compassion, understanding, even admiration, the existence of the file was a material testament to his persecution after all, but her expression was languid, dispassionate. What did he expect? She was giving out dozens of these documents every day, and, besides, this was history, times have changed, life marches on. He thanked her, and, embarrassed by his vanity, sat down in one of the multiple small booths occupying the remainder of the area, opened the file and started reading.

Sometime before coming to Bohemia, he had read in an émigré newspaper that all the State Security documents containing information on Czech citizens had been declassified and made accessible to the wronged individuals to view. He was not convinced there was much utility in inspecting a pitiful compilation of reports about his activities and behaviors, provided by the ever-present informants, and of comments and directives cobbled together by the secret police whose efforts proved to be so worthless, so irrelevant, yet so oppressive. Nevertheless, there was within him a sense of vindication, and certain perverse nostalgia about a threat that now ceased to exist, and a degree of curiosity about some occurrences and outcomes for which he had no explanation. In the end, he had decided to make contact with the innocuously titled Section of Archives, under whose auspices the documents were kept, to set up an appointment.

THE REPORTS WERE TYPED SEPARATELY, on single-sided pages, not arranged in any particular order. "*Michal: Hollander participated in the High Holy Days services in September 1977*," the first report read. Michal, Michal... Roman was aware that informants were assigned code names that were typically easily identifiable, often related to their professions or some other characteristics. Sometimes, the secret police simply utilized their first names. There was a Michal who used to attend some of the gatherings of Prague Jews, formal and less formal ones, a jovial middle-aged man with a distinctly sallow complexion whom Roman knew only superficially. This was a relatively harmless report; Michal could have belonged to the category of kindly snitches who purposefully reported irrelevant or intentionally discombobulated information.

Several pages of similarly insignificant reports followed. Then there was an account from work: "*The nurse: Hollander disparaged the security forces and the media during a chat in the nurses' station. He questioned the truthfulness and objectivity of the Czechoslovak press reporting on a police action.*"

Roman remembered that conversation. It had been a warm spring afternoon; the service was not busy, and several nurses in their sky-blue uniforms were sitting in chairs and on the sofa-bed in the nurses' station.

"So, Doc, have you read in the newspapers about the resolute action our security forces took yesterday in the Wenceslas Square subway station?" the charge nurse asked him, crossing her legs and pulling the uniform over her knees, ensuring they were completely covered. She was a Communist Party member, and she appeared to take her allegiance with utmost gravity.

"I read about it, but it was not explained who the perpetrators were or what crime they committed. And there was nothing about the specifics of the action taken by the police. Just that an action was taken and that it was successful. Do you have any more information?"

"No, I don't. I'm just proud of our security forces. I have no doubt they did the right thing protecting the public," the charge nurse replied.

"But don't you think that a little more information would have been helpful? The report didn't make much sense the way it was written. It gave the impression that facts were being concealed."

"Doc, I have no reason to question our journalists or our police and their motives. Frankly, you shouldn't either."

"You're right. Questioning them won't get us anywhere, will it?"

The nurse didn't answer. She grabbed the uppermost chart from a tall stack that sat on her desk, opened it, and started writing in it, muttering something under her breath. Brainwashed, or just convincingly playing the part, Roman recalled what he had been thinking at the time. And now he also knew that she had deemed the conversation worthy of reporting.

Next were the minutes of the interrogation that occurred after his arrest for the seditious comment he'd uttered in the bar. *He blames it on alcohol. But alcohol is a truth serum. We will squeeze him.* The fist blows were left out of the account.

I was contacted by the passport division, the comment on the following page read. *Hollander applied for an exit visa to France. They are asking for our input. We've been watching Hollander through the years. He just finished probation for subversion. He is not dangerous, but he is an irritant. A pain in the ass. A Jew. I will recommend that they issue him the visa. Let's hope he stays outside. They can have him. Signed: Lieutenant Nesvadba.*

So, Roman was right in his assumption. Letting him out had not been the result of a clerical error. They wanted to get rid of the undesirables. He thought about Nesvadba, with his pink face and side-swept greasy hair. What has become of him nowadays? Is he a travel agent, arranging sunny family trips to Corfu, Dubrovnik, Mallorca, ski excursions to the Swiss Alps, keeping tabs on the travelers' wallets rather than on their subversive potential? Did he open a restaurant or an art gallery in the downtown tourist section? People like him are adaptable. Has he been involved in politics, a fervent defender of democracy, a communist-basher?

Roman turned the page. Ah, here it is: *The Medic: Hollander shared with me that he had received four samizdat copies of Havel's Power of the Powerless. He did not divulge who gave them to him. He plans to distribute them at a party that will take place in the hamlet of Neblahovice on the evening of the twenty second of November at the house of a Petr Holík.*

Blood rushed to Roman's head, pulsating in his temples. *The medic* must be Honza Nečas, his good friend from medical school whom he had all but discounted as the potential source of the information on which the State Security goons acted when they barged in on the party. This was not a banal, harmless report, this was a serious denunciation that was meant to damage multiple people, foremost Roman himself. He evoked the memory of Honza's sincere open face, his hearty laugh. His relaxed, jocular deportment, his eagerness to help. It could have all been a pretense, but most likely it was not. He was an affable man without conscience. *Fucking bastard. Backstabbing son of a bitch.* Roman shut the file and abruptly stood up.

"Everything alright?" Ms. Šťastná smiled at him from her counter. He did not answer. She rose, adjusted her skirt and walked over to him. "I've seen quite a few people get very upset reading their files.

Some of them storm out of the room. Some of them cry." She was not indifferent after all.

"I just learned a man whom I considered a very good friend had been informing on me."

"That must hurt. The treachery," she said. Her presence made Roman feel calmer. "We live in a new era," she continued. "It's probably him who's in trouble now."

Yes, the list of erstwhile informants was recently published. It was so long it had to be printed in a book at least an inch thick. But Roman doubted that those people would face any consequences. Perhaps a fleeting period of public humiliation. But no consequences.

He sat back down. He thought about his reaction to Honza's betrayal. Why was he so enraged with Honza, yet so forgiving of Eva? Eva repented. But Honza may have repented too. It must be his guilty conscience over having asked Eva to join the CIA's risky undertaking that is making him see her deeds in a different light. He had misgivings about engaging her, misgivings mainly related to worries about her safety, yet he still went ahead and requested her help. He should not have done that.

Unsure that he was satisfied with his reasoning about the inconsistency of his emotions, he returned to the file. The last page dealt with the encounter at The Tiled Cage after the fruitless search for the samizdats at the house party. *I told him I would contact the dean of the medical school to have him expelled*, Nesvadba wrote. *I was bullshitting, but looking at his visage, he bought it hook, line and sinker. I scared the bejeebers out of him. He'll behave for a while.*

CHAPTER 31

THE HOTEL ROOM PHONE RANG. "There are two gentlemen down here asking to speak with you. They say they are with the police," the receptionist spoke in a hushed voice.

"The police?" What the hell was going on? He looked around the room. He grabbed the passport and the wallet and put them in his pocket. Chekhov's *Stories*, the book he brought with him for the trip, was lying on the nightstand. After a brief hesitation, he reached for it. He walked down the stairs to the lobby. Two younger men, mirror images of each other, with bland pale faces, both wearing a black suit and a dark blue shirt, rose from the couch with the reluctance of someone who was enjoying a comfortable respite and now had to get back to taking care of business.

"Mr. Hollander? I am detective Váša, and this is detective Rychlík." They flashed their badges and asked for his identification.

"What is this about?"

"We have some questions for you. It has to do with your recent trip out of Prague. Were you in the town of Borkovice three days ago?"

"Let me think for a second. It's difficult to keep track of time when you're on vacation. Yes, I was there three days ago. What does this pertain to?"

"They found a dead man there in the woods. Three days ago. Hacked up pretty bad."

"That's horrific."

"His name was Marcel Trkal. Did you meet a Marcel Trkal when you were in town?"

"I was sitting with a Marcel at the same table in the bar. I don't know what his last name was."

"What did he look like?"

"Very thin. A tear drop tattoo under his right eye."

"Same Marcel. Did you notice anything unusual in the pub? Anything suspicious?"

"Unusual or suspicious? I don't know if you would call that unusual for a rough and tumble bar, but Marcel and his woman, I think he called her Alenka, got into a bad argument. He threatened her with physical harm."

"What time did you leave the bar? Routine questions, Sir. No worries."

"I didn't look at my watch. Based on the amount of light outside, it must have been between eight and nine."

"Who did you leave with?"

"I was alone."

"Where did you go after you left the bar?"

"To the edge of town. I was a little drunk. I found an abandoned barn, I went in, lay down, and slept like a log until the morning."

"Something doesn't match here. Four people who were in the bar told us that you left with Marcel."

"What? That's absurd. That's a total lie."

"Alenka, Zoli the Gypsy dude, the waitress, and the bartender all said you left with him. Considering that, it looks to us like you were the last person to see him alive."

"It looks to me like I am being framed."

"We found the murder weapon. A big nasty curved dagger. We sent it in for fingerprints."

"You won't find my fingerprints on it. This is crazy. Think about it. Why would I have wanted to harm that man?"

"We don't know. Váša, I think we'll have to take him to Balvan." The two cops looked at each other, then they both turned to Roman with a vacant, watery stare.

"You're right, Rychlík," said Váša. "Mr. Hollander, we'll have to take you to Balvan."

"What's in Balvan?"

"The regional jail. You are under arrest on suspicion of murder."

HE WAS GOING TO THE SOUTH again but this time against his will, in the back seat of an unmarked police cruiser. In front of him were the mountains, looming larger as they were approaching them, rows of tightly packed parallel horizontal ridges arranged like giant steps rising up, first soft, round, furrowed bluish-green hills, above them yellow sandstone rocks with a smattering of pines precariously balanced on narrow ledges, then scarred bald maroon peaks of granite towering over the landscape. How vast. How free.

Roman's mind was in a paralyzing haze. Yes, it does happen, someone getting accused of a crime they did not commit. We read about it in the papers or hear it on the news; a destiny writhing in the current of a raging river of events. Now it's him.

They arrived. It's hard to get out of the car with the wrists handcuffed behind the back.

"I want to make a phone call. I have the right to call the American Embassy."

His request was ignored. The booking officers took his mugshot. They fingerprinted him and took away his clothes. Just yesterday he thought he had control over his life. It is astounding how quickly things can change.

THOUSANDS OF MILES AWAY, under the warm sun and blue sky, Andrea was heading to the coffeehouse after dropping the children off. She has been having strange intrusive thoughts since the early morning. Something had happened to Roman.

Customers were lining up at the counter, and she jumped in to help the baristas. Business had taken off lately, ever since they'd branched out to alcoholic coffee drinks and wine. Soccer moms would never shun a cup of Irish coffee or a glass of Shiraz. "Make me a medium caramel macchiato with three shots of espresso," a tall young woman placed her order. "I didn't get any sleep. The frigging dog was snoring in my ear all night long."

Roman is in trouble. Andrea was suddenly convinced. She quickly prepared the drink, disappeared to her back room and dialed the phone number of Roman's Prague hotel.

ROMAN SPOKE WITH HIS STATE-APPOINTED LAWYER, Marie Vránová, for the first time. They met in a visiting room with a window in the wall through which a guard watched.

"Doesn't look too good right now, Mr. Hollander. They found your fingerprints all over that dagger. What do you have to say about that?"

"I never saw that dagger, I never held that dagger. This murder accusation is so ludicrous that if I wasn't locked up, I'd be in stitches over it. Do you believe in dreams, counselor?" He told her about the dream he had when he was sleeping in the barn, of the gaunt Alenka rubbing his hands.

"It doesn't matter if I believe in dreams. What matters is whether the judge does, and knowing him, I think not."

"I had no motive to kill that guy. I assume that whoever bumped him off chose to do it on the night when I was there because they concluded, correctly, that I could be made into a convenient scapegoat. An alien in town, an intruder. People in these villages hate strangers, no matter if they are visiting for an evening or for a lifetime. The guy threatened his girlfriend Alenka in the bar. I'm sure that wasn't the first time he did. I suspect she killed him, or Zoli did, or they both did. Whoever did him in, or their accomplice, snuck into the barn where I was sleeping and wrapped my fingers around the handle of that dagger. They knew that I had been drinking quite a bit and that

I would be sleeping like a rock. Sounds crazy, but that's the only way I can explain the fingerprints."

"It does sound crazy, that is the problem. In five days, there'll be a preliminary hearing where the judge will decide if this goes to trial. I will cross-examine the witnesses, and I'll do my best to find any chinks in their armor."

Marie closed her briefcase. She was a middle-aged woman with streaks of gray in her thick brown hair. Her full figure, packed tightly into a burgundy nylon blouse and a black skirt lent her an air of confident, relaxed power.

"Do you need anything before I go?"

"Yes. Please contact the American Embassy and my wife. They would not let me call."

"FOR A STRAIGHTFORWARD CLEAN MURDER, they usually don't give sentences longer than twenty years," his cell mate said to him, a young fellow with a pustular face and sad ptotic eyes. "So don't despair. You're a spring chicken. You'll still have a life left after prison."

"There is a little problem though. I didn't do it."

"I've heard that before. We all say it. We're always innocent," the man laughed. "I started early. I stole a bottle of cognac from the grocery store when I was eleven. The plan was to drink it in the basement with my buddies but—"

The cell door opened. "Hollander, you have a visitor," a guard shouted and soon Roman was looking at Andrea through a sheet of plexiglass, and he almost broke down and cried.

She told him how she'd found out that he had been arrested by calling the hotel. She contacted the embassy just before getting a call from Marie, the attorney. Next day she was on a plane to Europe.

"Roman, please tell me you didn't do it."

"I did not. Do you believe me?"

"Of course I do." She gave him a long, tender look. "How are you coping?"

"Better already, now that you are here. Where are the kids?"

"Claudia offered to take them."

"That was very nice of her. What did you tell them?"

"I told them that you might be in trouble, and that I had to go to Czechia to see you and find out what was going on. Sebastian was very scared for you, but I couldn't make up a complete lie. It would not be good in the long run." She smiled. "We'll get through this. It may not even go to trial."

"You had a premonition about this trip, Andrea. You did all you could to dissuade me from going."

"I did, but we should not dwell on that now. Here is something you'll like to hear. A couple of days after you left, the owner gave his permission, and we put up the bird feeders in the yard. Birds of every color you can imagine fly in to feed. You'll be back before long to enjoy them."

Roman touched the plastic divide, matching Andrea's hand on the other side. "I know I made one good choice in life. You."

CHAPTER 32

THE CASE WILL GO TO TRIAL, Marie came to tell him. None of the witnesses caved in at the preliminary hearing.

"Some of these people are the perpetrators, Marie. We'll have to find a way to poke holes in their testimonies. Did you interview everyone who was at the bar that night?" He expected more from this self-assured woman. It seemed as if she wasn't truly working for him.

"Do you know the play Fuenteovejuna?" she asked.

"I do. A wall of villagers united behind a cause."

"Yes. Whatever the cause is they've united behind, it may be hard to break that wall."

AN OFFICIAL FROM THE EMBASSY visited, he reassured Roman they were watching the proceedings closely, didn't hang around for long. Andrea left with a heavy heart for the States to be with the children and to check on the business. She told him she would return for the trial. And Roman was sitting in an eight-by-eight cell with plenty of time to think.

Kohout had invaded his hotel room with the intent to kill him but changed his mind at the last moment. That brush with death had given rise to Roman's desultory peregrination across the city and the countryside that concluded with him making his way into the Borkovice bar. The encounter with Kohout was not random. But his presence in the bar and his interaction with the individuals there, which triggered the events that followed, was. Or was it really? Could it be that the false accusation, the arrest, were predestined, that it was a karmic retribution for the suffering he had caused Eva and Milan?

No, he cannot reason that way. He cannot let himself succumb to fatalism. He has to stay focused. The trial date is approaching.

ZOLI ON THE WITNESS STAND, a fine citizen in a white shirt and a tie. Then the bartender, the waitress. Then Alenka. "Did Marcel physically abuse you?" Marie asked on cross-examination.

"Never. He was a caring man."

"You're under oath, remember?" Marie warned her.

"He was a good man. The love of my life."

Then it was Roman's turn. "You are a violent man with a violent history," the prosecutor growled, his face a few inches away. "You beat up a bus driver. You tied him up, taped his mouth, and left him for dead. You illegally crossed the border, and two guards, not even twenty years old, paid with their lives because of your recklessness. Mr. Trkal can't tell us what happened," he thundered, his index finger piercing the air in Roman's direction," and you won't. But the evidence on the knife speaks for itself. You murdered that man."

Marie Vránová gave up fighting for his innocence and concentrated on getting a reduced sentence instead. It was over in two days. Fifteen years in a maximum-security prison.

Marie filed a routine appeal.

FIFTEEN YEARS. Much had taken place in the previous fifteen years. School, work, defection, CIA, love, guilt, new home in a new country, children. And now, fifteen years of oblivion ahead. He will be in his early fifties when he gets out, well into middle age. He will not see his kids grow up. There will be no trekking in the hills, no mountain views. No comfort of home, no calming cup of coffee with breakfast. There will be no freedom, the most obvious consequence just hit him, no freedom. If his stint in the military felt like prison, what will fifteen years in a real jailhouse feel like? He will miss Andrea terribly. He cannot expect her to wait for him. She will not put her life on hold for eternity.

Mornings are the hardest. It feels like he is being weighed down by a ring of stones hanging from his neck, like his chest has been placed in some kind of a compression device that is pushing the air out of his lungs. As the day advances the heaviness begins to lift hesitatingly, glimmers of optimism begin to tease him, a trace of resisting spirit emerges. New evidence will come to light. The appeal will succeed. And the next morning, agony sets in again.

But something astonishing occurred in this time of desolation. The pangs of consciousness, the nightmares began to retreat, to dissipate, until they completely vanished. No piercing thoughts about the past during the day and, after years of tortured sleep, no waking up during the night hollering, drenched in sweat, heart thumping.

"How are you holding up?" Andrea on the other side of the transparent barrier once more. It has been six weeks since he last spoke with her. Two weeks earlier his parents came, the warden made an exception, letting them see him in between Andrea's visits. They were trying their best to hide their devastation. Poor Mom, is she still writing her memoir? Does she still like what she sees?

"How are the children?"

"Cassie is fine for the most part. Sebastian has changed. He turned much more serious. He barely laughs. The day before I left, we went for a walk to the canyon, and he was crying because you were not with us. I am telling you this so that you know that he loves you. They both love you. And they will be with you soon, because you'll be back home soon. The embassy is in close contact with me. We are working on getting you a new lawyer. I spoke to the ambassador yesterday. He is optimistic."

"Andrea, the nightmares are gone. The guilty feeling is gone. Maybe it's the mind's way of coping. I don't know. This is what I was looking for, but not at this price. I do get a few hours of uninterrupted sleep, though."

Andrea's eyes welled up with tears. So, this is the resolution. This is what he came back for. Present suffering replacing past suffering. Family in shambles. The marriage may not survive. But all is not lost yet. "I'll be back in a couple of months, or earlier if there is a new trial," she said. "Be strong."

The heavy gate slowly closed behind her, and the guard led Roman to the prison yard. He sat down on the cracked concrete steps. A gray bird with sharp yellow eyes and a crimson crest landed near him on the pavement, let out a short trill and took off, disappearing beyond the barbed-wire fence. And Roman is inside the fence, his guilty conscience, his nightmares bartered off for fifteen years in prison. But that is life, isn't it? A continuous stream of tradeoffs, contradictions, paradoxes, compromises. Life is one giant quid pro quo. Everything comes at a price. Leaving gives rise to yearning. Freedom exacts sacrifice. Birth is inexorably followed by death. He is living through an ordeal while having made peace with the past.

The prisoners were filing back into the barracks, and Roman joined their slow-moving procession. He was hoping for another restful night.

NOTES

[1] State Security headquarters

[2] popular Czech beer

[3] gingerbread

[4,5] quoted from Bob Dylan's song "Sweetheart like You"

[6] A prison for political detainees in communist Czechoslovakia, located in a small unremarkable two-story building in the area of Prague Castle. It was infamous for using particularly brutal torture methods.

[7] West German armed forces

[8] the protagonist of Jaroslav Hašek's novel *The Good Soldier Švejk*

[9] České Budějovice, a city in Southern Bohemia, the site of the Budvar brewery, after which the Budweiser brewery was named.

[10] Vladimír Mišík, a Czech rock musician nicknamed "The Legend," persecuted by the communist authorities

[11] daring resistance group, active during the German occupation of Bohemia in World War II

[12] mercy columns erected in Europe after the Black Death epidemic

BIOGRAPHY

Ivan Zador always wanted to create with words, but it took him a while to write his first novel *No Saints Among Us*. Like the protagonist of his story, he hails originally from Czechoslovakia and is a physician. That is where the similarities between the two end. Ivan Zador lives in Colorado with his wife, Sandy, and a furry friend.